Something felt wrong . . . and evil

The quiet itself unsettled Rielle. Why could she no longer hear the festival? By unspoken consent, they moved along the passage, slowly, noiselessly, listening for that first telltale sound, any muted shuffle or scrape that would give them direction.

Adrian's fingers tightened around hers, and for a moment, Rielle was able to ignore the icy sensation that had begun to crawl over her skin. Fear . . .

The shadows had grown murkier, longer. The lamps flared then faded again, three times in quick succession, finally settling down to a lustrous glow. Soft yet eerie, the electric wicks burned with a peculiar radiance, like spirits trapped in opaque glass cages.

Rielle heard it then, behind her, a tiny almost imperceptible break in the silence. It could have been a rat, but she didn't quite believe that. Neither did her pounding heart or Adrian, whose body went suddenly taut against hers.

The Phantom!

D0888226

ABOUT THE AUTHOR

Although Jenna Ryan has worked in modeling and travel over the years, writing has always been her career goal. She loves whodunits, thrillers and old Alfred Hitchcock movies. She especially enjoys developing different characters, twisting the plot and creating a suspenseful atmosphere. When asked "Where do you get an idea?" Jenna replied, "A vivid imagination can be both a blessing and a curse."

Books by Jenna Ryan

HARLEQUIN INTRIGUE

Don't miss any of our special offers. Write to us at the following address for information on our newest releases.

Harlequin Reader Service
P.O. Box 1397, Buffalo, NY 14240
Canadian address: P.O. Box 603,
Fort Erie, Ont. L2A 5X3

Masquerade
Jenna Ryan

Harlequin Books

TORONTO • NEW YORK • LONDON
AMSTERDAM • PARIS • SYDNEY • HAMBURG
STOCKHOLM • ATHENS • TOKYO • MILAN

To my parents, Bill and Kay Goff,
who are always there for me.
And especially to my sister, Kathy,
whose contribution is invaluable
and whose patience and understanding go on long
after mine have run out.
Thank you all.

Harlequin Intrigue edition published November 1991

ISBN 0-373-22173-8

MASQUERADE

Copyright © 1991 Jacqueline Goff. All rights reserved.
Except for use in any review, the reproduction or utilization of
this work in whole or in part in any form by any electronic,
mechanical or other means, now known or hereafter invented,
including xerography, photocopying and recording, or in any
information storage or retrieval system, is forbidden without
the permission of the publisher, Harlequin Enterprises Limited,
225 Duncan Mill Road, Don Mills, Ontario, Canada M3B 3K9.

All the characters in this book have no existence outside the
imagination of the author and have no relation whatsoever to
anyone bearing the same name or names. They are not even
distantly inspired by any individual known or unknown to the
author, and all incidents are pure invention.

® are Trademarks registered in the United States Patent and
Trademark Office and in other countries.

Printed in U.S.A.

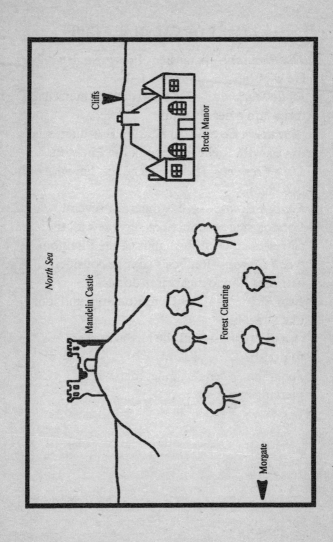

North Sea

Mandelin Castle

Cliffs

Brede Manor

Forest Clearing

Morgate

CAST OF CHARACTERS

The Phantom—A master of disguise. He kills. He vanishes.

Rielle Marchand—Helping a friend in need turns into a deadly affair.

Adrian Da Costa—An alluring Brazilian, who travels with Rielle to unmask the Phantom.

Luke Prentice—Rielle's friend left her with only two clues.

Reuben Bishop—A costumer for several London stage productions, he knew all the actresses killed at the hands of the Phantom.

Noah Bishop—Reuben's son, he considers actresses "annoying prima donnas."

Ivan Ragozcy—He's from Romania and looks like Dracula.

Ava Giordano—Will she be the next actress to perish?

Jonathan Lynch—A quiet man with piercing eyes.

Prologue

Smoke from a circle of medieval torches floated about Gabrielle Marchand's head, creating an odd assortment of shapes in front of her eyes. Lowering her lashes, she struggled to think past the pounding in her temples. Where was she? How had she gotten here? Why couldn't she move her arms?

With an effort she lifted her gaze from the huge chunks of rubble that littered the floor. Crumbling sandstone walls greeted her. And shadows, dozens of them. An assortment of sinister shapes shifting with each gust of wind that tunneled down the vast staircase. Thunder rumbled ominously in the distance, preceded by a blue-white flash of lightning that snaked through the ruined chamber. Even in her disoriented state, she realized she could only be in one place: the dungeon of Mandelin Castle.

"Oh, God," she breathed as her eyes slowly adjusted to the gloom. What a fool she'd been. What an easy mark. She'd walked right into a murderer's trap. He must have been waiting for her the whole time. Using the darkness as a cover, he'd crept soundlessly up behind her, grabbed her, then carried her deep into the bowels of the old castle and tied her securely to a stone column.

Why? she wondered frantically, twisting her head around to look at the staircase. He'd gone out of his way to catch her, yet the proof of his hideous crimes had to be back in his possession by now. Even if it wasn't, how could she possibly threaten him? Until he'd attacked her, she'd had no idea who he really was.

A terrified tremor ran through her. Whatever name he used, whatever mask he wore, he was no man. He was a monster, a fiend, a demon with no heart, no soul and absolutely no conscience.

Her throat felt dry and scratchy when she swallowed. Had he drugged her? She couldn't begin to imagine how long she'd been tied up down here.

Think, her brain commanded. Get away!

She squeezed her eyes closed and tugged desperately on the ropes that dug into her wrists.

A feeling of dread grew inside her as full consciousness slowly returned. He was crazy! This madman toyed with her, as he had each of his previous victims. And how many of those had there been? A dozen that the police were aware of, more if her instincts were to be believed. For all Rielle knew, he might be watching her right now from the depths of those huge, dusty shadows. A human spider studying the fly trapped in its web. She had to get out of here.

Biting down hard on her lip, Rielle rested her head against the stone pillar. Stay calm! But how? she thought frantically. She was at the mercy of a psychopathic killer.

Smoke continued to drift past her eyes, the harsh smell clashing with the scent of roses from the floral coronet she wore as part of her twelfth-century party costume.

The twenty-first of June marked the end of the Midsummer Festival in the village of Morgate on the Yorkshire coast. It was a time of celebration, the night of the elaborate masquerade ball on the grounds of Brede Manor. She should be there now, listening to the Gypsy minstrels strumming their lutes. She should be dancing and singing silly songs, staring in wonder at the sumptuous feast that would be laid out on the great sweep of lawn beyond the mansion. But she was here instead, imprisoned in the cellars of Mandelin Castle, unable to do anything except wait for a murderer to make his next move.

A soft, crunching footfall sounded on the stairs, and for a moment Rielle's muscles tightened. No, don't look at him.

Don't stare at those glittering eyes of his, those red lips pulled back into a hideous parody of a smile. Don't listen to the monster's voice.

Don't scream!

"So, you're awake, are you?" He approached with an unhurried tread, his slick tones rising above the hiss and crackle of the torches. "I am pleased. Once again the curtain shall rise for us."

In her peripheral vision, Rielle saw his hand slither out to trap several strands of her dark hair. She fought the urge to cringe. Creatures like him only fed on fear.

"The stage is set," he crooned very softly, savoring the revulsion she couldn't quite hide. "Soon all will be in readiness for the final act."

She swallowed the panic that rose in her throat. The final act. Final, as in . . .

No! She shoved the thought away. To her relief a thick veil of smoke obscured her vision, blotting out the sight of his glowing features. With obvious reluctance he released her hair and stepped away.

"Soon," he whispered as he melted into the backdrop of black shadows. "Prepare yourself, my dear. This will surely be your finest hour. When I return, we will play out the grand finale. And this time," he promised in a silky whisper, "I *will* have the last laugh."

As if to cement that statement, a low chuckle began to echo through the dungeon, a cruel sound that hung in the air long after he had departed the musty chamber.

Pulling up every scrap of her courage, Rielle worked feverishly on the knots that bound her wrists. She would not fall apart, she told herself, though the declaration felt suspiciously like a prayer. There was a way out of this draconian world. She wouldn't stop believing that.

The heavy ropes cut into her skin, bringing a cry of pain to her lips. "Damn you, Luke!" she swore as tears of frustration formed behind her eyelids. "How did you get mixed up in such a horrible mess? How did I get involved in it?"

Her mind jumped back three weeks in time. That's where the answers resided. This whole nasty affair had started the night her old friend Luke Prentice had come crashing back into her life, the night of the worst fog in London's recent history. The same damp and chilly night she'd heard those muffled footsteps closing in on her as she'd headed toward her flat off King's Road in Chelsea....

Chapter One

She'd made a very big mistake, Rielle thought. People of reasonable intelligence didn't stroll down deserted London lanes at ten-thirty on a Monday night. Particularly when the fog slinking silently across the Thames was quite literally thick enough to cut with a knife.

Masking a deep shiver, she picked up her pace, a problem in three-inch heels but wise considering that she'd been hearing intermittent footsteps behind her for the past five minutes.

A dozen pictures flashed before her eyes, the least comforting of which was a vision of Jack the Ripper stalking her with a giant butcher's knife. Melodramatic maybe, but there were other equally unpleasant possibilities.

With a shiver she passed beneath a creaking antique store sign in an otherwise silent Philbin Lane. No, not quite silent, her sharp ears amended.

She paused for a second by the shop door. The footsteps were still back there, making a soft leathery sound in the puddled lane and bringing goose bumps to her already chilled skin.

Ah, but she of all people shouldn't be afraid. Besides, she couldn't abide cowardice, especially in herself.

So she wouldn't run. Neither would she let some weasely-faced robber relieve her of the fifty or sixty pounds she had tucked in with all her credit cards. She'd earned this money honestly, a new enough phenomenon for her.

She'd been born with what her freighter captain father called a devious mind. His sister Lavinia, a painfully pious woman who looked like a nineteenth-century schoolmarm, put it a little differently. A criminal mentality was her sour-tongued assessment of Rielle's character. But then Aunt Lavinia was also known to drink a lot of sherry before, during and after her lengthy sermons. Who was she to criticize? Anyway, even if she did have a point, Rielle would hardly place conning people out of a little money on the same twisted level as rape or murder.

Saints only lived in mythology, she thought, refocusing on the matter at hand and stealing a quick glance into the mist behind her.

Nothing stirred. No doubt about it, this was the worst fog she'd ever seen in the city. And she'd lived through a great many London fogs in the past decade.

Actually she'd lived through a lot of things: from elegant royal receptions to sooty rooftop chases that could have come straight from *Oliver Twist*. She often thought she'd done it all—and on those rare moments when either her conscience or Aunt Lavinia's lectures got to her, occasionally wished she hadn't.

Friends with whom she seldom socialized these days still mourned her decision to get out of what was casually referred to as "the business." Sometimes she agreed with them. Money was awfully hard to come by these days. However, even con artists with high ethical standards could get caught. A lot of those old friends had spent time looking at London from the wrong side of a jail cell.

So she'd gone straight. And if a few of her less tolerant associates preferred the term *desertion*, that was their problem. There were no more professional cons in her repertoire, although she couldn't deny that life as one half of the up-and-coming Gabrielle Rousseau fashion design team had its shadier aspects. Still, duplicity in the ever-changing world of entrepreneurial anomalies was apparently quite acceptable.

The footsteps broke in again. Someone was definitely following her through the foggy streets of London. And that person was getting much too close for comfort.

If there was one thing Rielle knew about these fogs, it was the weird tendency they had to distort even the smallest sounds. Maybe those footsteps were really ahead of her. Maybe they were as innocent as her own.

She relaxed a bit, letting the tension in her body subside but keeping her senses alert. In the old days she would have found such a situation exhilarating. But then what did a wide-eyed eighteen-year-old, newly arrived from Baton Rouge, know about fear and danger? The word *mortality* hadn't even entered her vocabulary until she'd made her big career switch. Now she was a single woman on the right side of the law who understood all too well the basic concepts of life and death and who'd recalled too late the pitfalls of being out alone after dark in the city.

Taking one last look over her shoulder, she tugged her fashionably oversize trench coat tighter about her body and slipped from the lane, around the corner print shop to Clocking Row.

The fog was too heavy for her to see which windows were lit and which weren't. But it wasn't quite thick enough to cover the muffled noises behind, not ahead of her. And it couldn't prevent her from glimpsing the nondescript shadow that suddenly sprang out of the worn brickwork to block her path.

She suppressed a startled cry. The figure hovered for a moment, a shapeless silhouette, unmoving in the ghostly glow of a nearby street lamp. In the back of her mind Rielle registered the leathery footfall, then dismissed it swiftly when a pair of gloved hands came up to make a grab for her arms.

She hated being grabbed, hated even more being cornered. Maybe that was good. It kept her from being afraid. She held back an angry growl. Her heart pounded but that was good, too. It made the adrenaline pump.

Hands on her shoulders hauled her roughly backward. Fog still obscured everything. One chance was all she'd get at this.

Her breath stopped in her chest. Her fingers curled tightly about the only weapon at her disposal. Bracing herself both mentally and physically, she brought her purse around in a well-aimed arc—and succeeded in catching her would-be attacker completely off guard. She heard the dull impact with his head and would have followed up with a whack to his ribs if he hadn't managed to snag the strap and rip it from her fingers.

Rielle knew better than to panic. And screaming for help was pointless in the city.

Not that she'd have the chance to scream, she realized, alarm and annoyance slicing through her as the man's hand slammed down over her mouth.

"Don't—" he cautioned, but her elbow caught him in the stomach before he could finish.

Aware that her momentary advantage wouldn't last, Rielle twisted her head around just enough to move his palm. Working her mouth free, she sank her teeth into his hand and at the same time spiked his foot with her high heel.

Fear and a fresh surge of adrenaline shot through her. Mild surprise in there, too. This man was no mugger. Or if he was, he'd do well to find another line of work. She had much less trouble than she should have eluding the hands that would have grabbed her a second time.

"Wait," he croaked before she could kick off her shoes and start running. "Rielle, it's me. I'm not trying to rob you. I just want to talk to you."

"Luke?"

She was ten yards away by then and off balance, but even allowing for the disorienting effects of the fog, she recognized the strained voice. She'd been friends with Luke Prentice for eleven very long, very corrupt years. In fact, it was Luke who'd introduced her to a life of crime less than a week after she'd arrived in London.

She paused, righting herself. Eleven years? Had she really been a crook that long?

He'd called it nautical kismet, their first meeting in a slummy Lambeth pub. Her father had called it Cockneyland at its colorful finest. She'd called it a dive and let herself be plunked down at a dirty corner table while the only parent she'd ever known had ambled off to have a pint with his salty shipmates.

So she'd sat there, sipping warm lager and lime, peering through the smoke at all the whiskered sailors and trying to look tough. Or at least worldly. She knew she hadn't managed either one when Luke plopped himself down in front of her and asked if she was lost.

A born shyster, that's how he'd described her. Pretty with just enough sultry edges to throw suckers for a loop.

Sam Spade talk, she'd recognized it right off. But the words didn't matter. Only the meaning behind them. And the bright blue eyes that stared across at her. Beyond beautiful.

An angel had been dropped at her table. Surely for a reason, she'd told herself. Men who looked like Luke didn't just appear, not without a push from some higher power. This encounter, unreal though it felt, was meant to be; Rielle had had no trouble convincing herself of that. And after hearing a few of Luke's stories, she'd had no desire to walk away. Not for a very long time....

She sighed now, listening as he croaked her name again. A curious mixture of relief and regret slid through her, feelings that lasted precisely three seconds. She approached him with a residual trace of caution and no small amount of doubt, squinting through the fog until she spied his familiar features.

The angel hadn't changed. His golden blond hair was long, like rumpled silk. His raincoat, though fashionable, looked wrinkled as if he'd slept in it. Two of the tortoiseshell buttons hung by threads.

Drawing closer, Rielle stared at him. "What are you doing here, Luke?" she demanded. "Why are you following me?"

"I wasn't following you." He pushed his fingers through his long hair and straightened his rumpled coat. "I've been

wandering around in circles for the past thirty minutes trying to find your flat.''

Eyes not leaving his face, she continued to watch him. He
was lying, but she chose not to challenge that. ''Why?'' she
asked instead.

As always, his smile was dazzling, a ray of sunshine to
brighten an otherwise gloomy night. That was Luke Prentice's gift, or his curse, depending on how one knew him. To
Rielle he was part of the past, much loved and as often as
not, much more trouble.

''Just thought I'd drop in on my gorgeous Gabrielle,'' he
said, his winning smile not quite reaching his eyes. ''Any
harm in that?''

Plenty, she suspected. ''None,'' she said, and gave him a
circumspect smile of her own.

''Great. Let's go.'' Before she could object, he'd cupped
her elbow in his hand and turned her south on Clocking
Row.

And Rielle wasn't sure which bothered her more. The
nervous glances he cast around the deserted street. Or the
barely perceptible footsteps that trailed them along the wet
sidewalk to her flat.

''NOW I COULD BE WRONG, but I don't think old Topper's
going to be in any rush to work himself another mark.''
Luke poured a glass of Napoleon brandy and strolled to the
dormer window of Rielle's comfortably furnished second-
story apartment. ''Trust Bradley Chatsworth to turn a minor biff into an all-out battery charge.'' He sighed. ''Running scams sure isn't what it used to be.''

As far as Rielle was concerned, the whole business of
running scams had sunk to sleazy new lows of late. Scarcely
worth the effort anymore, or the risk. Old money was tight,
and the nouveau riche were much more cautious with their
bankrolls than the dilettante set who'd never been forced to
practice any form of self-denial. That left only the middle
class and the poor, and Rielle couldn't see the mental victory in conning them. For all her criminal tendencies, even
a Louisiana con artist could have a social conscience.

Even so, she could still dredge up a feeling of empathy for old Topper. Like Luke he belonged to a near-extinct species, a cross between Henry Gondorff and Robin Hood. Unfortunately both Topper and Luke were a little too trusting for their own good.

From the rich brocade sofa that had once belonged to her Creole grandmother, Rielle watched Luke's agitated movements. He was making her edgy with his pacing, and being on edge made her crazy. Enough of this.

She stood, skirted the Oriental wood chest that served as a coffee table and went to stand in front of him, arms folded across her chest, trying to look like Aunt Lavinia. "All right, that's it. What are you doing here?"

Luke swallowed half his brandy in a single gulp, his handsome Aryan features still locked in a smile. "I told you, I felt like talking to someone who cares about me. I hate to admit it, love, but you're pretty much alone in that category."

Not good enough, that lie. Something was terribly wrong. Resting her shoulder against one of the walnut-paneled walls, she asked, "Where's Paul?"

The question hit its mark dead-on. She knew by the way Luke immediately swung his head around. "I don't know," he mumbled. "Rome, maybe."

"Your partner's in Italy, and you're in England?" One delicate dark brow arched in suspicion. Luke Prentice and Paul Joubert were partners, thick as thieves for the past five years. They never took vacations. And anyway Paul wouldn't be caught dead in Rome in June. A rift, then? No. Which left only one alternative. "Okay, who are you two hustling this time?" she demanded wearily.

"No one, I swear. We're taking a break from the business."

"Liar," she accused.

"Skeptic," he retorted. "It's true. Paul said he needed a rest, and you know we only work together." Maybe his ingenuous expression would have convinced her if he hadn't tipped his empty snifter back, gulped a mouthful of air and promptly choked on it. Luke never could con his friends.

"You were saying?" Rielle said smugly when he stopped coughing.

He rolled his eyes. "All right, so maybe we're in a little trouble."

"Only a little?"

"Okay, a lot." He squinted out the window at the fog as if gazing into the past. A rueful smile touched his lips. "We kind of hooked up with the wrong person."

"So unhook yourselves."

"Not that simple, Gabi."

"Luke..." she warned through clenched teeth. She despised "Gabi" and he knew it, which meant he was trying to distract her. "Keep going," she said, and saw his smile widen a bit.

He continued to stare into the fog. "I can't tell you any more than that. It's too dangerous."

What was too dangerous? Rielle wanted to shout but knew that wouldn't accomplish a thing with Luke. "Where's Paul?" she tried instead, and this time he shook his head.

"Hiding, I hope. We're going to meet up in—well—soon. Somehow we've got to figure out what to do with what we have."

The first real ripples of unease slid through her. "Is what you have the reason you're so scared?"

"The word is 'terrified,'" Luke said, shocking her with the uncharacteristic admission. "And the answer is yes." His blue eyes darted from the fog to her face and back again. "Look, I'll tell you this much and no more. We have proof of a crime, a bad one. I'm not talking about your run-of-the-mill con here, Rielle. This is big. And messy."

Messier than a con gone wrong could be any number of things, none of them pleasant. "You could turn your proof over to Scotland Yard," she suggested with no idea what she was talking about.

He waved the advice aside. "Not possible, love. I have a record, remember? So does Paul. We can hardly trot into the Yard, pitch our proof down on some stuffy inspector's desk and expect to make it out unshackled."

"You could send this evidence to them with an anonymous note."

Luke's troubled gaze probed the swirls of mist beyond the window. "I thought about that, but there's an element of danger in that plan, too."

Pointless to push him too far, Rielle knew. Luke could be a stubborn creature sometimes. "Maybe I can help, then," she said softly. She turned her own eyes to the shrouded street below. Why did he keep looking out the window? Was someone down there? "I know a couple of people at Scotland Yard," she went on, unable to see anyone through the thickening billows. "Why don't you find Paul, come back here with your proof and we'll work things out from there."

Luke left the window to pick up his raincoat, considering the matter for a long moment. "How well do you know these people?" he asked at length.

She wouldn't lie to him. "Not as well as you're hoping, but they helped me when I decided to go straight."

"Go straight." He shuddered at the prospect, but didn't discount it, Rielle noticed. A faintly cynical smile crossed his beautiful mouth. "I suppose anything's better than being dead." He pulled open the door and took a quick look in both directions. "I'll think about it, Gabi," he promised, dropping a kiss on her cheek. Then he was gone. And for the first time in twenty-nine years, Rielle was too jolted to be annoyed.

A slow chill crawled down her spine. Something was worse than wrong here. Maybe worse than dangerous. The sound of footsteps in the fog came back to her with frightening clarity, mingling with the echoes of Luke's ominous parting statement.

Anything's better than being dead....

ONE WEEK LATER the horrible words were still running through Rielle's head. At that moment so was the sooty Lambeth fog.

She waved at the thick gray air with one gloved hand. No elegant designer labels today, she thought with minor regret. Her jeans were ten years old and torn at the knees, her

brown leather aviator jacket and boots were vintage WWII
and her long hair was tucked up inside a peaked cap. She felt
like a teenage toughie who'd lost her motorcycle—and
maybe her best friend.

Other thoughts came to her along with the low moan of
a freighter putting into port. In her mind's eyes she saw a
scrap of paper, a note she'd received from Luke the previous afternoon, hastily scrawled and stuffed in with a tissue-
wrapped key.

"Keep this for me, Gabi," it read. "I'll call you when it's
safe."

Rielle hunched her shoulders in the late-morning fog.
Message and key had arrived at her flat in yesterday's post,
a grubby package tied up with a ratty piece of string. There
was a hint of desperation in his handwriting; she'd sensed
it instantly.

Luke was in trouble; he'd admitted that much. He had
proof of a crime—and a fear of death that would never have
surfaced unless he'd felt truly threatened.

The street around her grew dingier, darker, the air thicker,
more sooty. Factory sounds filtered through. Smoke belched
from ancient chimneys, adding to the fog. This was the old
neighborhood. She knew people here. Former associates
who would help her help Luke, or at least fill in some of the
gaps.

She glanced around. Nothing to see really, not in this
weather. Still it amazed her how different her perceptions
were now that she was back on familiar turf. She'd thought
she might be mugged in Chelsea last week; the idea had actually frightened her. Yet down here by the river it didn't
even cross her mind. No one would hurt Gabi, not even
those who called her a turncoat.

In her mind Rielle pictured the key Luke had sent her.
Old-fashioned, like a room key, with a square of black-
rimmed silver attached to it. And stamped on that square,
two initials: B.M. A person, or possibly a place.

She'd locked the key away, of course, but not her curiosity. Luke was her comrade. She would help him—it was
as simple and as complicated as that.

She heard something ahead of her, a tiny scuffing sound in the narrow lane. Black wool garments and an old silk top hat took shape through the gloom. Beneath the hat she saw pointy tufts of white hair and a man's round, lined face. Topper, leaning against a filthy brick wall, smiling obscurely as if he'd known she was coming.

Probably he had. Rielle tugged lightly on the bill of her cap. Her instincts were minor league compared to this man's.

"Tell me the news, Topper," she said softly, coming up beside him and hoisting herself onto the lid of a dented trash bin. "What have Luke and Paul done?"

In his usual phlegmatic way Topper shrugged. "They're on the devil's path this time, Gabi," he told her in a cultured accent that never failed to surprise her. He stared off into the fog. "Word has it they're not alone, either. The grim reaper's right behind them. And he's mad as a bloody March hare."

Chapter Two

"Excuse me, are you Adrian Da Costa?"

Without breaking stride, Adrian continued walking toward his pit, tugging open the Velcro collar of his racing suit as he went. "No comment," he said flatly, unmoved by the subtle assertiveness of the voice that would have detained him.

Today's qualifying heat had been an unqualified disaster. He didn't need to sour his mood further by summoning polite responses to a lot of simplistic questions from a female reporter who wasn't even sure of his identity. He'd been a Grand Prix driver for more than five years now. If this woman blocking his path didn't know that much, she had no business asking him for an interview.

"I don't want a comment," she said, her composure not shaken by his abrupt dismissal. "I want to talk to you about your cousin, Luke Prentice."

Not by the flicker of an eyelash did Adrian react. But he did slide his dark gaze to her face. It was a striking face, delicately boned and framed by a long, elegant sweep of chestnut brown hair, with the fine features and fair skin that spoke of a European ancestry. Possibly French, though her accent fell somewhere between Deep-South American and British.

Unflinching blue-gray eyes returned his cool stare. She was wearing a press pass, but if she was Luke's friend, chances were she was no reporter. That didn't leave much in the way of alternatives. It did, however, bring him to a halt a good distance from his pit.

"How can I help you—" he lowered his gaze to her pass "—Rachel Masters?"

"Rielle Marchand," she corrected with no apparent concern for the deception. She waved a hand down the pit lane. "Security's very tight at this racetrack. Reporters are allowed in—fashion designers aren't."

"So for today the fashion designer is a reporter."

"Something like that," she said, and he caught the tiniest trace of an edge in her otherwise smooth voice. "I see no point in being coy about this, Senhor Da Costa. I'm sure you can guess that my past isn't exactly untarnished. Fortunately I've been told that yours is similarly disreputable."

He leaned one shoulder against the guardrail, fighting a glimmer of amusement he hadn't felt in years. "It's Adrian," he murmured. "And I would appreciate it if you would keep your voice down. I receive enough bad press as it is. The wolves don't need to draw blood from an old wound."

She held her ground in front of him, the shadow of a smile on her generous lips. "It isn't wolves I'm interested in. It's your cousin."

"Second cousin, twice removed," Adrian told her in a dispassionate tone. "Luke was born and raised in Nottingham, England. My home is in Rio de Janeiro, Brazil. As you might expect, we were not especially close as children." Hadn't even met until they'd reached their delinquent early teens, he was tempted to add but held off. This woman hadn't gone to the trouble of seeking him out at Silverstone two days before the Grand Prix on a whim. "Has Luke been arrested?" he asked, intrigued in spite of himself by her silver-blue eyes.

For the first time she faltered slightly, her dark lashes sweeping down to hide those glorious eyes. "I don't think so. At least if he has, my friends at Scotland Yard aren't aware of it."

"You have friends at Scotland Yard?"

Her lashes flew up, but her expression remained calm. "I have friends in many places. And they're all telling me the same thing. They've neither seen nor heard from Luke for ten days now."

Adrian shrugged. "Is this of some importance to me?"

"If you have any feelings for Luke, yes."

If he had any feelings at all was what she wanted to say, but of course she wouldn't. And he wasn't in the mood to set her straight. Let her believe a jaundiced media. He'd never bothered to set any of those people straight, either.

He opened his racing suit a bit more, allowing the soft June breeze to cool down his heated skin. It was an uncustomary eighty-two degrees today. He was hot and sweaty, irritated with his car's performance this afternoon and loath to show up at the press conference scheduled to begin in less than one hour. At the risk of becoming embroiled in a conversation his instincts cautioned him to avoid, he supposed he could give this woman a few minutes of his time. Especially since this woman had the most hauntingly beautiful eyes he had ever seen.

"I'm listening," he said, still lounging against the girder, oblivious to the curious stares being directed his way by the various pit personnel. "Why are you so anxious to locate Luke?"

"He's in trouble."

Adrian arched a mocking brow. "Is this unusual?"

She held back a sigh. "Topper says," she began, then seemed to reconsider the wisdom of revealing her source. "Well, never mind about that. To put it bluntly, the police think Luke killed someone two weeks ago, an actress by the name of Charity Green. Among other things her husband, Lachlin Green, is on the Bank of London's board of directors. He's very old, very staid and very wealthy, the antithesis of his wife in every way. According to her friends, Charity retired from the stage after her marriage five years ago, but she'd been growing bored with her chosen life lately and was considering a comeback."

"In other words, she was an easy mark," Adrian interpreted, accepting the bottled water someone handed him in passing.

Rielle conceded the point with an eloquent arch of her brow. "You have a good grasp of English idioms, Senhor Da Costa."

"Adrian. And understanding the idioms of any language is necessary."

"To say nothing of advantageous."

"That too." With deceptive indolence he narrowed his eyes. "Was Luke conning this woman?"

"Apparently. But I know Luke. He didn't strangle her."

Adrian took a long drink of water, his gaze never leaving Rielle's shuttered face. "I assume the circumstances surrounding Mrs. Green's death suggest otherwise."

"Would you like to hear the details?" she asked politely, and he didn't pretend to misunderstand her question or the carefully controlled tone in which she offered it. His reputation in print was less than charming. He could imagine that reality didn't strike her as much of a step-up. He could give her histrionics, of course; he did have that capacity. But his emotions were rusty these days, locked away in favor of the rigorous self-control that had become his trademark.

Pushing the damp hair from his forehead, he squinted up at the burning sun, though he could still see Rielle through his lashes. She was watching him. Closely. Patiently. God knew what she was seeing. Likely nothing more inspiring than an out-of-sorts race-car driver who was displaying a monstrous lack of concern for a blood relative. If he had any sense at all, he would give her the answer she was clearly expecting and focus his mind back on Sunday's race where it belonged.

"Were there any witnesses?" he asked instead, shrugging off the top half of his racing suit and tying the sleeves about his waist.

Her eyes flicked over his sweat-damp white T-shirt, then rose to meet his. "Several, but they only saw Luke running from the scene of the crime. No one actually witnessed the murder."

"Where was this woman killed?"

Rielle rubbed her arms with her palms, as if she were cold. Or frightened. "In the old Cobdon Theater," she said at length, choosing her words with care. "The one off Shaftesbury Avenue. It was boarded up after a fire in the lobby last year." She shuddered visibly this time. "The police found her body on the stage. She was in full makeup and Esmeralda costume, and the time of death coincides with the witnesses' accounts of the time they saw Luke running down the back lane."

Adrian held himself very still, turning her words over in his mind, weighing the possibilities and all the dark implications contained within them.

The newspapers had been full of similar stories lately. Chronicles of a madman's deeds, a phantom whose female victims now numbered close to a dozen. The killings had appropriately been dubbed "The Theater Murders" by the London *Times*. No tangible clues, no workable common denominator, nothing of investigative value to tie these women together. In each case an actress or former actress had been killed on some deserted stage, wearing costumes that ranged from Marie Antoinette's ball gowns to Esmeralda's peasant skirts and blouses. Yet the murderer always managed to vanish without a trace. Until now, it seemed.

Shaking the absurd thought aside, Adrian tossed his water bottle into a nearby green bin and took Rielle by the arm, guiding her away from the curious eyes in the pit lane. "Luke is no homicidal phantom," he said as they crossed the track to a relatively uncrowded section of the infield. "He has never even been convicted of conning anyone."

Rielle's delicate jaw was set in a determined line. "That may be, but it doesn't change anything as far as Scotland Yard is concerned. Luke's wanted for strangling Charity Green, and he was positively identified as he ran from the deserted theater where she was killed. No one else was seen leaving by any of the exits. Well, no one except his partner Paul," she added, another faint shudder passing through her.

Adrian frowned. "Paul Joubert was there, as well?"

She nodded wordlessly, and a portion of his tension subsided. This simplified matters enormously. "In that case," he said, "the detectives should focus their attention on finding Paul. He will talk. He never was as slippery as Luke."

"No, he wasn't," Rielle agreed, looking away. "Anyone could find Paul."

The skin on the back of Adrian's neck prickled, but he kept his expression even when he asked, "Has someone found him already?"

"I'm afraid so," she confirmed, her voice little more than a thread of sound in the hot afternoon air. Her gaze returned to his face. "Paul Joubert's body washed up on the south bank of the Thames four days ago. He's been dead for a week."

"Do the police also believe that Luke murdered his partner?" Adrian inquired, opening the door of a long, smoky-gray mobile home behind the pit area and motioning Rielle inside.

She paused just beyond the threshold to look around. Sparsely furnished with an excess of leather and chrome. Nothing lived-in here. Still, this was only a place to relax when he wasn't smashing old lap records on the track. While she might have been tempted to make some sort of personal statement with ornaments or pictures, Adrian Da Costa didn't really strike her as the type.

"That's the current theory," she answered finally, moving farther inside. She poked one of the Italian leather chairs. Buttery soft. Expensive. "I don't think they're looking too hard for alternatives, either. As far as the police are concerned, Luke's the Phantom. He killed those other actresses, he killed Charity, then he killed Paul. Now they say he's running from justice."

"And you would like to prove them wrong." Adrian poured two cups of coffee and handed her one. He regarded her with a trace of mocking tolerance. "Such a thing will be extremely difficult, you know. To find Luke when he has gone into hiding is never an easy task. He could be in the mountains of Nepal by now.''

"Maybe, but I don't think so."

Again that dark brow lifted in mild curiosity. "Is this a feeling you have, or did Luke tell you something you have not told me?"

Rielle hesitated. Funny, the sensations that swept through her, the desire to share her findings with this man, this stranger. Not really what she'd intended when she'd come here, but possibly the best thing she could do for Luke right now.

She took a sip of the strong coffee, grateful for the caffeine zing that sharpened her tired senses. "Luke's in trouble," she said. "He told me that much himself ten days ago. He also told me he had proof of some horrible crime that had been committed. I've been asking around. Those who should know say that Luke and Paul and a third person—a man, they think—were working a con on Charity Green together."

"Does Scotland Yard know about this third person?"

"Yes, however, since he's nothing but a Mr. X to them, and since they have absolutely no idea as to his identity, they're prepared to assume that Luke is the Phantom. I happen to believe the opposite is the case."

Adrian swirled his own coffee, watching her. "You think this mysterious Mr. X is the Phantom."

"It makes sense," she said simply, sliding one hand into the pocket of her linen jacket. "There's no law that says con men can't be duped. Luke would never murder a mark, not even at the risk of being arrested. And no one will ever convince me that he strangled Paul Joubert."

"Then there is no doubt that Paul was murdered?"

"None at all, not even in the minds of the Scotland Yard detectives. The problem is they think Luke did the strangling. I know he didn't."

"And you intend to prove it." Adrian repeated his earlier assertion, punctuating it with a frown and a vaguely impatient wave of his left hand. "What you suggest is madness. And futile in any event if, as you say, Luke is in hiding, and if," he added with a shrewd tilt of his brow, "it turns out that you're right about this unknown third person. Assuming this Mr. X is responsible for the Theater Murders and for Paul's death, as well, then it is only logical to also assume that he will be looking for Luke. A phantom wishing to maintain his anonymity could not allow someone who knows his identity to live."

"Which is why I have to find Luke first," Rielle stated, not swayed. "Luke has proof of a crime. Maybe it has something to do with the Theater Murders, maybe it doesn't. Whatever the case, I want to—no, I have to—help him."

Adrian regarded her through eyes too shielded to read. Dark, dark eyes with just a hint of the temper for which Latin-American men were famous.

He'd pulled on the top of his red racing suit but left it unzipped. He looked hot and tired and extremely sexy. Strange that she would notice such a thing. She could feel the danger in him, and something else. An odd sort of buzz that shot through her like a low electrical current. Maybe she should touch him to see if the charge came from the climate-controlled caravan or from some obscure place inside her.

A tempting thought, but she held off, fingering her coffee cup instead. "Obviously you disapprove, *Senhor.*"

Whatever its source the brief flash of emotion she'd glimpsed vanished from Adrian's eyes, and his features assumed their usual impassive expression.

"The choice is yours," he said, shrugging as if it didn't matter to him. A lie, though Rielle couldn't be sure how she knew that. He leaned against the chrome-edged countertop. "Just where is it you plan to begin your search?"

This time Rielle didn't hesitate. She pulled the key Luke had mailed to her from the pocket of her navy blue pinstriped jacket and tossed it to him. "As soon as I can decipher the initials on that tag, I'll have my starting point."

"B.M." Adrian read the inscription out loud, then closed his long fingers about the silver square. "Interesting. Maybe I will come with you to this place."

Rielle ignored the tiny shiver that ran through her, putting it down to the prospect of locating Luke. "You know what those initials stand for?"

Nodding, he tossed the key back to her, and for a moment she thought he wasn't going to tell her anything more. But then he moved a shoulder and pushed himself from the counter. "Brede Manor," he said calmly, heading toward the bathroom. "A remote place, but a poor choice of hiding spots, I think."

"Why?"

He glanced at her over his shoulder. "Because I know about it," he said. "And if I know, Paul would have known, as well. And that being the case, the person who killed him quite likely shares this knowledge."

"READY FOR QUALIFYING, Adrian?"

Someone in the pit garage shouted the question early Saturday afternoon; Adrian had no idea who. "Car's good," he answered, his sights focused on the narrow cockpit.

Acceleration, speed and power, all there at his command, under his control. Or were they? He'd almost spun off the track during the practice session that morning. His fault, and he didn't like it one bit.

Irritably he climbed into the cockpit. Balaclava, helmet and safety harness on, flurry of last-minute activity around the car's rear wing, tension thrumming through his body—it was time to set his mind on the matter at hand. He could not afford to be distracted. The smallest mental lapse could send both him and the car crashing into a guardrail, or, worse, one of his competitors.

A mechanic shook his clenched fist in front of Adrian's visor. He gave the man a thumbs-up sign and tried once again to empty his mind of all things not race related. No surprise really that it didn't work, that his thoughts continued to slide off in another direction.

Rielle Marchand. He had no trouble picturing that face. Beautiful silver-blue eyes, mane of dark brown hair, determination radiating from every part of her slender body—including her mouth, he recalled in faint amusement. She did make an impression, no question about it. But he didn't have to let her impress him into becoming involved in a situation that would almost certainly spell disaster. How could it be anything less? Paul Joubert was dead and Luke was in hiding, suspected of being the theater murderer. A ridiculous accusation admittedly, but Scotland Yard obviously believed they had a case.

The muffled whine of megahorsepower engines reached Adrian through his helmet. With uncharacteristic impatience, he pushed the sound aside, letting himself remember instead. Maybe if he didn't fight the past so hard, he could ease his thoughts back to the place where they needed to be.

Engines continued to roar around him. He let the sounds fade slowly from his mind. Very high-tech, this racing world, far removed from the world he'd known as a child. A born pickpocket, wasn't that what his mentor, Uncle Emile, had called him? Luke, he'd learned later, had never been able to master that particular skill, but Adrian could do it blindfolded. No wallet, watch or jewel was safe from his sticky fingers. He had even managed a few money belts on the beaches of Rio....

"Isn't he the cutest little boy!" the motherly European and American women would exclaim to their husbands. "Oh, but look at those rags he's wearing." Sympathy in their voices, Adrian had milked that for all it was worth, adopting the sorrowful expression he'd mastered by the age of two. "Give him money," the women would insist immediately. "He needs food. Don't you, sweetheart?"

The husbands always complied. Their mistake, of course, to show Adrian where they kept their cash, but what could wealthy business executives possibly know about life on the streets of Rio, or any other city in the western hemisphere?

He had five brothers, four sisters, a mother and a grandmother, living in two shabby rooms and sharing three beds. His father had taken off, and school, what was that? Adrian knew he should go and sometimes he did, but as Emile was so fond of pointing out, picking moneyed pockets put food on the table. And if his mother wondered about that sometimes, she never said anything. She just crushed him against her too-thin body every now and then and promised him that some day he would escape from this place, that of all her ten children he was the one who would make a name for himself.

Uncle Emile agreed, and on the morning of Adrian's eighth birthday appeared on their rickety doorstep with a shiny new go-cart in tow. "No questions, *meu filho,*" he had warned. "Go now and practice, and we will see how many things you can be good at."

Piece of cake to zoom around in his new cart. Maybe he should race it instead of picking pockets. Or maybe he should do both, Uncle Emile suggested with a sly smile.

Yes, that was logical. It took money to make money. It also took nerve, which Adrian had in abundance. To pick the pocket of a rich *turista* meant nothing to him—and less than nothing when, despite his best efforts to provide, his mother became sick two years later.

That's when he'd gone to see her. And she had looked so bad that all he could do was cry. She had managed to smile at him. "Be the best, *querido,*" she'd whispered. "You have relatives in England. You find them. They will help you."

She'd died the next day, Adrian recalled with a pang. His grandmother had not lasted much longer, and pretty soon people had started taking the babies away. Emile said it was better that way, but Adrian had missed them, still did. Only his mother's words stayed with him, though he'd never bothered looking for his English relatives. Emile told him they were no different than he was; they just acquired their money through more devious means.

"We use our heads not our hands." That's what Luke had boasted when they had met some four years later in Rio. "You've got the moves, cousin, you should try it sometime...."

A thick hand pounding on Adrian's chest brought him sharply back to the present. "Give 'em hell," his engineer was mouthing to him.

Another clenched fist, another thumbs-up. No time now to reminisce. His mother was right; he had made it out. And there was no damned way he would ever go back.

Chapter Three

Paul Joubert was as dead as a proverbial doornail, the man who sat alone in his boxy London flat thought. A scummy con artist who'd known nothing of the performing arts and even less about the art of illusion had been strangled in typical Phantom fashion. How confounded those poor Scotland Yard detectives must be by now. The "Phantom" they'd created preyed upon women. Actresses. One actress actually, but they couldn't know that. They didn't possess their Phantom's insight. They weren't privy to his secret voices, those soft, tragic whispers that came from a higher power to offer him guidance.

Where were the whispers now? he wondered a little hazily. Had Sybil in a spate of hell-born fury lured them away? Was she going to win the fight?

No!

The Phantom clenched his fists. Sybil would never win. He was a better performer than her, much more credible in his roles, with or without the whispers. She'd been a shrew who'd desperately needed a lesson in diplomacy. All her cruel taunts and derisive laughter had garnered her was an early grave.

Oh, she did her best to fool him, he reflected smugly. She'd tried to sneak back from the other side a dozen different times in many different disguises, but her clever masquerades never worked. He'd learned to see through all of them.

"You can't outwit me, Sybil," he whispered, the words dancing about the musty bed-sit like a sprinkling of faerie dust. "You have no sense of subtlety. You think in two dimensions of wigs and costumes, of putty and paint. Useful but not always necessary."

The faerie dust turned to soot at that strangely esoteric thought. He'd almost forgotten about his problem. Sybil's fault, as usual, but then she thrived on trickery. It took a master of deception to stay ahead of her. Fortunately the Phantom was up to the challenge.

Closing his eyes, he breathed deeply the harborside air that was more a product of memory than proximity. What had Paul Joubert told him in those last gasping moments before he'd drawn his final breath? Something about Morgate, a small village on the Yorkshire coast, and the rather bawdy Midsummer Festival celebrated there each year. He'd also mentioned Brede Manor, perhaps the place his partner, Luke Prentice, would run to in desperation.

Brede Manor. Quiet, out-of-the-way and open to a select number of paying guests in the summer months. The Phantom's lips lifted into an eerie semblance of a smile. He would find Luke there. And he would also find that which had been so rudely appropriated from him.

He must leave immediately, he realized, before Sybil returned to haunt him, to torment him. Maybe this time she wouldn't come back; there was always that hope. But he had his doubts about such a wish being granted. A cunning creature was Sybil Fawkes. No, she'd assume another form soon enough. And the Phantom would be called upon to kill her once more.

First, though, he must locate Luke. That meant waiting for the whispers to give him direction. He only hoped he could conjure them up quickly. Already in a distant part of his mind, Brede Manor called to him.

"Brede Manor . . ."

Rielle tested the name of the moldering Yorkshire estate on her tongue and found she liked it. She didn't like the idea that Paul's killer might have been able to extract that name from his victim, but then no situation was perfect. At any rate there was little to be gained worrying about things she couldn't change. Set it aside, she thought. Concentrate on the literary history of the area instead.

It was certainly rich enough. Count Dracula had conspired to settle in a decrepit Yorkshire abbey, and of course Heathcliffe had been spirited into oblivion by Cathy's ghost somewhere out on the windy moors. If it weren't for the somber nature of this trip to the northeastern coast, Rielle would have been excited by the prospect of it.

Unfortunately excited wasn't an accurate description of her present emotional state. Obvious concerns aside, she was all but running through a crowded London train station in an effort to keep her new-found ally in sight. And as for being an ally, Rielle wasn't convinced that such a word could rightly be applied to Adrian Da Costa.

He was shrewd, though—she'd learned that much in the past two days. And fast. A physical and mental speedster, he'd come up with the name Brede Manor less than five seconds after she'd given him the engraved silver key ring Luke had mailed to her.

"Percy Fagan owns both Brede Manor and Mandelin Castle," he had elaborated Friday night over a pint of lager in a cozy little pub in Northampton. "You must have heard of him. He was in your line of work once."

Rielle had ignored the mocking comment. Few things could truly ignite her temper. Besides, she'd already established that nothing this man said or did was likely to rile her.

He was too intense for her tastes. Too focused, too distant and much too self-possessed—although the last was probably an asset, given his choice of careers. He was also very Latin, with his narrow, faintly arrogant features, dark curling hair grown long at the back and an extraordinarily beautiful pair of brown eyes that would have been the undoing of a more susceptible female.

No problem there. She'd always leaned toward Nordic types in the past. Golden-haired princes, she thought sadly, calling up a picture of Luke.

She glanced at Adrian beside her on the busy platform. Unlike Luke, this man wasn't spectacular looking so much as he was strikingly sensual. Just under six feet tall and slenderly built, he moved with a subtle grace that was both rare and fascinating. Rielle recalled the race she'd watched earlier that afternoon. He'd blasted around the track like a creature possessed. If his car hadn't broken down halfway through the race, she had no doubt he would have crossed the finish line a full thirty seconds ahead of his nearest rival.

It was because of his engine's malfunction that they were rushing for this early train. While she'd been checking with her various London sources yesterday, Adrian had managed to wangle two rooms for them at Brede Manor. How, she wasn't sure and didn't really care. All that mattered was finding Luke before he wound up in the same state as Paul Joubert. At the moment, Percy Fagan's manor house seemed to be the best place to start their search.

"Fagan," she murmured, sidetracked yet fully aware that Adrian's dark eyes had come to rest on her face. Even so, he continued to thread his way effortlessly through the crowd.

"What about him?" he asked, drawing her along in his wake and momentarily forestalling her answer.

He was dressed casually in jeans and sneakers, a white polo shirt and red jacket. In leather pumps and a narrow black skirt, she was hard-pressed to match his long stride. Didn't he do anything at a sedate pace?

"Nothing," she answered. "I've heard the name before. I was trying to picture his face."

A derby-topped man with his nose buried in the *Times* cut across her path, very nearly tripping her. Reaching out, she grabbed Adrian's arm to balance herself. She didn't need to slam into that deceptively strong body of his to understand just how attractive he really was, and how little it would take to let that attraction build. Already she could feel a shimmer of awareness gliding through her as his hands came up to steady her. And always there were those hypnotic eyes of his.

For a moment she leaned against him, but only until she remembered where they were going and why. Given his high profile, there was no point trying to travel incognito. They'd kept their cover simple and straightforward: a young couple on a week's holiday who wanted to avoid the press and all the curious eyes that people in Adrian's profession just naturally attracted. She had to remember that and act accordingly. But not until they reached their destination.

"Shouldn't we hurry?" she suggested, righting herself with all the grace she could muster, which was considerable. "The train's about to leave."

He shrugged, a dismissive gesture that struck her as typically Latin. "We can board here," he said in his softly accented English. "Are you certain there is nothing more you wish to discuss?"

Sunday afternoon commuters continued to elbow past, and to anyone except Rielle his question might have sounded absurd. It would have been a lot easier to talk in the privacy of a train carriage.

Easier, yes, but not as safe. Eavesdroppers lurked in quiet places, and so, she thought with distaste, might a certain Phantom.

"I did some research on the Phantom," she said quickly. "If he is the third person Luke and Paul were mixed up with, Luke will have to watch more than just his back. They say this man's a master of disguise, that he could be the kindly old watchmaker in your neighborhood shop, a French marquis or a bag lady on the street. No one knows what he looks like or even how old he is. They only know he kills actresses."

"And that all of the actresses he has killed have at some point in time been associated with the Brittany Rhodes Academy of the Performing Arts," Adrian put in with a shrug. "This is well documented by now."

Rielle conceded the point. "But it still isn't worth much to the police. Everyone who's anyone in the theater from propman to producer has had or still does have an affiliation with Brittany Rhodes. It's a very prestigious school, you know."

"So I have heard."

"Maybe the Phantom thinks it's too famous," she theorized. "Maybe he went there once and didn't like it. Or maybe," she said with a sigh, "the school itself is irrelevant. It could be this guy just gets a sick thrill out of murdering female stage performers."

"And anyone else who gets in his way."

"Like Paul?"

"Like anyone, Rielle. Including Luke and all his known associates." Adrian ran a hand around the back of his neck, massaging the muscles beneath his hair. "He might prey on actresses, but I do not think this Phantom lives by a strict set of rules."

"No, but Luke does," Rielle defended while the crowd continued to whiz by. "He wouldn't murder anyone. He doesn't even like fox hunts."

Adrian arched a dark brow. "You sound very sure of yourself."

She stared at him in mild surprise. "Aren't you?"

"I would not be here if I weren't."

Well, that much she could believe. As for anything else, she could only guess. If he would just smile. He had such a wonderful mouth, full lipped and sensual. His smile would be positively devastating.

Then again, maybe it was better that he maintain his stoic expression. More devastation in her life she really didn't need.

"You are involved with him, aren't you?"

"I beg your pardon?" Rielle dragged her mind back to their conversation, her eyes back to Adrian's impassive features. The tiniest hint of a smile grazed his mouth. She'd been right to amend her earlier thought.

"You and Luke are more than friends," he repeated in a musing tone. "I had not thought of this before."

Why would he have? Luke, for all his endearing affections, was not her type at all. "We were good friends only," she said now, then realized in horror that she'd spoken in the past tense. Luke was not dead. She refused to think that way.

"You were friends?" Adrian repeated before she could correct herself.

She managed a shrug of her own. And a shudder. "Slip of the tongue," she told him. "I have a lot on my mind."

"I can imagine."

Again she caught the softly mocking edge in his voice, and again she ignored it. Certain things weren't worth fighting over. "Our relationship isn't important," she reminded him. "Finding Luke is."

A nod was Adrian's only response, but Rielle was perceptive enough to recognize the coupling of distant amusement and rigid determination behind it.

A tremor that was as much anticipation as terror ran through her. Paul was dead. Luke was missing. Now to complicate matters even further, she was about to embark on a Phantom hunt with a man whose ascetic reputation could scarcely be considered a comfort. The intuition she'd relied on all her life told her there was more to Adrian Da Costa than met the eye. Something dark and dangerous and intriguingly obscure. Much like this trip to the Yorkshire coast.

She would have to be very, very careful.

THE JUMBLE of red-roofed cottages, fishing vessels and cockle stalls that comprised the town of Scarborough rushed by in a collage of color and seaside mist. Only a few minutes now until the train pulled into Morgate station, presumably a few more until they reached Brede Manor. Rielle sat up straighter in her seat, pushed aside the doubts that had been plaguing her since they'd left London and looked at Adrian across from her in the private compartment.

Not unexpectedly he wasn't looking back. Nor was he contemplating the hazy patch of faerie-tale forest through which they were passing. He was staring at someone in the corridor, a man of indeterminate age whose black hair had been slicked back to form a prominent window's peak above his narrow forehead. Ebony eyes glittered beneath a pair of bushy brows that very nearly joined at the bridge of his nose. His skin was uncommonly pale, his manner of dress somber and his aquiline features, though banal in expression, nevertheless struck Rielle as vaguely sinister.

"He should have fangs and a cape," Adrian noted dryly, and she bit back a smile as the man moved on.

"If he did, we'd have reason to be worried." She nodded toward the misty moors. "The sun's beginning to set."

Amusement played on the corners of Adrian's mouth. "Does this mean you would like to return to London?"

She frowned. "Of course not. Why would you think that?"

He shrugged. "Because I have been watching you. The closer we get to Morgate, the more guarded your expression becomes."

He'd been watching her? She must be losing her touch. She usually knew when someone was staring at her, even when the staring was being done under cover of the thoughtful silence they'd shared since leaving the city. Aloud, she said simply, "My expressions or lack thereof aren't especially telling, Senhor Da Costa. Don't forget, I'm no stranger to deception, and you know what they say about old habits dying hard."

This time there was no mistaking the glint of humor that sprang up in his dark eyes—and no eluding the hand that shot out to trap her unsuspecting wrist. "Adrian," he murmured, drawing her forward as he slowly brought her fingers to his lips. "Say it, Rielle."

The command was quiet but clear. Rielle felt his warm breath on her skin, his dark eyes on her face and had to brace herself not to react to either one.

Lashes lowered slightly, she met his gaze. "For the sake of our temporary working relationship, I will," she agreed, her serenity intact on the surface if nowhere else. "First, though, let me say this. With very few exceptions, I don't follow anyone's orders but my own. So you can take your dominating attitude and all your Latin charm and go straight to hell with them—" she forced a smile "—Adrian."

Except for the rhythmic clacking of the train's wheels, dead silence reigned in the coach. Rielle half expected the grip on her fingers to tighten, but then, this man wasn't known for overt displays of temper.

She didn't move, didn't drag her eyes or her hand from his. Let him get good and angry if he wanted to; he wasn't going to tell her what to do.

He wasn't going to get angry, either, she realized a second later. The spark of amusement she'd glimpsed earlier passed through his eyes again as he lifted the side of her hand to his lips. "I think I already have," he said against her skin.

It took her shocked senses a moment to understand what he meant, a little longer to decide whether or not she should be offended. She had, after all, just told him to go to hell. "You think I'm some sort of monster?" she questioned finally in an attempt to lighten things up.

"I think you are very beautiful."

"Thank you." Why was he still holding her hand? "It's not an evil quality, you know."

"No?" He arched a skeptical brow. "You have never used your beauty to con people?"

"Sometimes," she admitted. "But I never conned anyone who couldn't afford to play the game."

"So I have heard."

She hesitated, torn between curiosity and a growing desire to pull her hand free. Curiosity won. "From whom?" she asked, aware in the back of mind that the train was slowing behind the fog-shrouded Morgate station.

Standing, he brought her smoothly to her feet. "You are not the only one with connections in London. Many of Luke's friends are my friends, as well."

Rielle pictured a few of Luke's more colorful confidants. No, she couldn't see Adrian in a smoke-filled underground pub, sizing up possible marks over a warm pint and a plate of sausage and mash. Still, she didn't know him very well, did she? And he must have been a fairly good hustler at some point in his young life. Word had it the teenage Adrian had swung more crafty deals than Dickens's Artful Dodger.

How old was he now, she wondered, stealing a look at his face as they made their way through the nearly deserted coach. Thirty-one maybe, no more.

She considered asking him, then thought better of it as he helped her down onto the damp, misty platform.

To be more precise, the thought flew from her head. How could she hope to hold something like that in surroundings like these?

The eeriness of it caught her off guard. So macabre, the atmosphere. And a silence so thick she could almost hear it. And there was the oddest sense of darkness, though it really wasn't dark at all. Nothing moved, either. Not people, or animals, or even the fog itself. It was positively creepy.

Backing up a pace, Rielle held tight to Adrian's hand and looked around a platform that had all the earmarks of a Gothic horror film. The kind where spirits wandered, werewolves prowled and phantoms could all too easily hide. Where one Phantom could all too easily kill.

Chapter Four

Rielle disguised a shiver. Such a spooky feeling, but who could blame her? It was as if she'd been dropped into a ghost world, a place where nothing was real with the possible exception of the fog. Far in the distance, an animal howled.

An image of something not quite human flashed through Rielle's mind. Good thing she didn't believe in werewolves, better still that Adrian was standing at her elbow looking totally detached, as if all of this was no more or less than he'd expected.

She admired his stoic attitude, his unperturbed stance. Did she give a similar impression? Probably not. This wasn't exactly Paddington Station. It wasn't any station she'd ever seen. Swathed in layers of gauzy mist, the old wood-and-stone building appeared to fade in and out of existence, never quite vanishing from sight, yet never seeming to take on the properties of a solid structure. Even the people who finally came into view had a surreal air about them. Like vapors, Rielle thought, accepting her unease as part and parcel of the eerie setting.

She studied the seven wandering souls in front of her, disregarding the two porters and the wizened old station-master and trying to figure out why the remaining four, a woman and three men, struck her as so peculiar.

"These people look dead."

Adrian's low voice in her ear unsettled her, but no more than the remark itself. It had to be a trick of the fog that they appeared so unnaturally pale. No, not pale, she amended, biting her lip. Bloodless.

"Night of the Living Dead," she murmured out loud as the man they'd seen earlier on the train, the one with the widow's peak, floated past. "Maybe Morgate's really some ghoulish aberration of Brigadoon."

Before Adrian could respond, the lone female, a slinky-looking woman in her late thirties, drifted listlessly across the platform. "Good evening," she greeted them in an affected British accent. Her tone was deep and seductive, her brown eyes sultry, her red mouth pouty and a little too large for her narrow face. She was draped in layers of camel and black, colors that only accentuated her pallor. Her dark, burgundy-tinted hair was cut in a super short Parisian bob, and from her ears dangled a pair of delicate crystal earrings that tinkled lightly when she moved.

The woman's restless eyes shifted to Adrian's face, then back to Rielle as she continued, "My name is Ava Giordano. Perhaps you've heard of me."

"And if you haven't, rest assured she'll be happy to remedy that situation." A man of sixty or better joined them. With his tweed jacket, peaked cap and deep-bowled pipe, he might have been taken for a modern-day Sherlock Holmes. His nose was hawklike and slightly skewed, his face angular, his gloved fingers long and thin. But at least he was smiling.

Smiling with sharp, pointed teeth, Rielle noticed, edging closer to Adrian.

"Reuben Bishop," he said cheerfully, extending his right hand. "Costumer for many a Paris and London stage production."

Ava's lips lifted in a condescending smile. "None of which I've had the pleasure of performing in."

"You're an actress, Ms. Giordano?" Adrian inquired once the introductions had been dispensed with.

"In many a Paris and London stage production," she mimicked Reuben, then moved her too-narrow shoulders in a bored gesture. "In point of fact, I'm beginning to find the trappings of the theater a trifle tedious. The same role night after night. Would you believe I've been playing in *The Scarlet Pimpernel* for two entire seasons now?"

"And was there ever a more charming Louise?"

A second man strolled over. He was tall and fortyish with blond hair, thinning a bit at the temples, and eyes the color of powdered silver. A slight limp interrupted an otherwise even gait. He was handsome enough, Rielle decided, but like the others, much too pale. A gray cape that should have belonged to the as-yet-unmet man with the widow's peak swung about his knees as he drew alongside Ava and treated her to an admiring stare.

"Please allow me to introduce myself. I'm Jonathan Lynch, actor and most devoted fan, Ms. Giordano. May I say again, you were a delightful Louise. However, I do feel your talents would have been better suited to the part of the heroine, Marguerite."

Ava's head rose to a haughty level, her earrings jingling with the motion. "I see nothing wrong with playing a secondary character if that is one's choice. At any rate I don't recall hearing your name being bandied about the Haywagon, Mr. Fynch."

"Lynch," he corrected with a small bow. "And if I've offended you, please accept my apology. As I said before, I'm a most devoted fan."

And the third strange person Rielle had met in as many minutes. She glanced up at Adrian, who didn't seem the least fazed by any of this. "Maybe we should see about hiring a car," she suggested. "I can't imagine that Brede Manor is within walking distance."

"Brede Manor?" Jonathan's gray eyes lit up, and he offered her a smile that would have done the Cheshire Cat proud. "Why, that's my destination."

"And mine," Ava put in, flicking at her asymmetrical fringe of bangs with a scarlet-tipped fingernail. "How coincidental that the four of us should arrive in Morgate on the same train."

"The five of us," Reuben announced, baring pointy incisors in a disquieting smile. "Though I expect it's not so much coincidence as a simple matter of logistics. The London train stops here but twice a day on weekends, only once on the other five days. Also, one must remember that the Midsummer Festival is about to commence." Smoke from his pipe mixed with the fog to curl around his nostrils. "Those of us who are familiar with this heathen celebration wouldn't want to forgo any part of it. Even my son, pragmatist extraordinaire, has at last been persuaded to cast aside his misgivings and join me here for the festivities."

Rielle's gaze shifted to the ebony-eyed man hovering soundlessly beside the station. "Is that your son?" she inquired, not bothering to hide her distaste. But Reuben merely laughed.

"Not at all, my dear. Noah will be driving up from his home in the Chilterns later this evening. Which will please Ms. Giordano to no end, I'm sure."

"Noah Bishop is coming to Morgate?" Ava ignored Reuben's heavy sarcasm, just as he'd ignored hers a few moments ago. "How wonderful. Perhaps he'll let me read for him." She fingered the tips of her icicle-shaped earrings. "I was told the power of the crystal is considerable, but I had no idea it would work so well. And so quickly. I only got into this crystal thing recently, and already my fortunes are improving." To Rielle and Adrian, she waved an airy hand and explained, "For those of you who are uneducated in the names and faces of the theater, Noah Aloysius Bishop is an extremely talented young director. The Alfred Hitchcock of the stage, if you will. Some might even say the master of death, though I think that's a rather inappropriate description in light of all the nasty Phantom business we've been hearing about lately."

Unless the master of death and the Phantom were one and the same person, Rielle's morbid mind supplied. It was an unfair, completely unfounded notion, one she wished had remained in her subconscious. No need to make this situation any more unpleasant than necessary. And no point jumping to unsupported conclusions.

"Pardon the intrusion, ladies and gentlemen." A man's gruff Scottish brogue cut through the fog, silencing the group on the platform. "I'm Fergus McBrecken. Mr. Fagan sent word from the city instructing me to fetch ye back to the manor."

Rielle fixed her gaze on a shaggy-haired man with a thick white mustache who'd materialized behind the swirling mist. "You mean Fagan's not in Morgate?"

The old man turned his piercing blue eyes on her. "No, lass. Mr. Fagan's been in London for some time now. Three weeks or better, I'd ken."

"The devil, you say," Reuben declared, knocking the bowl of his dead pipe against his palm. "He might have seen fit to get in touch with me."

"Are you a friend of Mr. Fagan's?" Jonathan asked, saving Rielle the trouble.

Again Reuben's lips drew back in a pointy-toothed smile. "We went to school together," he acknowledged.

"Old Gooseberry's Academy of Debauchery and Dirty Deals, no doubt," Ava put in under her breath as the porters finished loading up their luggage onto a pair of rusted trolleys.

Rielle studied the woman's wan features. "I take it you and Reuben Bishop know each other."

Using her bloodred nails, Ava made a motion of indifference. "By reputation mainly, although I did catch a glimpse of him several years back when I played a summer session of *King Lear*."

"One of the Brittany Rhodes productions?" Rielle asked, interested now.

Ava regarded her, clearly affronted. "Is there any other?" Before Rielle could come up with an answer, she went on. "At any rate Reuben Bishop was there that year, trying to finagle a deal, I've no doubt." Her smile was less than complimentary. "They say he'd sell his own mother for nothing more than a few quid and a pint of ale, a tale I'm inclined to believe. They also say he bilked three or four underwriters on his way from Whitechapel to Picadilly. Still, one shouldn't condemn the man, I suppose." A calculating gleam slithered into her dark eyes. "Particularly when that man's son has the wherewithal to create a star."

"This way, if you please," Fergus McBrecken interrupted, turning from the platform. "Penelope's right out front."

Rielle looked back at Adrian. "Penelope?"

Taking her chin between his fingers and thumb, he turned her head toward a patch of darkness barely visible through the thickening fog. A black shadow that took on the properties of a positively ancient Rolls Royce limousine the closer they got to it. "Penelope," he surmised while Fergus, ahead of the group, fiddled with the stubborn rear-door handle. "This should be an interesting trip."

"It has been so far," Rielle agreed, and felt that increasingly familiar sense of fearful excitement start to build again as Fergus at last coaxed the door open.

Pushing her feelings down, she let the uniformed Scotsman assist her onto one of the two opposing velvet seats in the back of the Rolls limousine. Across from her, Reuben, Ava and Jonathan sat like marble statues, watching as Adrian slid into the car with his customary fluid grace. Moments later Fergus's heavy brogue reached her ears.

"Are we all set, then?" he asked.

"All set," a low, whispery voice to Rielle's left answered.

A chill as damp and cold as the wind on the moors swept across her skin. She knew what was coming. She knew, and still she had to look.

Slowly and very much against her will, she turned her head to regard the man beside her. Although his face was half in shadow, there was no mistaking the pronounced widow's peak that marked his forehead or the coal black eyes that burned with an almost febrile intensity.

"Good evening," he greeted, his heavily accented voice deeper now, more beguiling. "I am Ivan Ragozcy from Lupeni."

"From where?" Rielle asked without much hope.

"Lupeni, Romania," he clarified. "In an area you call the Transylvanian Alps."

VAMPIRES, CON ARTISTS and gypsies, Adrian thought with
a shake of his head. He huddled deeper into his jacket as the
sea breeze swept up and over the rugged cliffs to reach him
on the rear terrace of Brede Manor. He'd seen the colorful
Gypsy bands camped out in a forest clearing between the
Elizabethan manor house, with its stark Gothic flourishes,
and the twelfth-century ruin that was Mandelin Castle. According to Reuben, they'd come for the Midsummer Festival, a bawdy celebration involving the ghost of a medieval
knight, a diabolical faerie ring—the exact definition of
which still eluded him—and a whirl of passion and revelry
he had no desire to participate in.

Why? he wondered, momentarily diverted. He had the
blood of his Latin ancestors in his veins, didn't he? He'd
been passionate enough once, and he was certainly no
stranger to lust—or any other basic urges for that matter. Of
course, he'd been much younger when he'd felt those
things—and hungry for a taste of the world.

Well, he'd had his taste and more, he reflected wearily,
willing the pounding that had started up in his temples to
subside. He missed his native Brazil, but beyond that the
pattern of his life was exactly as he wanted it. His world was
structured and well-ordered, unpredictable enough to hold
his interest, yet not so erratic that he lost his focus.

And not quite focused enough to win today's race, his
mind put in with a trace of self-derision. And for what? A
blown engine and an early train.

If he was honest, he'd admit the mechanical breakdown
had been a stroke of luck. Could he have held on to the win
with half his concentration tied up in another arena of
thought? Maybe, but he still resented the lapse. To be second best wasn't in his nature. To be distracted was unpro-
fessional. And to lose because he couldn't keep his mind
fixed on a simple objective was unthinkable. Above all else,
his goals, both personal and professional, meant a great deal
to him.

As much as a distant relative to whom he hadn't spoken
for close to three years? Jamming his hands into his jacket
pockets, he hunched his shoulders against the briny wind

that continued to whip up from the rocks below. Did those same goals mean as much as a striking dark-haired woman with the eyes of an enchantress, the face of a storybook heroine and the mind of a criminal?

He swore softly, the wind stealing the words from his mouth and flinging them back against the mansion's venerable stone walls.

A feeling he couldn't shake gnawed at him, threatened to consume him if he wasn't careful. A feeling with a name. Gabrielle. She was a Deep South beauty, and for all her adopted British reserve, American through and through.

Too outspoken, though, for his tastes. Go to hell, she'd told him and undoubtedly meant it. She'd also said she didn't take orders from anyone, although he suspected she'd probably been referring more specifically to anyone in her former profession.

Her convictions were her own business, but Adrian wasn't accustomed to dealing with such strong-willed women. He was sure he didn't want to.

Eyes closed, he pushed his misgivings aside and raised his face to the bunched black clouds overhead. The fog, like a curtain in some weird ghostly play, had begun to lift the farther Fergus McBrecken had driven them into the country. A heavily wooded section of the country that brought back strong memories of childhood and all the magical bedtime stories his mother and Uncle Emile had told him. Fantasies about dragons and dancing brooms, poison apples and beautiful maidens who slept for a hundred years.

There were faeries in one of those tales, he recalled, allowing himself a small smile. There were also faeries here in Morgate, and more specifically in the fabled forest between Brede Manor and Mandelin Castle. At least that's what the old legend claimed.

He hadn't caught the whole story, but he had heard Ivan Ragozcy mention the Midsummer Festival several times before they'd reached the manor. He'd also heard something about a good faerie and a bad one, a mortal named Sir Arundel and a veritable witch's cauldron of local lore and superstition. Maybe Rielle had picked up on the details.

He'd been too busy answering Reuben's questions about auto racing and his reasons for coming to Morgate to listen to Ragozcy's ghoulish ramblings.

Releasing a pent-up breath, Adrian rubbed the aching muscles in his neck and stared out over the jagged Yorkshire cliffs. Faeries, festivals—why in God's name was he here? Because a Phantom wanted for committing the Theater Murders might be, likely was, after Luke? Or could there be another reason for his coming, a simpler one that had nothing to do with curiosity or obligation or even a latent sense of fealty?

"Thanks for helping me ward off the vampire."

Rielle's voice reached him from the double balcony doors, cutting short Adrian's thoughts and pretty much answering his question. Damn, though, it wasn't the answer he wanted. She was only pretty, and he could find women like that anywhere.

Clamping down on a twist of emotion he knew better than to analyze, Adrian sent her a dispassionate look over his shoulder. "You seemed to be handling him just fine."

"I'm a good actress." She pushed herself from the narrow door frame, sidestepping a stone lion with a winged faerie on its back to join him at the edge of the terrace. "During my senior year I played Mina Harker in a Baton Rouge stage production of Bram Stoker's novel. Who knows? If I hadn't chosen to pursue other interests, I might have been another Sybil Fawkes, queen of the London stage and star of three Paulo Scholotti films. A multitalented shrew, that's what a number of her spurned lovers called her, though I suspect they were being polite for the press."

Adrian's impassive gaze touched briefly on Rielle's mouth before rising to meet her eyes. No matter where he looked, he was in trouble, his instincts and a hard knot of resistance in his stomach told him. He turned back to the turbulent sea. "Sybil Fawkes is dead," he stated unnecessarily. "Hers was the first of the Theater Murders."

Rielle glanced over her shoulder. Checking for eavesdroppers, Adrian assumed. She wouldn't find any. He wasn't so far removed from his youth that he'd forget something as basic as that.

"Killed by the Phantom, I know." Convinced that they were alone, Rielle wandered over to the stone lion and ran her fingers along the faerie's wings. "I've been looking around. I think the key Luke sent me might belong to one of the guest rooms. Unfortunately, this being a private home and not a hotel proper, none of them are numbered."

Adrian looked up at the four-story mansion, noting idly the tall pointed windows, steep roofs and discolored stone gables reminiscent of medieval lances. "We'll have to try as many locks as possible later tonight. Do you know if Fagan is expected back soon?"

"Gretchen Wolfe, his housekeeper, says he is, but I don't trust her. She reminds me of someone."

"Who?"

"I'm not sure."

A frown pulled at the corners of Rielle's mouth. Despite a strong caution from his brain, Adrian was tempted to reach out and run his thumb over her lower lip. Actually he was tempted to do much more than that, but his control kicked in as it always did, allowing him to calmly shrug the urge aside. "Maybe you have seen someone who looks like her on television."

"Or in the movies." She gnawed thoughtfully on the lip that Adrian still wanted to touch. "I don't think she's Fagan's regular housekeeper. As a matter of fact, I don't think Fagan's even met her."

A flash of movement in the shadows beyond the terrace doors alerted them both to a third person's presence. In a single deft motion Adrian grabbed Rielle's wrist, spinning her like a dancer and pulling her firmly back against his body.

She knew how to work a con; he'd give her that. No angry protest came from her throat. She didn't struggle or even go rigid in his arms. She simply rested her head on his shoulder and waited for the shadow to resolve itself into a human being.

"Pardon the intrusion," Gretchen Wolfe's gravelly voice announced from the doorway. "But dinner will be served at eight o'clock."

"Boris Karloff," Rielle said under her breath before stepping gracefully out of Adrian's embrace and turning to face the solidly built woman. "Thank you, Gretchen. Will Fagan be arriving in time to join us?"

"He's here already. Mr. Fagan and another guest."

"Noah Bishop?" Adrian asked, resting his shoulder on one of the scarred pillars.

"I believe so. I'm not good with names."

Rielle kept her expression pleasant. "Have you worked here long, Gretchen?"

"Six days, miss," the housekeeper replied stonily, folding her large, square-shaped hands in front of her. "Mr. Fagan's permanent housekeeper was called away early last week on a family emergency. Before she left, she arranged for me to take her place. Will there be anything else?"

Rielle shook her head, and with a stiffly polite nod, Gretchen moved off.

She did look like Boris Karloff in one of his more sinister roles, Adrian thought. Solemn, daunting and as tall as he was in flat shoes.

"I've seen friendlier mannequins," Rielle noted, returning to the stone wall that rimmed the terrace. She studied his features consideringly. "Have you ever met Fagan?"

Adrian shrugged. "Once, many years ago in Brazil. He won't recognize me now."

"Have you changed that much?"

"I was fifteen, with bare feet, torn jeans, hair down to my shoulders and a head full of get-rich-quick schemes."

"Something must have worked for you. You got rich."

"Not by picking pockets."

She sent him a surprised look. "You were a pickpocket?"

"I was many things, Rielle," he murmured, squinting at the pounding waves. "A thief is a thief."

"Thanks," she muttered in a sarcastic undertone. "I was wondering when I'd have time to feel guilty today."

"We are guilty."

She stared at him in exasperation. "Of conning people, not killing them. What are you doing, vying for sainthood or something? Because if you are, you're selling it to the wrong person. I know how much money you make racing cars, and I'm also well acquainted with the clever little tricks you people use to avoid paying the kinds of taxes certain governments think you should. Don't talk to me about guilt, Adrian Da Costa. We're all censurable one way or another." Her lips curved into a guileless smile. "Even Amelia."

He arched a dark brow, undisturbed by her candor that contained no real bite. If anything it added to the appeal. "Who is Amelia?"

"Sir Arundel's faerie lover." Rielle motioned toward Mandelin Castle and the four decrepit turrets visible above the forest treetops. "Sir Arundel was a knight in the noblest sense of the word. Early one evening as he was returning home, he found a fire pony caught in a patch of nettle and saw a small band of nymphs desperately trying to set it free. They told him the winged pony belonged to the faerie queen, Amelia, and that he must be released before the moon came full and Amelia's counterpart, Odessa, arose. Odessa was a Metamorph, able to change form at will. Apparently her treachery knew no bounds. She was known as much for her ability to transform herself as she was for her evil nature."

"Amelia was not the evil faerie?"

"No, she was the good one. Of course, she wasn't perfect."

Adrian hid a smile. "Are you trying to make a point with this story?"

"Yes." She eyed him closely. "Am I succeeding?"

He started to move a shoulder, then stopped and slid his gaze to the cracked stone ledge directly above Rielle's head. Had he glimpsed something up there? A shadow? A tiny flicker of movement?

His eyes told him no, an answer the shifting clouds seemed to confirm. Giving himself a shake, he pulled his gaze away. His instincts, so finely honed on the racetrack, had begun to play tricks on him. Not a good way to stay healthy, he decided, a slight frown invading his features.

Running a hand around the back of his neck, he glanced upward once again—and almost choked at what he saw. That was no cloud-shadow perched precariously on the edge of the crumbling sill. It was a marble statue, a carving of a black-robed faerie whose bloodred eyes for a brief moment seemed to glare at him . . .

. . . As it plunged directly down toward Rielle's head.

Chapter Five

One minute she was standing, the next she was flying across the terrace, too startled to really know why. She landed on her back, more or less, with only a distant awareness of the hands that kept her head from slamming into the stone wall and the sound of something hard smashing against the cobbles, shattering into a thousand pieces.

Had she seen a pair of red eyes? The picture seemed locked in her mind, but it made no sense. The eyes staring down at her were brown. Beautiful. Sexy. She must have hit her head after all.

"Are you hurt, Rielle?"

She squinted through dust and dusk and sea mist, then realized with a start that she wasn't breathing. Not entirely surprising. She felt as though someone had punched her in the small of her back, knocking the air from her lungs.

She took a tentative breath. It hurt, but only a little. "I don't think so," she managed to croak. She stared up at Adrian's slender face. He looked different up close, more sensual, not older exactly, although there were lines bracketing his mouth, fanning out from the corners of his eyes when he smiled. So why didn't he smile more often?

She felt his breath on her skin and forced herself to remember where she was. "What happened?" she asked uncertainly.

"One of the statues fell." Adrian's lips moved against her cheek as he levered them both to a sitting position. "Or was pushed."

Rielle knew she should be shocked, but she wasn't. She glanced at her scraped knees, wondering absently how she'd done that. Then reluctantly she let her gaze shift to the broken black statue.

Odessa, the evil faerie. A Metamorph whose eyes remained red no matter what form she took. A bloodthirsty killer in her own mythical world. Had she been pushed from the ledge by a greater evil? A Phantom?

No, not possible. Even dazed, Rielle refused to believe that. She felt Adrian's strong hands helping her to her feet and allowed herself another brief look at him. Why did she want so badly to fall against him? To see if she could coax a smile from him. Maybe even to explore that fascinating mouth of his with her fingertips.

She shoved the thoughts away with uncustomary frustration. Now was not the time for fantasies, and besides, he wasn't her type. Not to mention that she'd almost been killed. Maybe they both had.

"Are you sure nothing is broken?" Adrian asked, and she smiled to herself.

Only the strange spell he cast, she thought sadly, shaking her head. "My pride," she admitted. "Nothing else." She lifted her gaze to the cracked second-floor ledge twenty feet above them. "Is that where it fell from?"

He nodded, his eyes narrowing as something stirred in the spreading gloom. A figure at the balcony doors, stepping out of the unlit corridor onto the terrace.

"Ragozcy," Rielle muttered under her breath, and didn't mind at all that Adrian's warm, lean body was pressed against her from behind. "Good evening, Ivan," she said in a louder voice.

Did he give a surprised start? She couldn't tell with all the shadows out here. It seemed—though surely it had to be her imagination—that those shadows clung to him as he approached.

"I thought I heard something fall," he said softly, indicating the shattered statue. "My room is directly above this terrace. These old buildings can be most unpredictable. Mr. Fagan must be told, of course." Ragozcy's black eyes impaled Rielle. "I trust you are all right, little one."

At five foot eight, Rielle hardly considered herself to be little, but she let the remark pass as Adrian returned the man's stare. "It could have been worse," he said. "We will talk to Fagan at dinner." He paused, arching a dark brow. "Which room is yours?"

"I am on the third floor," Ivan told them, his silky red lips drawing back into a knowing smile. "Since you are both unharmed, perhaps you will join me in the sitting room for a glass of wine. The other guests have not come downstairs as yet."

Rielle masked a grimace. Red wine, no doubt, and a conversation with a vampire. This was very bizarre. Thank God for Adrian Da Costa.

And that, she realized in mild astonishment, was the strangest thought of all.

IT WAS DARK in the underground Moroccan café. The man with the shaggy brown hair, flat brown eyes, red fez and black mendicant robe shuffled across the smoky room with great care, and a prayer on his lips that he wouldn't trip over the lolling dogs that were stretched out on the floor at their masters' thonged feet.

The hiss of hookah pipes reached his ears along with the tink of tiny finger cymbals that struck the oddest note of familiarity in his mind. No one appeared to be looking at him, which was good, but then he couldn't see much more than three feet in front of his face. The tinted contact lenses weren't helping one bit. Someone else's prescription; of course he'd be half-blind in them. But blue eyes were a rarity in places like this.

The smoke grew thicker, but Luke persevered, plodding across the chipped floor, through a beaded doorway and over to the first empty table he could find. Whiny snatches of music penetrated the din. God, what he wouldn't give to hear Donovan's "Epistle to Dippy" right now. What he wouldn't give for a pint of good stout ale and a cigarette, a smoke that didn't have to be sucked through water into a hose.

Shaking his head in rueful acceptance, he peered through his mop of dyed hair. Still no one watching him, at least not openly. What did that prove? The Phantom was as subtle as he was masterful at disguising himself. How had he looked the last time Luke had seen him? Gray hair and a beard. Black eyes. Distinguished and articulate, but how old? In his thirties? His sixties? And what was his real name?

Luke had known him as Gustav, which meant absolutely nothing. This Phantom had as many names as he did faces. Maybe he even used the real name and face on occasion— who knew? He was a fox, a con artist, a killer. He was also a raving lunatic. And he was after Luke.

Actually he was after what Luke had stolen from him, but it would be all the same in the end. Find the proof, then kill the thief who'd taken it and run. He'd already murdered Paul; that was old news by now. Even the Cockney clip artists had heard the tale. But thankfully none of those hungry grifters knew where to find Paul's partner.

That didn't mean the Phantom wouldn't catch up with him, Luke realized, lifting the cloudy amber drink that had been plunked down in front of him and taking a tentative sip. No poison. So far so good.

He relaxed a little, watching the smoke curl in great lazy circles about his head. Yes, the Phantom could still catch him, but that wouldn't help him retrieve his lost proof. The proof was safely out of reach of Phantom fingers. Luke had mailed the key to Rielle earlier in the week, and if there was one person in the world he trusted it was Gabi.

His insatiably curious Gabi...

He hesitated, then brushed the thought aside. No, she wouldn't do that. She'd never go traipsing off blindly to Brede Manor. As far as Luke was aware, she'd never even heard of the place. His active association with Fagan had ended long before he'd met her. In fact, the only person other than Paul who might conceivably make the connection was Luke's cousin, Adrian Da Costa, and he was probably off celebrating a victory in the German Grand Prix right now.

Again Luke shoved the uneasy thought aside and took another sip of his diluted drink. No point worrying over such things. What were the odds of Rielle and Adrian hooking up? Might be interesting, though, he reflected in absent amusement.

Sobering memories of Paul and Brede Manor and the Phantom crowded in on him. Bad mistake to let a stranger talk him into working a con on the late Mrs. Charity Green. Paul had died because of that mistake.

Had he talked first, Luke wondered? Could be, though it shouldn't matter. Paul had known their rendezvous point, not where the proof was hidden. While the two were synonymous, there was little chance that anyone else would realize that.

Luke finished his drink slowly, sweating under his beggar's robe. He would stay in Morocco for a few more hours, then he'd have to move on. Eventually he'd risk phoning Rielle, but that could wait. The Phantom didn't know about her, and even if he were to make the unlikely link, he'd have no reason to go after her.

A shudder passed through Luke's body. What a mess he'd made of things.

Please, God, he prayed, let Rielle and that key be safe.

"IT'S THE SOLSTICE," Percy Fagan explained. "Midsummer magic." He waved a hand toward the terrace. "Either that, or Odessa's statue was too far out on the ledge. I am sorry, though, Rielle. It wasn't much of a welcome to my home." He crossed the carpeted sitting-room floor like a weasel on the lookout for a fox. Quick, slippery movements, eyes combing every shadow, wiry muscles taut, reflexes fit for a man half his age.

So this was Luke's mentor, Rielle mused, this agile sixty-year-old character with the wispy pointed beard, thin lined face and sparkly blue eyes. He was the epitome of a Dickens character right down to his droopy black suit and half-fingered gloves. A deliberate resemblance, she suspected. Obvious but effective.

"Ah, the solstice," Fagan exclaimed again, spreading his nimble fingers. "So many things we can't explain happen at this time of year." He slanted his guests a sly look. "The Druids were big on this, you know. All things earthly fascinated them. Used a lot of oak trees in their rituals."

"Sacrificed a few people to honor them, if I'm not mistaken," Reuben added, lighting his pipe. He glanced at his bored-looking son beside him. "You could write yourself a good script up here, Noah. Blood's still big at the London box office."

Noah's only response was a shrug as he drained his third glass of port and avoided Ava's devouring eyes. He was beyond handsome, really—blue eyed, fine featured and slender, an inch or two taller than Adrian, but with the same dark, curling hair. There was something else, though, Rielle realized, studying him covertly. Something about his thin-lipped mouth that struck her as faintly cruel. Of course that was hardly a fair judgment to make, but the look was there, a minor flaw in an otherwise outstanding face.

She shifted her gaze to Adrian, lounging in a wing chair by the hearth. His dark head was slightly bent, his deep brown eyes intent on his own glass of port. He hadn't spoken much during dinner, responding only when he was questioned directly. With the possible exception of Ava and Ivan, everyone present seemed to recognize him, both by face and by name.

He didn't want to be here, she thought with an irrational twinge of annoyance that vanished the instant he lifted his head to stare at her. Cool eyes, unreadable, with an underlying fire she couldn't begin to understand. Did he care about Luke? About anyone? She pulled up short. No, she wouldn't do this. What did she know of his upbringing in Brazil? Not enough to question his motives, or his values.

"I hear there are a number of Gypsies camped out on your grounds, Mr. Fagan," Noah remarked, already halfway through his fourth glass of port. "Do you think that's wise?"

Fagan's smile was positively wicked. "Wiser than it would be to turn them away."

"Itinerant thieves," Ava stated flatly with a disdainful flick of her bangs. "I saw a group of them begging apples at the kitchen door."

"Better begging than stealing," Reuben pointed out. His lips twitched as Jonathan, blond hair slicked back from his angular face, limped over to the embroidered sofa and sat down beside Ava. She ignored him as studiously as Noah ignored her.

Mind games, very intriguing but not the kind Rielle wanted to play that night. With Fagan and his guests gathered down here in the sitting room, now would be a perfect time to sneak away and try the key Luke had sent her in a few locks. If she could sneak away.

"Full-blooded," Ivan was saying, his whispery voice bordering on passionate. "These Gypsies will know how to celebrate your Midsummer Festival, Mr. Fagan. Such a lust for life they possess. Such rich blood."

He had a weird fixation with that word, Rielle decided. And an even more disturbing fascination with her throat. She fingered the black turtleneck of her cashmere dress and saw the immediate spark of humor that passed through Adrian's eyes. If nothing else, she could amuse him. Holding back a sigh, she stood smoothly.

"If you'll excuse me," she said, sending Adrian a deliberately provocative smile, "I think I'll take a walk around the grounds."

"Brave girl," Ava drawled. She stretched out like a contented cat on the sofa, still ignoring Jonathan. "I wouldn't leave this lovely fire for anything, certainly not for a chance run-in with a sweaty Gypsy." She shuddered. "What a vulgar thought. Must you let them stay, Fagan?"

"Color, Ava," Fagan said. "They have panache and spirit and a sense of the solstice no other group can match. They adore to dance, to make music. The untamed airs they call the faerie songs. They are the essence of the Festival, as you will soon discover." His sigh was one of pure delight. "It's all so pagan, a feast for the soul. You can almost taste the passion. Gypsy flash and fire, faerie lore, banquets like nothing you've ever seen—you'll be enchanted, all of you. You could do nothing less.''

"Exactly when does all this enchantment begin?" Noah asked, his tone sour.

Fagan regarded the glimmer of distant campfires, visible as a deep orange glow against the night sky. "This will be your only evening of true peace and quiet," he said, seeming to relish the thought. "Best relax and prepare yourselves for the coming festivities. I think perhaps a movie might be in order. Something fantastical . . ."

With Adrian close behind her, Rielle exited the sitting room. The key Luke had sent her was similar to her room key, which made the general starting point for their search an obvious one.

"We should try Ragozcy's lock first," she said in a low voice, and in the dim entryway light saw Adrian's lips twitch slightly.

"I think you read too many vampire stories, Rielle."

She didn't deny it. Instead, she led the way up a wide staircase to the second floor.

Dark, polished wood gleamed in the golden light of a dozen wall sconces. There were tapestries everywhere, rich with color and texture, as well as several ornately framed portraits of kings and medieval courts, Druid feasts and soft elysian dreamscapes. The carpets were Persian, the fixtures marble and brass, the chandeliers Italian crystal. To say these things must have cost a fortune would have been a profound understatement. So how, Rielle wondered, had an allegedly reformed crook came up with such a vast sum of money?

"Probably the way you would expect." Adrian replied when she put the question to him.

"Not legitimately?"

"Not likely." His long, fluid stride carried him down a hallway brightened only by a few electric lamps. "In fact, I am not even certain that he is retired. Luke might know."

"Did Fagan recognize you?" she asked as they reached the first locked door.

After making certain they were alone, Adrian took the key she handed him and inserted it. "I doubt it. If he recognizes my name, it is likely because he has heard it more recently in connection with my racing career."

The key proved ineffective, and they moved on. "You don't like this, do you?" she questioned softly, leaning against the wall and watching him with thoughtful eyes. "All the recognition, the interviews, the intrusions into your private life?"

He shrugged and tried one of the storage closets to no avail. "I am used to it."

"That's not an answer, Adrian."

He raised his head to look at her. God, but there was something about him when he did that, brought those dark eyes into focus on her face. She wanted to reach out and push the hair from his forehead, to run her fingers across his cheekbones and jaw, down his neck to his shoulders. His wasn't a broad build in any way, but then she'd never really been attracted to brawn. Come to think of it, she'd never felt this kind of attraction to any man. Now that was a disturbing thought.

"I do not like intrusions into my private life," he said calmly, and for a moment Rielle had the uneasy feeling that he was reading her mind, responding to what he saw there. But no, he had to be answering her earlier question. She still knew a thing or two about masks.

She remembered to check the hall for eavesdroppers. It appeared clear, and she wandered to the next door. Noah's, if she wasn't mistaken. "Were you ever a con artist?" she asked. A brazen question, considering what he'd just said, but that was her nature; she'd given up trying to change it a long time ago.

He didn't seem upset, massaging a muscle in the back of his neck as they moved from Noah's room to Ava's. "In a way, I was. But it is different in Brazil than in Europe or the United States. We do not like to steal from our own. So I would wait and set up the wealthy *turistas*. Carnival was the best time. People relax, become careless, often drunk. I was small as a child, very slight, and such children elicit sympathy. I would watch these people, let them see me, learn their habits. Sometimes I would intercept them as they came out of the hotel elevators and offer to take their room key to the desk.''

"They let you do that?'' Rielle was amazed. "How delightful.''

He smiled a bit. "They would watch, but yes, they let me do it. For pocket change. I would turn in a key, not theirs, to the front desk, and they would smile and leave. Then I would go up to their room and clean it out.''

"Sweet child.'' Rielle studied his implacable features. Still no visible sign of emotion. "Ambitious anyway. Tell me, did you ever get caught?''

He shook his head. "I was very fast.''

"And very thorough, I'll bet.''

"That too,'' he agreed, trying another door, again without success.

As they worked their way slowly down the long hall and finally up to the third floor, Rielle did her best not to stare. It shouldn't have been difficult, yet for some reason it was. Impossible, really. Why? Because she kept seeing a grubby-faced urchin with soulful brown eyes and a mop of dark, curling hair in her mind's eye? She grinned to herself. What a sucker she would have been for his little scam.

"Have you thought about what this key might lead to?'' Adrian inquired, bringing her swiftly back to reality.

She nodded, checking the hall once more. "Some. I know it won't lead us to Luke, so the only other answer I can come up with is that it will take us to the proof he told me about in my apartment.'' She paused. *Be all right, Luke,* she prayed, then collected herself. "He said that he and Paul were planning to meet somewhere. So Luke must have come to Brede Manor when they first split up, hid the proof and left again, intending to stay out of sight until it was time for their rendezvous.''

"Which might also have been set up to take place here, if in fact this is where Luke hid his proof.''

"It's possible,'' Rielle conceded, rubbing her arms to ward off the sudden chill that crawled over her skin. Her gaze roamed the empty hallway. "Whatever the case, I only hope Paul didn't mention the name Brede Manor to the Phantom before he died. I'm still not convinced that statue of Odessa wasn't pushed from the ledge." By Ragozcy, she was tempted to add but didn't. She'd had her fill of vampires for one day.

Beneath Adrian's deft hands, she heard a muffled click, the sound of a lock springing open. Not Ragozcy's room, she realized, straightening in anticipation from the wall. She'd memorized the guest quarters earlier. His was farther down and on the other side of the corridor.

She glanced in that direction, past a brutal-looking display of medieval weaponry to the shadows that strangely enough seemed thicker on the third floor. She heard the sea in the background, a great roar of water—and then beneath it something else. A sound that was closer, stealthier. Something...

Without warning, Adrian's hand came down over her mouth. He gave her no chance to react or even catch her breath, but pulled her through the door he'd just opened and into a pitch-black room.

She heard it a second later, above the rapid beat of her heart and the sound of Adrian's breath in her ear. A tiny groan, barely audible, followed by a creak of hard leather.

Someone's shoes! But was the person in them coming or going? And how much if anything might he or she have overheard?

Adrian left the door open a crack, just enough for Rielle to see out into the corridor. What she saw brought a chill to her skin, a soundless gasp to her lips.

The housekeeper Gretchen Wolfe was walking silently along the carpeted hall. Thin lipped. Grim faced. And carrying a huge medieval mace in her broad, capable hands!

Chapter Six

She stopped in the middle of the hallway, her gray eyes cold and unblinking, her fingers tight about the spiked club. She was listening, Adrian knew, possibly considering her next move.

The seconds ticked by with no one making a sound. Sea and silence clashed forces. The shadows appeared to deepen. Rielle shifted against him but didn't struggle to get away. Adrian kept his arm around her waist, his hand over her mouth and tried to ignore the feel of her slender body in his arms, the scent of Eternity perfume that clung to her skin, the silky texture of the hair that brushed across his cheek.

With Gretchen Wolfe standing less than fifteen feet away, armed for medieval combat, it should have been a simple enough task. That it wasn't, while it came as no great shock, still had the power to annoy him. Or would have if the housekeeper hadn't suddenly turned those steely eyes of hers in their direction.

Rielle stiffened, pressing herself back into him. He felt the tension that thrummed through her, through him. Gretchen had drawn to within ten feet of them, raising the mace as she came. Her lips were a colorless slash; her sensible black shoes made no sound at all on the carpet.

Adrian drew Rielle deeper into the blackened room. He could no longer see the housekeeper, only the shadow she cast on the wall and floor. Arms reaching, fingers curled like thick claws around the mace, lifting it higher and higher. Until . . .

Something clicked beyond them. He heard a muffled bump, saw the shadow shift. More soft thuds, another click and then—nothing. Only a heavy silence that seemed to enfold them like a funeral shroud.

Rielle held herself perfectly still in his arms. He felt the uncertainty that pulled at her, the tendrils of fear. What was Gretchen doing with that damned mace? he wondered, his head ready to explode from the slamming in his temples.

The answer came clear in a creak of hard leather shoes and a shadow that slowly began to fade. And in Rielle's relieved whisper. "She hung the mace in the display case with the rest of the weapons. She's leaving." Her head dropped back onto Adrian's shoulder, her body collapsing into his. "Thank God."

Adrian closed his eyes and forced his tightly strung muscles to relax, ignoring the bands of pain that compressed about his skull. He allowed Rielle to step away with nothing more than a glimmer of disappointment. Evidence of his growing misery, to let her go and not even care.

They should have done this tomorrow. It might have mattered then. Right now all he cared about was falling facedown on the nearest bed, letting his unconscious mind work on the pressure inside his head.

The door closed with a soft click in front of him, and he opened his eyes wearily to a lighted room. Thick damask curtains in deep artists' tones hung at the windows. There were oil paintings of the Roman Fountains at Bath and others of bacchanalian delight, a hand-painted carpet from the Orient and the strong scent of lavender wax in the air. Much like his own room actually, though this one clearly had no occupant. Yet. He moved toward the window and the campfires beyond, aware that Rielle was watching him yet disinclined to meet her assessing gaze.

"You look awful," she said, leaning against the heavy door.

He shrugged, uninterested in sympathy. "I have a headache. It is not a problem." He turned away and began prowling through the room. Unoccupied from all outward appearances. Clean, a little stuffy and equipped with a huge four-poster bed.

"You're starting to look like the rest of the guests."

He tested the mattress with his hand. "Vampiric?"

"Pale, anyway." She left the door and wrapped her fingers around his arm, tugging gently. "Why don't you sit down for a minute?"

"Because I would prefer to get this search over with and go to my own bed."

Her response was genial but firm. "Tough, amigo. Either you sit down, or I'm going to phone all your favorite press people and tell them what a hustle artist little Adrian Da Costa really was."

A hollow threat, but he let her push him onto the bed anyway, tipping his head back and massaging the cramped muscles in the back of his neck. It didn't help.

She hesitated, then sat down next to him and pushed his hand aside, replacing it with her own surprisingly deft fingers. "Does this happen after every race, or is Brede Manor getting to you?"

"Midsummer magic." He repeated Fagan's words, moving a stiff shoulder and letting his head drop forward as she worked the worst of the tension from his abused neck muscles. "It is the race. The G-forces are very strong now, very difficult. Not so much at the track we were on today, but there is a problem even on some of those corners."

"Why do you do it?" she asked, and again he shrugged.

"I like to race."

"Not for the money?"

His mouth curved into a slow smile. "The money is good, but unimportant now, Rielle. I have no expensive toys, no costly habits to support." No family, he was tempted to add, but such a comment might bring questions about the brothers and sisters he'd lost more than twenty years ago, and that was something he wasn't prepared to discuss. They were, for the most part, happy. He'd paid dearly to learn that. They knew who and what he was; he'd even spoken to them on occasion. But twenty years was a very long time, and time and distance, he'd discovered, were often stronger than blood ties.

He felt her push his hair away. The cool air touched his skin, making him wince. How could air hurt? He kept his eyes closed and tried to think, but even that was difficult. And probably not worth the effort. Maybe he should give in, go with his feelings for once.

A cynical spark of amusement passed through him at that thought. Yes, he had feelings, but no, he was not yet ready to go with them, to show them to anyone. Not even to this woman with her wonderful fingers and glorious eyes. He could want her without wanting to share any part of his emotional self with her.

"You might try relaxing a little," she suggested, and her breath shimmered across his skin with a warmth that definitely didn't hurt. He had to admit, though, there was a certain element of discomfort in the desire that washed through him. Yes, he could want her.

He swallowed a groan, keeping his features calm, unrevealing. "I think this is not the best place for either of us to relax," he said, lifting his head a fraction but still tempted to topple back into her. "We should be searching the room while we have the chance."

She pressed her thumbs firmly into one knotted muscle at the nape of his neck. "Are you always this practical, Adrian?" she inquired, and he shuddered as her fingers slid around his throat. So gentle, her touch. So soothing. But then he let so very few people touch him these days.

"Not always," he replied, lulled by the drowsiness that swept through his body. It felt good. "In this case, however, I think it is wise to be practical. We still do not know what or who we are dealing with."

"Tell me about it." Sighing, she combed his hair back in place with her fingers. Absently, he suspected, and found himself wanting to believe otherwise. "We got lucky with Gretchen. But I don't suppose that really means much, does it?"

No answer expected. Adrian straightened his shoulders, both relieved and disappointed that she no longer touched him. He pressed down on a nerve above his collarbone and averted his head to look at her, offering a faint smile of thanks for her efforts. She was still so close, so tempting to him. Surely a sign of some sort, though he was in no shape to figure out what.

She gave his hair one final stroke with her fingers, then rose with a reluctance he might or might not have been imagining. "There isn't much here," she said doubtfully, strolling over to the painting of Bacchus. "Of course, it doesn't help that we have no idea what we're looking for." She wandered toward the entertainment center each room boasted and began poking around behind the television and VCR. "I only hope that whatever this proof of Luke's is—if it is in fact hidden in this room—it isn't something we can destroy simply by touching it. What if it's a silver cigarette lighter with a fingerprint on it?"

"A fingerprint would prove nothing, Rielle. The Phantom would know this." Adrian left the bed to flip through a stack of outdated newspapers and magazines. Only five victims for the notorious Theater Murderer in these articles. That made them more than six months old, and likely useless in terms of information. He moved on to the bookshelves while Rielle attacked the closet. Dickens, Chaucer, the Brontë sisters and one Shakespearean play: *A Midsummer Night's Dream,* printed in 1865. Interesting but insignificant. Or if it was, he didn't see it.

He searched the nightstand and dresser, then joined Rielle, who was now going through the compact discs and videocassettes Fagan provided for each of his guests. "All the classics from Bach to Wagner," she told him of the CDs. "And movies ranging from *Abbott and Costello Meet Frankenstein* to *The Yearling.* All alphabetically arranged except for these three—*Dr. Jekyll and Mr. Hyde,* Hitchcock's *Dial M for Murder* and Paulo Scholotti's cult classic *Marionette.*" She indicated the out-of-order items and the streamlined VCR with an unconcerned wave. "This is really discouraging, Adrian. There isn't even anything stuffed inside the machine. No envelopes taped to the bottom of anything that I can see. Nothing under the bed or rolled up in the window shades. And all I found in the closet were two feather pillows, an extra quilt and three boxed parlor games. From all outward appearances, this is a fruitless undertaking. It doesn't tell us where to find Luke, or whether or not the Phantom might have found him first."

"In other words there is no point searching any more tonight," Adrian translated. He glanced out the windows. The Gypsy campfires were dwindling in number. Eleven o'clock, his watch informed him.

He reached for Rielle's hand. "Let's go," he said. "The other guests will come soon. They should not see us prowling around the third floor."

"Might not be a good idea," she agreed, then stopped and frowned, her gaze riveted to the carpet beneath his feet. "What's that?"

He looked down. "What is what?"

Bending, she scooped something up. "It's a button," she exclaimed. "A tortoiseshell button."

He raised a questioning brow, and she clenched her fist, a gleam of hope lighting her eyes.

"Luke had buttons like this on his raincoat," she stated with certainty. "Five on and one missing. I remember noticing that."

"You notice unusual things."

"I'm a fashion designer. I pay attention to clothes—probably the way a Grand Prix driver does with cars." He conceded the point with a slow smile, and she went on. "Luke was here, Adrian, in this room, I'm sure of it. And so is his proof."

The conviction in her voice was most appealing, Adrian decided, raking his fingers through his hair. He tried not to wince. Maybe when his head didn't feel like it was going to blow up, he would have to discover just how many other things about her might also appeal to him.

He caught himself quickly, before the idea could get out of hand, dragging his thoughts back to the ruthless reality he'd come to prefer in his life. Fighting a wave of blackness that threatened to overcome him, he avoided her eyes, focusing on the button instead and nodding. "I think Luke's proof is here," he said, "although we might not know it even if we came face-to-face with it."

She shivered, and her hand suddenly felt quite cold in his. "That's not the only thing we won't know." She succeeded in capturing his elusive gaze. "What if Paul did know something, Adrian? What if he said something to the Phantom?"

"In that case," Adrian said in his most prosaic tones, "we had better hope he does not know of our connection to Luke, or we might both end up as Paul did." He ran his knuckles lightly across the skin of her throat, his eyes now staring deeply into hers. She needed to hear the words. "Dead, Rielle. Murdered by a man who is perhaps as brilliant as he is mad."

THE PHANTOM'S FINGERS crawled slowly up the wall. He watched them in fascination, while the silky soft whispers droned on in his head.

Tedious business, this eavesdropping, but worthwhile. Too bad the whispers couldn't do it for him, but of course that was impossible. Whispers didn't have ears.

A smile played on his red mouth. His fingers continued to creep up the wall. Fools. They'd thought they were alone outside Rielle's room. Unobserved, saying goodnight, talking in muted tones. From his hiding spot he'd managed to catch a few significant words. Enough to understand that Rielle and Adrian were Luke Prentice's friends. A most interesting discovery. Maybe they could be used to lure Luke out of hiding.

Yes, but what were they doing at Brede Manor? the Phantom wondered, and in his mind the whispers that had been with him since early that evening took on a smug air, startling him as they often did when they changed tone.

"Dear Phantom," the layered voices chided, louder now that they had his undivided attention. "They're looking for Luke. What other reason could there possibly be for their presence here? They cannot know about that which Luke has stolen. No, such a thing is extremely unlikely. They've come here to find their friend, nothing more."

The Phantom considered the idea, accepting it finally because he really didn't care. Unless Rielle was really Sybil come back in a new form. Now, there was something he hadn't considered before. Another thought to torment him. And there was that other woman, too; he mustn't forget her. She wasn't pretty like Rielle, but Sybil could be uncommonly sneaky with her disguises.

"No! Listen to me," the whispers ordered sharply, breaking up that thought quickly enough. "This is not about Sybil. This is about Luke and now these other two who have come to find him." The words slid out in a cool evil hiss that ended on a cruel note of laughter. "Maybe, though," the musing continued, "we will let them find a Phantom instead."

"SHE IS EVIL, this Odessa. A Metamorph. A bloodsucking faerie, kin to the Glaistig, who are each part woman part goat." A female voice floated upward to Rielle's bedroom, catching her attention. "Ah, but Odessa is so much stronger," the voice continued, "so much more devious. Eyes of deepest red, soul of a hell-born demon, she is a creature of the night, of the moon. Her eyes betray her form, but only the light of the sun can truly destroy her. 'Come, dance with me,' she whispers to the men who are her victims. And when they do, she feeds upon their life's blood. The fatal seduction. Once lured into her faerie ring, there is no escape."

A black-haired Gypsy dressed in a fringed shawl, spice-toned skirt and braided headband stood at the rear of the manor house, just outside the kitchen door, her dark eyes challenging as she worked her own brand of magic on a highly receptive Percy Fagan.

Rielle was already perched on her open windowsill, enjoying the fresh sea air. She discovered that if she was very careful, she could lean out just far enough to see Luke's shifty mentor.

She looked at him now, her fingers curling about the stone ledge. Strange. Why would Fagan be dumping two loaves of bread, a gallon jug of milk and a dozen red-cheeked apples into the Gypsy's empty burlap bag? And what was the Gypsy handing him in return? A soft cloth pouch of some sort, but what could possibly be in it that Fagan would want?

"My band champions Odessa at the festival," the Gypsy announced in a prideful tone. "The evil is more intriguing to us. Provocative in its magic. Always the Metamorph will triumph. She will choose her dark disguise, and that is the form she will take. Only her eyes will give her away. But this does not matter. The solstice will come, and Odessa will once again thwart the plans of Amelia and her mortal lover, the good Sir Arundel."

Fagan's smile was artful, giving nothing away. "A fascinating tale, I agree, my dear." He tucked the pouch inside his baggy jacket, then waggled his half-gloved fingers at the woman. "Now, you'd best be gone before my guests wake up and see us bartering our wares. Some of them might not approve, and disapproval is bad for business."

"As you wish." The Gypsy's brightly painted lips parted consideringly. "I warn you, though, friend Fagan, be careful that you do not misuse the magic I have given you. Perhaps you will not like the results."

Fagan merely continued to wag his fingers at her, and with a swish of her skirt the woman whirled around, vanishing, burlap bag and all, into the early-morning mist. Below her Rielle heard the kitchen door click shut, leaned out a little farther, then had to smother a gasp as she almost tumbled onto the lawn two floors below.

Her curiosity would get her killed one of these days, she thought shakily, sliding from the sill and shedding her white terry bathrobe.

She gave her damp hair a shake as well as her mind, reaching absently for a pair of old Levi's jeans and a pale yellow T-shirt. *Don't misuse the magic I've given you,* the Gypsy had said. Rielle tugged on the jeans. Cheap magic to be paid off in bread and apples. But cheap didn't necessarily mean harmless. And according to Adrian, Fagan was no stranger to subterfuge. Who knew what the old fox might be up to.

She pulled the faded shirt over her head and considered waking Adrian. Her eyes landed on the old-fashioned alarm clock by her bed. 6:30 a.m. He'd be dead to the world for another two hours because of the prescription painkillers he'd taken.

Relief ran through her. There was something so disturbing about that man. Or maybe it was her reaction to him that bothered her. She kept wanting to touch him. His hair, his face, his skin. Kept wondering what it would be like to kiss him, to have his mouth on hers, his hands on her body.

It was more than that, though. She felt the most curious surge of emotion when she was near him. Sensations that were foreign to her, or had always seemed so in the past.

A hint of vulnerability—that's all she ever really saw in him, and she'd managed to glimpse just enough of it to be drawn closer. And that's when she got lost, when things no longer made sense.

She did want to touch him, quite badly at times. Last night, for instance, she'd touched then found herself wanting to take him in her arms and hold him, to be that one person he would allow himself to trust. Silly fantasy, she knew. And definitely not a comfortable point to linger on.

Jaw set, she turned to look at a reflection in the mirror that stared back at her in complete bewilderment.

With determination she combed her fingers through her hair in an attempt to untangle both it and her thoughts. It worked to a degree. But she was still sorely tempted to slip across the hall to Adrian's room and... to catch him all sleepy eyed and sexy and underclothed, with his dark curls rumpled and his guard down.

She didn't dwell on it. Instead, she concentrated on her reflection, braiding her long hair and telling herself that she'd crawled out of bed at this early hour for a specific purpose. Luke.

The proof he'd spoken of had to be in that room. It followed, therefore, that he wouldn't want anyone else staying there. Indeed, he would have taken steps to prevent such a thing.

So, reasonably, all she had to do now was get her hands on Fagan's reservations list. If she was right, if Luke was in fact holding the room for himself, that would pretty much bear out her conviction that his proof was hidden there. Maybe Adrian was even correct in his theory that Luke and Paul had planned to meet here at Brede Manor.

What a nasty batch of images that conjured up. Rielle hunched her shoulders. Terrifying to think the Phantom might have learned of that meeting, that he might be sleeping just down the hall from her, eating from the same china, sipping the same aged port.

Fear crawled over her, but she wouldn't give in to it. Spine stiff, she took a deep breath, exhaling slowly, then stopped and frowned as a tiny thread of sound reached her ears. Music. Faint, but definitely there. And extremely familiar. A soft rock beat, floating in not from the corridor but through the window on the morning mist, so softly she thought she might be imagining it.

But no, it was a man's voice all right. Donovan Leitch, mystical hippie folk rocker from the late sixties. And the song was "Mellow Yellow," Luke's favorite.

Brows still knit, she ran to the window, poking her head out and trying to locate the source of the song. It seemed to be coming from a stand of shrubs beyond the garden wall.

Luke's name was on the tip of her tongue. She managed to keep it from slipping out. A feeling of optimism took hold of her. Maybe Luke was down there, sending her a signal.

Then again, it might not be Luke at all.

She paused, her instincts cautioning her not to do anything rash. But was it really so rash to go downstairs and out into the yard in broad daylight? Surely not, she decided, grabbing her Reebok shoes and pulling them on as she hopped toward the door.

The old house was as silent as a tomb and about as dark, thanks to the heavy curtains that had been drawn over the windows. Rielle kept her footsteps light, her eyes and ears alert for any sign of life, but even the three resident cats Fagan had appropriately named Odessa, Amelia and Arundel were nowhere to be found. She cut through the sitting room to the glass doors that opened onto the terrace, pushed them back carefully and stepped outside.

Fragments of Odessa's broken statue still lurked near the stone wall, but Rielle managed to ignore them, fixing her attention instead on the silvery strains of music that continued to drift along on the morning mist. Was it coming from the shrubs or the cliffs beyond them? Was she a fool for trying to discover the source?

She knew better than to answer that question and, giving the doors behind her a decisive tug, moved across the balcony, hoisting herself up and over the wall and dropping to the wet grass below.

The song played on, low in volume but loud enough to pull her forward. Like one of the Pied Piper's rats, the criminal part of her mind offered in sarcasm.

She found her feet slowing on the damp, spongy ground. Maybe she should go back and wake Adrian. But then the music might disappear and what would she have accomplished? Besides, seeing Adrian at such an indecent hour was bound to mess up her thought processes.

Biting her lips together, she shoved all thoughts of a certain sexy Grand Prix driver from her head. The mist was dispersing gradually with the rising sun. For the first time since her arrival, Rielle felt the warm rays on her cheeks and with them a clearer sense of where the music was coming from. The cliffs, it had to be. Below ground level, possibly from one of the many caves that dotted the Yorkshire coastline.

She made her way carefully along the hedgerow until she reached a vine-covered gate she hadn't noticed before. The manor house loomed behind her, a brooding leviathan that seemed to watch her every move. Glancing over her shoulder and straight up, she scanned the pointy, Gothic windows. Still curtained, every last one of them. So why did her skin crawl when she turned her back on them?

She shivered despite the strengthening sunlight. Did the creepy feeling come from inside her, or from a more sinister source?

Swallowing her uneasiness, she wrapped her fingers
around the wooden guardrail that ran along the upper edge
of the cliff. Below her the sea smashed against the rocky
shore, sending up a salty spray and momentarily blotting out
the singer's voice. But the beat never stopped. *Please God,
let it be Luke,* she prayed, pushing away from the rail and
starting slowly down a narrow stone path that zigzagged
steeply toward the water.

It was not a trek for the faint of heart, she realized,
clutching at each slippery boulder she skidded past. Yet at
some point, long ago, this must have been a walkway of
sorts. Portions of a railing like the one above still stood in
lopsided fragments. For what it was worth, that probably
meant this path led somewhere specific, though, she hoped,
not to a watery grave.

Halfway down the side of the cliff, Rielle stopped to catch
her breath and regain her balance. The music was still below her, repeating itself for the second or third time by now.
The sun, having more or less broken through the haze,
shone directly into her eyes; the air was sticky with salt and
moisture. That, together with the difficult descent, brought
a light film of perspiration to her skin.

With one hand she pushed back the damp tendrils of hair
that had come loose from her braid, using the other to
steady herself on a weathered section of rail. The ground
under her feet was fit for mountain goats, not humans. She
knew that just as she knew she shouldn't rely too heavily on
the guardrail for support. But she kept seeing Luke's face in
her mind's eye, and more distractingly Adrian's, as well.
And those two images made it impossible to concentrate on
anything else. Or would have if a whisper of movement behind her hadn't suddenly set every nerve in her body on
edge.

Rielle's head jerked up. The mind pictures vanished instantly. She saw a shadow on the stones. Misshapen. Moving. And then she heard another flap. Of what? Cloth? Her
eyes rose sharply to the sky. No clouds. No reason for a
shadow to fall. So where had this one come from?

Her muscles went rigid, her hands gripping the rail with all her considerable strength. What could she do but turn and face the thing behind her? Prying the fingers of one hand free, she collected her courage, spun around and found herself face-to-face with . . .

Her entire body went limp. A rosebush! She'd almost given herself heart failure over a scrawny little plant that had managed to take root between two boulders.

But it pointed out the dangers of this little jaunt, didn't it? Like it or not, she had to go back.

Decision made, Rielle worked herself around on the path and tugged experimentally on the railing. It seemed secure enough, and risking one more pull, she used it to propel herself upward. Rather, she started to.

It came out of nowhere, a sickening rending sound that scarcely had time to make an impression on her brain. She was quick, yes, but not fast enough to compensate for the support that was suddenly, startlingly, no longer there. It was as if the earth opened up beneath her. The ground tilted sharply, her sneakers began to slip and her fingers had nothing of substance to cling to. Only a piece of broken, rotted wood and whatever bits of vegetation could survive on such a rugged expanse of rock.

She felt her hand close about something, the rosebush, felt a part of it tear off. And then she was falling, sliding along the steep embankment. Down the slippery face, over pointy stones and mud and moss. Tumbling toward the pounding waves. And almost certain death.

Chapter Seven

She screamed as she hurtled downward. Screamed Adrian's name out loud. But he wasn't there to hear her; no one was. And there was nothing for her hands to grab, no cracks wide enough for her to wedge her feet in and break her fall.

A desperate cry was torn from her throat. She couldn't think about the pounding her body was taking as she struggled to keep her muscles from going stiff. She had to stay limp and roll.

Rielle had no idea how far she tumbled, only that it hurt. She banged her hip on a blunt rock, her shoulder on a clump of earth and stone, her chin on who knew what. The sea was an angry roar in her head, the ground slimy but rough, coated with barnacles or some other form of marine life. She swallowed a sob as her elbows scraped across the scabrous surface. Painful, but she realized quickly that it slowed her down.

With a grunt she dug her heels in and at last felt them begin to grip. More and more, though her downward momentum didn't stop until she succeeded in hooking her fingers around a yellowed vine that resembled a piece of withered sea kelp.

It would never hold, her brain warned, but she refused to panic, would not allow herself to consider that she might die. Not the resilient ex-con artist. Not even the upscale fashion designer.

She could almost hear the vine groaning as her fall came to an abrupt, arm-wrenching halt. Would it be strong enough? Breath held, she risked a hesitant upward glance, prepared for the worst. But though the vine looked delicate, it was actually quite ropy, tough enough to support her weight until she could get her feet under her.

She groped for a toehold and finally found a crevice she could squeeze both feet into. That accomplished, and having more or less managed to steady herself, Rielle rested her forehead on her arms, fingers still clinging tightly to the vine. Her heart thudded against her ribs, a belated reaction she couldn't suppress. Thank God her family had no history of coronary problems.

She let her breath out in a huge, shuddery sigh, not daring to look down. She couldn't move just yet. She was shaking, and her body felt like one giant bruise. And the music was gone. She noticed that in the back of her mind but couldn't really say it surprised her. This had to be the Phantom's handiwork, didn't it? How it would benefit him to harm her she couldn't imagine, but that must have been his intention.

Frissons of fear shot through her. He was here at Brede Manor; she knew it. Paul must have told him something. But what?

A stream of dreadful possibilities slithered through her head. Too frightening to contemplate such things. Her skin was icy despite the hot sun on her back. Maybe she was wrong. The Phantom might not be responsible for any of this. But if not him, then who? And why?

Outside sounds slowly began to penetrate; the cry of a hungry seagull, the crash of waves below, the wail of a distant freighter's horn. Her father still captained trans-Atlantic freighters. Why couldn't that be his ship out there? Why couldn't he come to rescue her?

No chance of that, she thought, and allowed herself a brief moment of self-pity. Tears she never permitted formed behind her eyelids. Her father drank too much, played poker constantly and remembered his daughter only when she was standing in front of him—or tripping over him. Sometimes not even then.

So why wasn't it his face that haunted her now? Why not Luke's, or even a Phantom's mask? Why did she see dark piercing eyes and features so remote in expression that they could never be read? Why did she want to run straight to the man who possessed them?

Around her the seaside cacophony grew louder. The wind picked up, nearly blowing her from her tenuous perch. This probably wasn't the best time to get maudlin. She had to climb out of here before anything else happened.

With an effort she shut away the dark confusion in her mind and lifted her head. She hadn't fallen as far as she'd thought, only twenty feet or so. Using the vine as an anchor, she hauled herself up two of those feet to a small rock ledge, huddling there for a moment to give her sore arm muscles a rest. When she could lift them again, she reached for another jut of stone overhead—and promptly choked out loud when it seemed to shift beneath her fingers.

She snatched her hand away, recoiling so fast she almost lost her balance. But it wasn't fast enough. Someone's fingers had closed about her wrist. Fingers that were cool and strong and not entirely gentle.

Her head jerked back, her eyes landing on the person who held her. Dark, curling hair, narrow features, lashes lowered against the glare of the sun. Adrian!

She started to breathe easier, then felt her blood chill as her gaze slid down his face. No, not Adrian. She didn't need to see the color of the man's eyes or the white turtleneck sweater and impeccable navy blue blazer he wore to realize that. The faintly cruel line of his mouth said it all. And the grip on her wrist that bordered on painful.

"You appear to be in some distress, Rielle," Noah Bishop said, his lips curling into an emotionless serpent's smile. What was it Ava had called him? The Alfred Hitchcock of the theater? The master of death? She shivered, and his fingers tightened perceptibly, cutting off her circulation. "Be a good girl," he coaxed softly, "and give me your other hand." The smile broadened. "We wouldn't want you to fall from this ledge and break your pretty neck, now, would we?''

"I SAW A MAN stumble off the side of a cliff once, hit a rock, plunge into the water and recover sufficiently to play a polo match the next day.''

Noah kept his hand firmly planted in the small of Rielle's back as they made their way through the mansion's lower level. His voice had a dreamy quality to it that Rielle found extremely unnerving, but she could hardly run from the man who had just saved her life. If not that exactly, he'd at least pulled her to safety—which was not to say that he hadn't lured her to the cliff in the first place, but she knew that idea might simply be her paranoia surfacing. Even so, she kept her spine stiff and tried not to limp as they passed through the deserted entry hall.

"That happened in Mexico, though," Noah continued, sounding almost visionary, as if the subject enthralled him. "Fall into the sea hereabouts, and you'd die quick enough. I wonder how many souls these old waters have snatched.''

By percentage, probably not as many as the Phantom. Rielle hid her distaste and trudged on toward the grand staircase, glad enough to see one of the other guests, even if it was only Ivan Ragozcy streaking past her in a whirl of black. He was going up, and in a big hurry, it seemed.

"One assumes the sun has risen.'' It was Ava who offered the droll comment as she slunk like a sultry vapor out of the second-floor shadows. She waved a slim hand in the direction Ivan had taken, the persistent tinkle of her crystal earrings for some reason grating on Rielle's nerves. "Time for all good Transylvanians to be in bed.'' She summoned a coy smile exclusively for Noah's benefit. "I trust you found your own bed comfortable, Mr. Bishop?''

Who cares, Rielle's outraged mind wanted to snap. She settled for a low snarl, not liking Ava Giordano one bit. Why didn't the Phantom set his murderous sights on her? She was an actress, wasn't she? Even her trusty crystal power would be hard-pressed to save her from that creature's clutches.

The idea, deliciously vindictive though it was, brought a frown to Rielle's lips. Who said the Phantom wouldn't go after Ava?

Behind her she heard Noah's indifferent response, but that didn't faze the persistent Ms. Giordano. She intercepted him neatly, hooking a determined arm through his and forcing him to halt midstride.

Rielle set her morbid thoughts aside and took the opportunity to slip away from her rescuer. *Find Adrian,* her brain commanded. *He'll help you make sense of things. Maybe he'll even care.*

Would he? The question hung there, unanswered. So tenuous, the feelings that slid through her. She wanted to know them, to understand them and explore them as she did everything else that made no sense in her life. She might have, too, but just at that moment she happened to look down.

From the upper landing she saw Reuben Bishop quietly letting himself into the house, entering through one of the many sets of glass doors that opened toward the sea. His step was brisk on the carpeted floor; his long gaunt face wore a satisfied expression.

A frown touched Rielle's lips. She strained for a better look. What was that thing in his hand? Not his pipe— something smaller, softer, possibly made of cloth. She jerked back as if she'd been slapped. It was a pouch, just like the one the Gypsy had given Fagan outside the kitchen. And that wasn't the worst of it. Reuben's long stride had brought him much closer now, well within Rielle's auditory range. And when he passed beneath the landing, she recognized instantly and with an icy chill of dread the tune he hummed softly to himself...

"Mellow Yellow!"

ADRIAN WOKE, not in his usual clearheaded way, but slowly, fuzzily, his eyes bleary and unfocused, his mind a network of thoughts and dreams and long-buried recollections that went all the way back to his childhood. Lying on his stomach, he rested his cheek on the pillow and squinted at the few sticks of furniture he could see. Brocade chair, bowl of overripe fruit sitting on a linen-draped table, circle of winged faeries staring down at him from the wall—where was he?

A frown crossed his mouth, but he didn't bother to move. His head felt good, and the bed was comfortable enough. He'd remember when the painkillers wore off. Until they did, he might as well go back to sleep and dream some more about Rielle.

Impossible to forget such a woman, even in his confused state. Long limbed, yes, and slender but strong, with sleek, elegant muscles, a soft, kissable mouth and always those dark blue eyes. Those eyes that were beginning to haunt him.

The eyes of a criminal. Beautiful, but she could not be trusted. He had heard about her in London, from those people he'd spoken to about Luke. Gabi would steal a man's heart, they'd told him, and break it without a second thought. For a purpose, always, but who could know that? Not her marks, maybe not anyone, not even Luke. Possible that she had changed now that she'd gone straight?

This was no problem, Adrian had thought then. No woman could get to him, and trust was not something he gave easily. In fact, he seldom gave it at all.

He turned his face into the pillow, not entirely resenting the knock on his door that forced his mind away from a dangerous train of thought—and replaced it with the picture of an old English manor house, and the memory of a falling statue that still made him shudder inside.

The pounding persisted, growing louder when he lifted his head. He grunted a low, rather rude response in Portuguese and reached for his jeans on a chair by the bed. He made it to a standing position, dragging them on and tugging at the zipper that got stuck halfway. With a shrug he left it partly undone, not bothering with the snap. People who banged on his door at eight in the morning on the day after a race should not expect him to care about offending their sense of moral decency.

Raking his fingers through his hair, he stifled a yawn and opened the door. And almost got hit with Rielle's clenched fist. She pulled back just in time or she would have caught him in the throat. Not that he would have noticed. He was too astonished to do anything except stare at her.

She'd braided her long hair, but it had come loose, forming a cobra's hood around her face. Her features were smudged with grime, her jeans torn at the knees. Her pale yellow T-shirt was streaked with mud, her lightly tanned arms scraped and already showing signs of bruising.

He reached for her, but knew the mask had dropped instinctively into place over his face. He couldn't prevent it from happening. It was simply not possible to change a twenty-year habit in five short seconds.

"What happened to you?" he demanded, drawing her into the room as he brushed the last of the cobwebs from his mind.

She didn't pull away, nor did she stumble against him. Somehow he hadn't expected that she would. But he had expected something. Not panic or hysteria or even anger; no, those things wouldn't fit this woman. Which was perhaps why she showed him nothing. Because she was more curious right now than upset, still not sure what to make of him. She stared back at him, studying his shuttered expression as if she knew it was a sham, yet wasn't sure what to do with that knowledge.

"I have no idea what happened," she said finally, and reaching around her he pushed the door closed. Her stare became a look of perplexity. "It was so strange. I heard music below the cliffs, a song Luke loves. I went to investigate, but the guardrail broke and I fell. Noah Bishop pulled me up. Of course, the music had stopped by then...." She furrowed her brow, glancing away, toward the window. "Anyway, when we got back to the house, he started talking about death as if the subject fascinated him. I thought he must be the Phantom, but then I saw Reuben. Or more correctly, I heard him. He was humming the same tune that drew me to the cliff—and stuffing a pouch, just like one a

Gypsy woman gave Fagan earlier, into his pocket." Her frown deepened. "I wonder what that's all about?"

She seemed to shake herself mentally then, a belated note of urgency entering her voice when Adrian, unable to come up with a suitable response, offered no comment.

"Do you hear what I'm saying?" she demanded, then paused and sighed. "God," she murmured, "I'm starting to sound like that seagull in *The Little Mermaid.*" Her eyes caught his. "Is this making any sense to you at all?"

She brought her hands up, undoubtedly intending to grab hold of his shirt and shake the full import of her story into him. Except that he wasn't wearing a shirt, a realization that seemed to surprise her. And that surprise didn't diminish as her gaze dropped to the unfastened waistband of his jeans.

He would have smiled if he hadn't understood all too clearly what she'd just told him. "You think someone tried to kill you?" He wanted to be absolutely certain of this before he said anything more.

"Yes...no." Her eyes slid again to his waistband. "I'm not sure." She bit the inside of her lip. "Uh, I don't want to seem like a prude or anything, but wouldn't you be more comfortable if you were dressed?"

This time he did smile, a little. Calmly he placed the side of his hand under her chin and tipped her head back. Or tried to. Full of surprises, this one. She resisted the action much more than he would have anticipated, though surely that was unintentional.

"You Americans are so modest," he said when at last he had her attention. "I think you could not live in Brazil with such a chaste attitude."

Amazing to him that she didn't slap his hand away. Instead, she arched a cool brow and retorted in a deceptively sweet tone, "This isn't Brazil, Adrian. My attitude is correct not chaste. Now, either put some clothes on, or go stand on the other side of the room."

Again, not what he'd expected from her. Or from himself, he reflected in irritation. What kind of conversation was this to be having when she was standing there all bruised and filthy... and irresistible even so.

He brushed her lower lip with his thumb, his eyes looking deeply into hers. "You must leave here," he murmured, dismissing their banter and returning without preface to the more serious topic. "To pursue this Phantom is dangerous, perhaps deadly. And do not try and convince me that I am wrong," he warned when she would have opened her mouth to protest. "You could have been killed today."

She lifted his fingers from her lips but didn't step away. "Today and on a thousand yesterdays," she reminded him. "I'm not an innocent, Adrian. A little rusty, maybe, but I seldom repeat the same mistakes twice. I intend to help Luke, and not you or anyone else is going to stop me."

Amusement played on the corners of Adrian's mouth. "Yes, you have mentioned this before."

"I know. Do we understand each other now?"

He said nothing. Still smiling slightly, he brought her hand to his lips, but at the last second changed his mind and reached for her mouth instead, covering it with an insistence that left him feeling both astonished and faintly amused. Wanting more...

Hands planted firmly on either side of her head, he held her steady, deepening the kiss, savoring the taste of her in a way he hadn't done with any woman for years. Maybe not ever.

His tongue dipped into her mouth, finding hers, and he groaned in the back of his throat. Delicious, the sensations that raced through him, that he felt without meaning to, without even fully realizing what he'd done. Then it hit him, and he drew back almost instantly, mask in place, unwilling to know her reaction beyond that split-second response he'd sensed so strongly in her.

Lips pressed together, he turned away. "No," he answered her quietly over his shoulder, moving toward the private bathroom and the first-aid kit there. "I think we do not understand each other at all."

Whether she intended for him to hear her or not, he caught the smug "Not yet anyway" that she murmured in his wake.

And for the first time since his mother's death, Adrian could not entirely contain his fear.

"I SHOULD HAVE TOLD Adrian about this," Rielle muttered as she slipped across the first-floor entryway behind the housekeeper who was walking to Fagan's private study. Still, there hadn't really been time, had there? Or opportunity, either, come to think of it. Unless of course she'd wanted to burst in on him in the shower, which was a tempting enough thought, given the way he'd kissed her moments before, but not in Luke's best interests.

Right now she looked at Gretchen's ramrod-straight spine from the cover of a large potted palm.

"Fetch me a copy of *Ivanhoe*," Fagan had instructed the woman moments ago on the lower landing while Rielle had been making her way back to her room one flight up. "There's one in my study." He'd wagged a warning finger. "Mind, though, my dear, that you lock the door when you leave. I keep important documents in that room."

Rielle had done a quick about-face in the hall, forgetting for the moment about her torn and dirty clothes and the dozen or more scrapes that Adrian had cleaned and patched in an introspective silence she had yet to understand.

Well, she could work on that puzzle later. Right now she had other concerns. Gretchen, key in hand, was letting herself into the locked study, and one way or another, Rielle intended to sneak in behind her.

Maybe her luck was changing for the better. It wasn't a difficult feat to manage at all. Gretchen left the door wide open when she entered, and the door very considerately opened in. Rielle had no trouble concealing herself in the shadows until the housekeeper exited the room.

And probably locked her in...

Rielle winced when she heard the telltale click, then breathed a sigh of relief as her eyes landed on a second key, one that thankfully resided in the lock. Good. Now to see what little gems she could latch on to in here.

Rubbing her grimy palms together, she turned her attention to the quite spacious chamber. Paintings on the paneled walls, huge Elizabethan desk by the window, damask curtains drawn back to reveal a broad expanse of lawn and shrubbery and the most enormous oak tree Rielle had ever seen. And there was also that lovely brass key ring hanging boldly on a tray of papers atop the blotter. My, but Dame Fortune was a wonderful creature.

Or so she thought until she tried the keys in the desk drawers. They worked, but the drawers they opened yielded nothing except a stack of plastic pens with the name Brede Manor stamped on them, six reams of typewriter paper, a million paper clips, a ledger book whose entry dates were older than she was and three open-fingered gloves, all in different colors. Definitely worth keeping under lock and key.

She pushed her unworthy sarcasm down and the last drawer closed with her hip, then returned the keys to their hook. Her eyes traveled about the room.

What about a safe? her mind offered. There should be one of those somewhere in here. And where better to hide a safe than behind an oil painting?

She hastened across the carpet to the wall, tugging lightly on the first frame that came to hand. To her dismay it didn't budge, even when she gave it a much harder pull. What did Fagan do, nail his precious paintings to the paneling?

She considered the possibility of a spring-loaded device, the kind that allowed wood and canvas to effectively secrete wall vaults, then rejected the idea when she discovered that all the paintings were in exactly the same fixed state. She couldn't pry any of them loose, couldn't even move them when she stood to the side and pushed with both hands.

Frustrated, Rielle stepped back, tugging on her dark braid and gnawing on her lip. This was not turning out to be the simple search she'd envisioned. Trust a crafty little con man to make life difficult.

She tipped her head to one side. Where would be a good place to hide valuable documents? Not a lot here, really. Maybe she should go through the glass-fronted book-cases . . .

... Then again, she amended, stopping the thought short as her ears picked up on a muffled noise in the corridor, maybe she shouldn't.

She spun around, swearing softly under her breath. Forget hidden documents—she had to hide herself. Fast. And naturally this study didn't boast a single closet.

She heard the doorknob twist behind her, followed by a cheerful humming sound that had to come from Fagan's throat.

Rielle almost groaned out loud as she ran for the desk and dropped to her knees on the far side. Fagan, singing a song from *Oliver.* There had to be a shred of irony lurking in there somewhere.

The door opened—and closed again with an ominous click that wiped any trace of amusement from Rielle's mind. Footsteps on the carpet scuttled in her direction. The humming stopped. But so, it seemed, did Fagan's feet.

Rielle's heart thumped. She scrunched down farther. Had he seen her? No, not possible. She couldn't see him, and besides, he was talking to himself, a distracted muttering about timetables that had nothing to do with her.

He also held something in his left hand, she realized, risking a quick look around the corner of the desk. A leather-bound book with the word Register printed in big gold letters on the front cover.

The guest register, she assumed, carefully shifting position. If he had a particle of decency, he'd dump the book on the blotter and scurry back out the door before her abused muscles cramped up even more.

She should have known he wouldn't be decent about it. Still muttering absently to himself, he whipped around the desk—the side opposite to the one where Rielle was crouched—to the padded leather chair there. He opened the top drawer, dropped the register inside and sat down, rubbing his fingers together and reaching for the telephone. Rielle got no sense that he'd spotted her. Nevertheless, she kept a close eye on him as she crawled cautiously to the front of the desk.

The sound of a telephone being dialed behind her echoed in the silent room. She counted the rotations. Long distance. And someone Fagan called Edison on the other end.

Did she recognize that name? Rielle searched her memory. It might have a familiar ring to it, but she couldn't remember.

"Women, Eddie," Fagan was saying pleasantly into the receiver. "We need several attractive women if we hope to pull this off."

Rielle's head shot up.

"Actresses? My good man, of course they must be actresses." The chair creaked as Fagan leaned back. "Raid the academy, Eddie. I have a list of names for you. Only three to start with, but we need these ones for sure. The others you can select." A pause, then, "Yes, he agrees with me on the choices. In fact, he helped me find them. That's what partners do, you know. Now, about that list, these are the three women we simply must have."

Rattle of paper followed by a trio of names, one of which Rielle recognized. Myra Jenkins, a stage actress of some repute. And that brought a chill to Rielle's skin that no amount of heat could dispel.

Then words of closing issued from Fagan's mouth. For whatever reason he was working with a partner. And someone named "Eddie" Edison, as well. Possibly a contact in London. Almost certainly the academy he'd spoken of must be Brittany Rhodes, and hadn't every one of the Phantom's victims been connected to that institution?

Actresses not actors. Fagan and his partner wanted women and three specific ones at that. Rielle's head spun with questions. Who was Fagan's partner? Reuben Bishop? That made sense in that the two men were old friends, but beyond that, who knew?

Rielle's body stiffened. Fagan had hung up the phone, pushed back his chair. And mumbled something about food.

Please, she begged, let him leave and go raid a refrigerator.

He stood slowly, chuckling to himself. Rielle swatted at the strands of hair that clung damply to her cheeks and forehead. The room had become unbearably stuffy. Claustrophobic. A film of perspiration covered her skin, a combination of heat and terror. Was Fagan the Phantom? Was he setting up a scam in order to trap his next victim?

A shudder ran through her. Leave, she implored him silently. And thank heaven, this time he obliged. She had to crawl back to her original hiding place as he skirted the desk, but those kinds of maneuvers were old hat to her. They came back fast enough even with all the confusion and fear that swirled around inside her.

She heard the key in the outer lock, and was finally able to let out an enormous sigh of relief. It didn't last. The uncertainties returned like a black cloud to haunt her.

Ignoring her scrapes and bruises, she scrambled to her feet. Adrian had to know about this.

Percy Fagan was up to something. And that something could very well be murder.

Chapter Eight

"Is he still following me?" Ava detached herself from the crowd gathered on the extensive grounds beyond Brede Manor, joining Rielle and Adrian under one of the blue-and-white-striped canopies that lined the perimeter of the clearing.

Rielle, her eyes glued to Fagan, who never seemed to stand still for more than two seconds, waved a hand toward the forest. "If you mean Noah, he's sitting under an oak tree, scribbling something on an old theater handbill." She caught herself before naming the play. No need to let Ava know she'd been spying on Noah Bishop for the better part of an hour. Reuben, too, though he'd proved to be even slipperier than Fagan.

Prime Phantom suspects? Maybe Fagan and Reuben were partners in something. Maybe that thing was a scam of some sort. And maybe it even involved a small group of stage actresses. But Adrian had made a valid point when he'd reminded her that Fagan and Reuben were not the only two people staying at the manor. True, one or both of them might be a killer. But what if they weren't?

"We should watch everyone, Rielle," he had cautioned after she'd cornered him in his bedroom for the second time that morning. Fully dressed on this occasion and not sounding too pleased about the episode in the study.

"You must be more careful," was all he'd murmured, coming to stand in front of her. With his fingers he brushed the hair from her still-smudged face. "You are too impulsive, although I do not suppose my telling you this will change anything."

Would he kiss her again? Rielle stood still, waiting, wanting to know. But while his dark eyes had stared into hers for several long seconds and his thumb had moved in a subtle caress over her cheekbone, he hadn't touched her. At least not with his mouth. He had smiled, though, and that tiny curve of his lips still baffled her.

Movement in Rielle's peripheral vision brought her back to the present. Ava making a sound of disgust in her throat, fanning herself with a cloth napkin. She was dressed in a pair of gray linen trousers and a long-sleeved satin blouse. She'd wrapped a silver scarf around her head, draped a burgundy one over it and topped them both with a boxy little hat. Like a wimple, Rielle thought, though no one could look less like a postulant than this woman.

"I wasn't referring to Noah," Ava said now, her tone snappish enough to make Adrian cast her a dispassionate sideways glance. "I meant that pest, Jonathan what's-his-name. He's been trailing me around like a lovesick puppy all afternoon."

"Jonathan Lynch," Adrian supplied. He didn't sound very interested in her problem. Resting his shoulder on a well-anchored tent pole, he returned his attention to the milling horde.

There were too many bodies in too confined an area. Rielle sighed in mild frustration while Ava plucked an antipasto from one of the sterling trays. They'd come in droves to watch the mock tournament Fagan was staging as an adjunct to the Midsummer Festival. For a fee, of course. Whatever black secrets their host might harbor, he did know how to turn a profit. In a few minutes the symbolic black and white knights would mount up to begin the joust. A dazzling spectacle, but Rielle had no time for it. Or for Ava, who still complained loudly in her ear.

"First Gypsies and now a never-was actor. I can't take it. Noah Bishop notwithstanding, this isn't what I had in mind when I decided to come up here."

"Why did you decide to come up here?" Adrian inquired.

His eyes, shielded by sunglasses, continued to scan the crowd. No hint of emotion on his narrow face, nothing to betray his feelings. And nothing really new about that, Rielle thought, chewing on her lip. Except for that one very significant fact she couldn't seem to stop thinking about. He'd kissed her, an impetuous act if ever she'd seen one. Disturbing, too, in ways she'd do well to leave alone—but knew she wouldn't.

A feeling of puzzlement washed through her as she recalled her startled response to that too-brief contact. And yet why should one little kiss throw her emotions into a state of total chaos?

No question, this attraction was a complication she didn't need. Still, what could she do about it? Except maybe see just how much further she could push it. And him.

That delightful notion floated quite freely through her mind. Dangerous, such an idea, but awfully tempting. Good thing Ava chose that moment to swallow her canapé and emit a disdainful snort.

"What made me decide to come here, indeed," she scoffed, licking her fingers. "In a word, Gilbert." Her long-suffering sigh said it all. "My devoted husband had to travel to New Orleans on business." Her contempt for the Louisiana city and America in general was obvious, but while Rielle was tempted to push her face into a tray of raw oysters, she managed to shrug instead.

"That still doesn't explain why you came to Morgate of all places. You don't sound as though you're especially taken with this festival."

"I'm not. This whole Midsummer thing was Gilbert's idea. Not that I don't think he meant well, but I never have been, never will be a faerie fan... Oh, hell," Ava interrupted herself impatiently. "Speaking of fans, there he is." She appealed to Adrian. "Be a love and tell him I've contracted some dreadful tropical disease. You're from Brazil, you must know them all. Just pick one with a contagious-sounding name and give it to me."

Adrian's features remained impassive. "It would be a pleasure," he said politely.

Subtle sarcasm. Ava missed it completely as she did the mocking smile that played on the corners of his mouth. Rielle leaned against the table, wishing she had time to stick her tongue out at the woman's departing figure. But already Jonathan was limping into sight, and the realization that he really was following Ava brought a much more chilling thought to mind.

What if he pursued her, not as a romantic interest, but as an intended victim? Rielle pushed herself away from the table, moving closer to Adrian as Jonathan, nattily turned out in a white silk shirt, beige vest and trousers, made his way under the canopy.

It was a warm, muggy day, better suited for the jeans and off-white polo shirt Adrian wore than the linen and silk favored by Fagan's other guests. Even Rielle's one-piece coral pantsuit was cotton. Poor Jonathan. His thinning blond hair was damp with perspiration, his face red from exertion, the smile he offered them positively wilted. Few men in their prime would look this drained—unless of course they'd been following someone around the grounds all afternoon....

"Pardon me," he panted, mopping the back of his neck with a handkerchief. "But have either of you seen Ms. Giordano? I thought I spotted her passing this way."

Was spotting stage actresses his game? Rielle edged closer to Adrian. "Ava did stop by a few minutes ago," she replied placidly enough. "I'm not sure which direction she took when she left."

"She mentioned something about blackwater fever," Adrian put in, moving a shoulder. "Possibly she has gone in search of a Gypsy who can cure this most lethal tropical disease that she would have her more ardent admirers believe she has come down with."

Jonathan looked shocked, then confused and finally concerned. "I beg your pardon, are you saying that Ava is ill?"

"It's nothing," Rielle murmured. "Probably just a headache. You know how dramatic people in the performing arts can be." At his blank look, she sent him a meaningful look. "You do know how dramatic they can be, don't you, Jonathan? I mean, as an actor yourself, you must deal with histrionics all the time."

Did he glance away for a second? Falter slightly? It seemed to Rielle that he did. She peered closer at his innocuous features. "Of course," she went on before he could respond, "you're not like that yourself. No false pretenses for you, I've noticed. As a matter of fact, I don't even recall you running down your list of credits last night at dinner. Ava did."

"So did Reuben and Noah," Adrian added, helping her out. Then he rested his forearms on her shoulders from behind, and she promptly lost her train of thought.

Resisting the urge to shove an elbow into his ribs, Rielle fixed her attention on Jonathan's face. "Even Ivan Ragozcy did his share of bragging," she managed to say. About some very weird-sounding stage productions, she had to admit, but then she didn't speak Romanian, and it went without saying that she didn't frequent Transylvanian theaters. "Don't you ever talk about your accomplishments, Jonathan?"

This time he did look away, rubbed his bad left knee and appeared to squirm a little. His voice took on a rather evasive air when he said, "I'm really not one to boast about my achievements. Suffice to say that I'm capable of handling much greater roles than those I've been awarded."

"Have you ever played the Cobdon Theater?" Rielle pressed, then immediately regretted her indiscreet tongue. The bruises on her body made their presence felt every time she moved, evidence of just how dangerous a careless attitude could be. Particularly where the Phantom was concerned.

Thankfully, for all her lack of caution, Jonathan gave no sign that he found the question unusual. He merely blinked his pale eyes and nodded slowly. "The Cobdon Theater.

Yes, that name does ring a bell. I believe I played *Les Misérables* there a few months back."

"Good show," Rielle said. She studied him from under her lashes. He was lying, obviously, but why? Wouldn't the Phantom be more inclined to deny having worked the old theater? Maybe Jonathan's career was simply on the skids.

"Must have been an interesting production," Adrian murmured, and again Jonathan shifted his weight, clearly uncomfortable with the conversation.

"Yes, quite." Straightening, he tucked away his handkerchief and motioned toward the grandstand. "If you'll excuse me, I think I'll take my seat for the tournament."

"As we should all do," a man's cheerfully familiar voice stated.

Fagan materialized beside the table as Jonathan limped off. The old man's smile was rife with mischief. Too bad they couldn't come right out and ask the crafty little crook about Luke, or about his telephone conversation in the study.

"Mustn't miss the tournament. It's tradition, you know," Fagan continued, pleasant as always. He ran his gaze around the swarming grounds. "The crowds get bigger every year. And all because of a faerie tale. Lovely little fable. Now, if we could only get Odessa and Amelia to put in an appearance, we'd really be onto something." His eyes sparkled. "You're familiar with the story, I trust. Ready with your St. John's wort and all."

Rielle stared at him. "Our what?"

"St. John's wort." Fagan picked up a chocolate filled with orange cream, popping it into his mouth and reaching for another. Such dexterous fingers he had. True pickpocket material. And maybe more? "The wort's a flower, my children, a charm worn by those who support the fair Amelia at the festival."

"Support her in what?" Rielle asked.

"In her bid to be reunited with her mortal lover, Sir Arundel." He perused the luscious assortment of pastries before him, finally rooting out a banana cream puff. "Amelia is the good faerie, a creature of the light, while

Odessa, her evil counterpart, rises only when the moon is out. It goes without saying that they're enemies, rivals if you prefer. Queens, both, and powerful, though only Odessa has the ability to change her appearance."

"In other words, she's good with disguises," Rielle murmured.

"Exactly." Fagan's smile was a mask in its own right. "Every year on the eve of the summer solstice, Amelia is said to return in the hopes that her lover will cross over from the other side. Together forever and all that fantastical nonsense. Ah, but as goes Amelia, so too goes Odessa, whose goal of malice is to prevent this reunion from ever taking place. And," he added with a wink, "to feed upon those poor, unfortunate souls foolish enough not to protect themselves with a talisman. Thus the wort." He finished his tale with a flourish worthy of applause and bit into another sugary biscuit. "Bourbon cream." He sighed. "Thank heaven for my Charlotte. The woman's a treasure, and the best cook in the realm."

Rielle didn't recall meeting anyone by that name at Brede Manor. "Charlotte is . . . ?"

"My housekeeper." Fagan flicked a crumb from his pointed beard. "A true shame about her sister taking ill so suddenly, but these things happen. At least she was good enough to hire a replacement before she left. I should hate to have returned from London to a houseful of guests—minus two as it turns out—and had only old Fergus to help me cope."

Rielle felt Adrian's muscles constrict, her own anticipation mount. Careful, though, a voice in her head cautioned.

"You had two no-shows, Fagan?" she said. "Isn't that a little odd?"

"Not so very." Fagan dismissed this idea with a flap of his hand. "Things happen, plans change. They may turn up yet."

Who were "they"? Rielle wanted to know. She opened her mouth, hoping some cleverly phrased question would come out, but the words never formed. Adrian, still close behind her, still making her crazy with that warm, hard body of his, rested his chin on top of her head and inquired with absolute innocence, "One of those people would not be Rafael Sebastian, would it?" At Fagan's uncomprehending expression, he shrugged. "Rafael is also a Grand Prix driver. When I told him I was bringing Rielle here, he said he would like to attend such a festival himself. I thought he might have decided at the last minute to come."

"No Sebastians," Fagan stated, taking the bait. "Just a Fortesqueue and a Lamont. Mr. Fortesqueue, I'm told, summers in Odense, his wife in Southampton. Possibly they got their signals crossed."

"And the other person?" Rielle prodded.

"Haven't the foggiest, my child. I seldom know who's coming until they show up. Charlotte handles all the reservations. Gives me a chance to spend more time down in London." He dropped a handful of powdered rum-balls into the pocket of his baggy jacket and looked over at the rapidly filling grandstand. "Come along now," he urged, starting out from under the canopy. "The parade of participants is already underway. Old Fergus is playing the part of the black knight. Loves to be the villain, he says, but then don't we all?"

No response possible to that, and with a final beckoning crook of his gloved finger, Fagan scuttled into the lines of tournament goers streaming toward the canvas-covered bleachers.

Rielle waited until he was out of sight, counted to five for good measure, then spun to face Adrian, grabbing the front of his polo shirt in her fists. "Lamont, Adrian," she declared, shaking him. "That's one of Luke's aliases. Daniel Lamont. He borrowed it from the *The Shadow*. It's an old American radio program—Luke loves it. We used the name once when we were conning a real-estate broker up in Liverpool." She shook him again, trying to convey to him some portion of her excitement. "This is good, don't you see? It proves that Luke did intend to come back here, undoubtedly to meet Paul."

She caught her breath suddenly as a far darker thought occurred to her. "Maybe it isn't so good after all," she amended, wishing she hadn't known Paul's weaknesses quite so well.

She regarded Adrian's narrow features, expecting some sort of a response, even if it was only the slightest hint of a frown. She got nothing, saw nothing, except a glimmer she couldn't read deep in his eyes.

Or could she read it? Had she maybe even seen it before? This morning, perhaps, in his room, right before he'd kissed her.

Rielle felt herself sway a little, saw the glimmer in Adrian's eyes deepen and knew she should probably step away while she still could.

But that was silly, wasn't it, she thought, giving herself a firm mental shake. One might even say cowardly—and Gabrielle Marchand was certainly no coward.

Grinning to herself, Rielle loosened her grip on Adrian's shirt. Let him step away if he wanted to. Let that gorgeous body of his tense up. Let the chips fall where they may, her mind put in, and from the faint curve of his lips it seemed he might have heard the thought. Still, he didn't move. And that, she decided, was good enough for her.

Deliberately Rielle pushed all thoughts of the Phantom aside. Then reaching up, she slid her hand around Adrian's neck, her fingers through the dark hair that curled over the collar of his shirt. And brought his mouth firmly down onto hers.

RIELLE DIDN'T KNOW what she'd hoped to gain—or prove—by her impulsive action. Whatever it was, something told her it backfired. If she'd caught Adrian momentarily unaware, he was quick to recover.

With a start of surprise she realized that his mouth was open on hers, that he was kissing her back, and in a very demanding way. Kissing her with his lips, his tongue, his teeth, drawing her forward into his arms until she could feel every part of his body, every bone and muscle, every inch of heated flesh, even his breath, hot and moist on her face.

No mistake, she thought, too stunned by her own reaction to care about anything as insignificant as logic or wisdom. She felt the urgency in Adrian's touch, the wanting, but also the control he seemed determined not to shed. An undercurrent to those other things, but always it was there, the impregnable emotional armor of his.

A legion of questions filled her mind. Did she really have the right to try to force from him the response she wanted, to call up things he might not want to feel?

No answer came to her, and suddenly it no longer mattered. He was a big boy; he could push back if he really wanted to.

Shoving aside her doubts, she went with her own feelings. The muscles in his neck were taut, sinewy, the hair between her fingers surprisingly soft. The scent of him made her tremble inside. Clean, warm and completely, undeniably male. His taste? Intoxicating. She could get lost in these sensations so very easily.

Far in the back of her mind, in a corner only dimly recognized, Rielle felt the first tendrils of panic. Dangerous to give in to this attraction. Her brain knew it even if her instincts ignored it.

To her regret—or was it relief—he must have been thinking the same thing. Pulling back with obvious reluctance, he slid his lips to the corner of her mouth, kissing her gently and raising his head just enough to look at her.

His breathing was unsteady. An inner sense of self-preservation told Rielle she didn't want to know any more than that right now. She'd never felt so confused, so shaken. Probably just as well that enigmatic mask of his dropped into place.

"You should not have done that," Adrian murmured in his low voice, seducing her all over again, making her hot inside and out. His thumb stroked her cheekbone. "I am Latin American, both in character and in temperament. Maybe I do not like aggressive women."

"Maybe not," she agreed, her fingers still clutching the hair that curled softly over his neck.

His dark eyes looked down into hers. He touched the side of her mouth with his fingers. "I think I should not kiss you again."

She smiled with a serenity she thought she might never feel again, wondering distantly why neither of them had moved. "I kissed you, Adrian," she pointed out. "But you're right. It probably isn't a good idea."

Amusement, unmistakable and utterly enchanting, lit his narrow features. "You are more troublesome to me than all my racing competitors combined. You shouldn't be, and I cannot begin to understand why this is so."

"Because I'm a woman?" she suggested.

"Possibly," he said, and probably meant it.

Sighing, she shook her head and was finally able to step back. Out of range, but not of out of danger. God, life was complicated.

"Sexist," she accused mildly, not upset by his attitude. He'd come around eventually. "I think we'd better change the subject and get out of here before we end up in a joust ourselves."

"That might be interesting."

A smile curved his lips, but faded away when he glanced at the grandstand and the more serious threat there.

Rielle followed his gaze. Her mind became a tangle of morbid thoughts. The Phantom might be in that mob. Or he might be off chasing Luke. Who could know for sure? Yes, suspicious things had happened, but then she was looking for them, wasn't she? Maybe exaggerating some of them out of fear. And yet . . .

"Charlotte makes the reservations." She repeated Fagan's words thoughtfully. "We have to get back into Fagan's study, Adrian. Try to find the guest registry. If Charlotte also writes down the dates those reservations are made, we could find out which of the guests booked a room within the past two weeks. That would narrow the field considerably. Assuming for the moment that the Phantom is staying at the manor and that he isn't Fagan, he wouldn't have known he was coming until after he'd killed Paul."

Adrian wrapped his long fingers around hers. "That's true," he acknowledged. "But I would not count on such a detail being included in Fagan's register, and it is not worth the risk you took this morning in any event. Brede Manor is not the Ritz. Besides," he said, shrugging, "the Phantom is no fool. He, too, might have thought of this, found a way into Fagan's study and altered the records to suit his purposes."

"It's still worth a try," Rielle insisted, letting him pull her into the line of stragglers and all the noise and color that only added to the festivities.

She was silent for a time, watching but not really seeing the huge horses that cantered past en route to their designated field positions. Armor clanking, chains rattling, bridles jingling, the knights and their mounts filed by in a clattering stream. Then came the two combatants, the chauffeur Fergus McBrecken in black and an unknown commodity in white, heading toward them at a decorous trot. Pomp and pageantry. Who knew, this tournament might last the rest of the afternoon. And in the meantime the manor house would be empty....

Rielle tugged on Adrian's hand as another idea occurred to her. "Why don't we skip the joust and go back to the mansion?" She had to shout now to make herself heard above the noise. "No one will be there. We can search Luke's room. And maybe a few others, as well."

Adrian concealed a grin. "Don't you have any scruples, Rielle?"

She considered that for a second. "I don't believe in violent crime," she said at last.

"But anything else is fair."

"Say 'justifiable,'" she corrected with a shrug. "And if you're going to start in on your con-artist-turned-saint routine again, spare me. If I'm beyond redemption, I'd really rather not know about it."

Adrian's grin became a smile that shocked her with its beauty. A fleeting thing, but she wasn't wrong. She watched, intrigued, as his features settled back into their usual remote cast. "If you are beyond redemption, you're certainly not alone." His eyes shifted to the approaching knights. "I thought about searching the guests' rooms myself."

"Does that bother you?"

"Not at all." He turned back to her, arching a meaning-ful brow. "*That* is what bothers me."

She laughed. "Once a crook, always a crook, Senhor Da Costa. Or so my Aunt Lavinia insists."

"Your aunt is a wise woman."

"She's a lush. Let's go." Rielle pulled him around a tall, skinny woman in a cabbage rose tent dress.

The combatants drew closer. She glanced absently at the approaching black knight—and in her preoccupation only narrowly avoided bumping into the man in front of her who was chatting and waving his walking stick like a sema-phore.

Even so, she found it difficult to look away. All things medieval enchanted her. And this black knight, this vision of darkness, was such an evil specter, with his visor pulled down, his gauntlets on, his lance tucked securely under one mail-covered arm. And the horse he sat was enormous, menacing in a way, Rielle decided, tipping her head back for a clearer view. Of course it would have to be big to carry so much weight.

The thought had scarcely formed when something flashed brightly in front of her. Not a camera—it was sharper than that, more jarring. And it hit the black knight's armor full in the chestplate.

The effect was visually painful. Blinding. Sunlight glanc-ing off metal and directly into her eyes.

Into the horse's eyes!

A collective gasp erupted from the people around her, with everyone stopping too quickly, groping off balance for support. Rielle sensed rather than saw the animal beside her jerk. Alarm rippled through her, a slow-building dream, real yet not real at all. Beyond her control. Ominous, even be-fore it unfolded.

Confusion surrounded her suddenly on all sides. She felt someone topple into her arm, felt herself bump hard into Adrian. And then she heard the sound, the horrible night-mare noise that was really a jumble of separate things: a terrified whinny, a crash, a shouted warning, unintelligible above the thunder of iron-shod hooves.

Panic. She heard that, too. But she still couldn't see. The field had become a giant sea of yellow. And there were bodies banging into her from all sides.

Where was Adrian?

Something slammed hard into her back, knocking the breath from her. Something else landed on top of her. In her peripheral vision she saw flowers. Big pink roses, screaming in fear and pain. She'd fallen on the woman in the tent dress, who'd fallen on Adrian. And there were other people down, too.

She swallowed her rising fright. What was happening here? How had it happened?

A man tripped over her legs, falling to his knees on the grass. Bodies everywhere, some scrambling to get up, some crawling under the canopy, others too shocked to move at all.

"Look out!" This time Rielle understood the cry—and the reason for it.

The ground beneath her shook. Not an earthquake, her horrified brain informed her. Worse than that. Deadly if she didn't get out of the way.

Far above them all, the black knight's horse reared, as high as he could with the weight on his back. Flailing hooves hit the ground near Rielle's arm, near a stranger's head. The animal reared again, so close now she could see the nails in his shoes, feel the clods of earth and grass that showered down onto her face.

She couldn't move; there was a person half on top of her. Remarkably though, she could think, even through the frantic uproar, the noise and confusion and fear. Or maybe it was just grim, instinctive knowledge that pushed its way into her mind, past the dread and the panic she couldn't quite master.

The Phantom had caused this monstrous thing to happen. The Phantom was here, a foul presence, hidden in the crowd. Watching for Luke. Waiting to claim his next victim.

Chapter Nine

It was a cruel world, Luke decided with a sigh. What were the odds of his train derailing in the middle of—where was this place anyway? Somewhere in Bulgaria, a village whose name he couldn't pronounce and whose elderly female inhabitants still wore babushkas, black shawls and stockings and grave looks of suspicion on their otherwise unrevealing faces. The men were even worse, refugees from another century with their handlebar mustaches, fat pipes and starched white collars.

Starched convictions, too, Luke reflected, pleased when a young woman in a print peasant skirt and white blouse smiled shyly at him. He was walking along the main street of the village, a dark little hole in a remote region of the Bulgarian Mountains, and the way these people were staring you'd have thought he was the count on the prowl for a midnight snack. They'd probably never heard of a telephone, which was what he really wanted and the chief reason he'd left the train two miles back. That, and it was strictly verboten to stop moving when one was on the run—and undisguised.

He'd stripped off beggar's robes and brown dye that morning, swapped them for denim and leather and his own mane of golden blond hair. He grinned as an elderly woman in black clogs scuttled past, clutching her collar tightly around her throat. No doubt where her fears lay. Actually, though, if these people were going to take him for a creature of the night, they might want to go for the more contemporary character, the one he really did resemble.

Of course, if they were smart, they'd concern themselves less with bloodsucking bats and more with a bloodthirsty Phantom who might well be hot on Luke's trail at this very moment.

Yes, but what if he wasn't? The question and all its nasty implications gnawed at Luke. What if Paul had blurted out everything he knew? Not just about Brede Manor, which Luke figured he probably had, but also about those few people Luke trusted enough to turn to when he needed help. God knew, the Phantom was a devious creature. If Paul had done the unforgivable and mentioned Rielle's name...

Luke shuddered. Best not to dwell on what horrible things said Phantom might do to try to worm from her the information he sought regarding Luke's whereabouts. In all likelihood that hadn't happened, but Luke had no right to take such a risk, not with Rielle's life. He had to get in touch with her, and the sooner the better.

The sun had set behind the mountains. The resulting shadows made the village appear even gloomier, a throwback to a more fearful age. Few of the timbered shops and houses he passed looked inviting. Wooden shutters had been closed and bolted fast, and if this place boasted a single streetlight, Luke couldn't see it. In fact, he couldn't see anything clearly except for one somber building with a sloped roof and lamps burning low in two of the windows. The local inn, he assumed.

He bounded up two small steps and into an uncrowded room, a tavern, with dark plank walls, scarred tables and a big silver crucifix hanging over the bar. The bartender, a robust man, stared at Luke's blond hair, leather jacket and biker's boots as if they'd been fashioned by the devil himself. He whispered something and crossed himself quickly.

Fascinating, all this fear and superstition, but Luke had no time to study it. With his hand he made a miming motion.

"Telephone?" he asked in English, not holding out a great deal of hope. "Do you have one? I need to make a call."

"Telephone is in back."

The response, thickly accented though it was, left Luke momentarily startled. Then he laughed and shook his head. You just couldn't pigeonhole people these days, not even in isolated Bulgarian towns.

Of course, that was a lesson he should have learned by heart, he thought soberly, acknowledging the icy shudder that passed through him as he made his way to a functional if not fancy phone booth. He'd taken the Phantom—Gustav to him—at face value, and look where he'd wound up. On the run, mourning the death of his partner and scared stiff that he'd screwed up again by sending Rielle that damned key.

He prayed silently under his breath as he dialed and waited for the operators to work their transcontinental magic, which thankfully they did. Luke tapped his fingers in agitation. No answer. And no answering machine, he knew. Not that it mattered. He wouldn't dare leave a message anyway.

He banged the receiver down, more out of concern than anger. Darting eyes glanced at him, but he ignored them. Why was he so panicky all of a sudden? Was there some hidden snippet lurking in his subconscious? Some detail it remembered about the night of the murder that he couldn't?

He ran the whole ugly scene again in his mind. The old Cobdon Theater, he and Paul ambling in. The place had possibilities for future cons—might as well check it out. Their misfortune to show up at that particular moment.

He scrunched his eyes closed and pictured the dusty stage, the shadows, the movement within. And Charity Green dressed as Esmeralda, obligingly conned by Luke and Paul. Pawns, all of them as it turned out—putty in the Phantom's cold white hands.

The Phantom had wanted to kill her from the start; Luke was sure of it. He'd planned the whole thing to achieve that goal. Why? Had he known the woman before? Hard to say—the Phantom was a modern-day Lon Chaney in terms of theatrical disguise—but Luke didn't think that was the case. This Phantom had set his crazed sights on the late Mrs. Green, all right, but not because of any past relationship.

Because of what, then? Luke frowned in frustration. What was it that he couldn't quite see in his mind's eye? The detail he couldn't seem to catch and hold. Would the proof he'd hidden but not had time to examine provide the answer to that question?

He continued to tap the phone, then impulsively snatched up the receiver. More money in the slots, another number relayed to the London operator. Four rings this time, followed by a woman's businesslike "Gabrielle Rousseau Designs."

Rielle's designing partner, Lisa Rousseau. Luke winced. Lisa didn't like him much, which, depending on her mood, could make worming even the most trivial information from her about as easy as conning the royals. Taking a deep breath and deliberately not identifying himself, he asked to speak to Rielle.

"She's not here," Lisa replied with that cool, elegant tone of boredom she reserved only for him. "She left the city Friday, Luke."

"Left the city!" Luke fought a fresh ripple of panic. "Where did she go?"

"I can't imagine."

"Lisa, this is important, life-and-death important," he growled, then lowered his voice when the bartender crossed himself again. "Tell me where she went. Please."

He heard her release a weary breath. "I don't know where," she said finally. "I only know that when she left here Friday morning, she mentioned the name Silverstone."

Luke's blood froze. "Silverstone, the racetrack?"

"If that's what it is, yes." She paused, her voice laced with distrust. "Luke, who's really in more trouble here? Rielle or you?"

And Luke, visualizing the Phantom's strong fingers closing about Charity Green's throat, wished to God he could say.

"I DINNA KNOW what happened," Fergus McBrecken maintained steadfastly. He sat erect in Fagan's private study, along with Rielle and Adrian and a constable from the village who was making notes in his little black book. "Something shone in my eyes, brighter than a light, I'd ken. A reflection maybe. Spooked Lucifer as ye can surely understand it would. Did me nay good, either, I must say, but at least no one was hurt."

Well, that was a matter of opinion. Rielle covered a grimace of pain with a polite smile as the constable glanced back at her. She'd been hovering around Fagan's desk since she'd sweet-talked their host into letting them use this room ten minutes ago. The register was right in front of her; she'd found it where he'd left it: in the top desk drawer. Now if this skirt-chasing bobby would only stop leering at her torn pantsuit for fifteen seconds, she might be able to get a look at the thing.

"You have never seen a flash of this type before?" Adrian pressed, and without meaning to, Rielle let herself be distracted by him as he crossed the parquet floor to lounge against the door.

Hot, rumpled, dirty, probably as stiff and sore as her since practically everyone in the vicinity had managed to land on top of him during the melee. And yet for all of that, he struck her as more attractive than ever. Bruised and sexy, possibly approachable in pain, though she knew better than to test that one out. She'd touched him last night when he'd seemed somewhat vulnerable, and she could still feel his warm, smooth skin beneath her fingers, the silk of his dark hair, the knotted muscles....

Not again, she groaned to herself, taking a step closer to the register. For God's sake, Rielle, let it go. You'll only mess everything up if you—what? Fall in love?

A tiny shock passed through her as her fingers closed tightly about the register's gilt-edged cover.

Adrian continued to lean against the door, eyes hooded, looking tired, maybe a little pale. Rielle dragged her gaze away, but even that took a huge effort. He had a certain way about him, an air of solitude that bordered on loneliness. And that she understood.

She'd been if not lonely, certainly neglected as a child. He might hide his emotions well, but this was one mask she could see right through—and half wished she couldn't. The feelings it called up were more than a little disturbing.

With careful deliberation she blocked the thoughts and flipped the register open—then quickly slammed it shut again when the constable lifted his head. She smiled, and he blushed and immediately returned to his writing.

Klutz, she chided herself. *You weren't this awkward as an eighteen-year-old apprentice. Get the information you want and get out of here. And forget about sexy Latin race car drivers.*

"Might have been a reflection of some sort," Fergus was saying now. "From a mirror or a silver goblet."

Or a silver tray, Rielle mused idly as a grim-faced Gretchen marched into the study carrying a platter of tea and frosted cakes. She'd been shifting trays in the tournament tents with the impersonal efficiency that was fast becoming her trademark. Maybe she'd shone one of them in the horse's eyes. But why?

Rielle sighed. Well, nothing else made sense here, did it? One more unanswered question was hardly significant.

She waited until the housekeeper had gone, then reached for the register. Adrian was watching her. He held the other men's attention with his usual coolness.

The names were easy to find. It was an alphabetical listing. Unfortunately no dates had been entered, only the anticipated arrival and departure times of each guest. Disappointing, but then Adrian had warned her not to get her hopes up.

Rielle slipped the book back into the drawer and wandered to the window, pushing it open a crack. The sun had dipped below the forest treetops. Shadows of a gnarled oak tree fell across the carpet of lawn before her, an eerie sight with so much daylight left.

She heard the Gypsies in the distance, singing, preparing for the feast. Tambourines rode the warm summer breeze, floating through the webwork of deepening shadows. Almost pagan, the sound. Dark, faintly sinister. But melodic, stirring, the kind of rich, throaty music that pulled at the soul.

Reaching up, she started to shut the window. But her fingers went suddenly cold on the latch. Below the music, the voices, the jingle of the tambourine, she caught a sound. Laughter—soft but unmistakable. A very low, very dry chuckle, coming from the giant shadows, drifting slowly away into the forest.

It was a man's chuckle, nothing more. And yet there was a great deal more, looming just beneath the surface. Something that made her heart hammer in her chest, her mouth go absolutely dry. She might have stopped breathing. It didn't matter. Only the laughter was important. That silky echo that wouldn't fade even though its source had long since gone.

No, not gone, not really. Evil never simply disappeared, and that sound had been pure evil. And there was no doubt in Rielle's mind that it had come from the Phantom's throat.

"I AM ODESSA. I am evil." A woman wearing a long brown robe and white porcelain mask materialized in front of Adrian. Smoke hung around her like a filmy white cloak, making the red eyes of the mask appear more malevolent than they really were. "I am the Metamorph. And you are...?"

"On my way to the castle," Adrian said with a shrug that precluded further conversation. He moved smoothly past her, his long stride slowing a bit as he took in the spectacle that was the Midsummer Festival.

The celebration had been going on for hours now, since before sunset. Bands of people—many of them Gypsies— dressed in plain wool robes, their faces covered with smooth-featured masks, circled small fires, holding hands and singing softly, chanting, calling out to the faerie spirits. There must have been twenty such fires, and an equal number of human rings surrounding them.

They weren't the faerie rings, Adrian knew. Those were larger, much less solemn, and there were no fires burning in their centers.

His gaze strayed to a group of bare-chested men in tights, prancing like wild mythical creatures before a fascinated audience. The moon was out, almost full, suspended above the ruined castle turrets, shining ghostly white in the clear night sky.

No cool Yorkshire mist coming off the moors this evening. And no peace to be had in all of Morgate, Adrian thought in faint amusement, though he'd been told earlier by Reuben that Mandelin Castle was the crux of all faerie-related activities.

It was an interesting display, Adrian had to admit. And elaborately staged. The castle was a glow of gold against the sky, lit up as it must have been in medieval times by hundreds of torches that fluttered and danced in the breeze. Lyrical faerie airs swirled around him, carried on the delicate layers of wood smoke. Tambourines, flutes, violins, guitars, all these instruments melded together, creating a song that was as enchanting as it was unrestrained. The grounds were alive with motion, with dancers and acrobats and mimes. And color in profusion, despite the earth brown robes worn by Odessa's supporters and the gowns of wispy white in which those who championed the faerie queen Amelia were dressed.

"It is rich, is it not, my young friend?"

The sound of Ivan's voice beside him on the grass path caught Adrian by surprise, though he had no trouble hiding that reaction. Keeping his expression placid, he offered a small nod of agreement as the man in black fell silently into step with him.

"Your friend from America," Ivan continued in his whispery tones. "She will not be joining us for cocktails at the castle?"

Adrian cast him a speculative sideways glance. "You sound disappointed."

White teeth gleamed in the glowing bowls of firelight that formed a columned circle around the clearing. "She is quite lovely, this one. Full-blooded and passionate. Like the Gypsy. It is rare to find such a woman these days."

Suppressing a snarl, Adrian nodded again and made a show of redirecting his attention to Mandelin Castle. The evening had retained much of the day's heat. Jeans and sneakers and a long-sleeved cream polo shirt were all he needed to keep warm—and they had an added benefit, subtle but effective. They gave him that unassuming air he'd adopted naturally as a child and still enjoyed in situations like this.

Quiet, casually dressed, unresponsive—few people put their guards up against such a combination. He had learned a great deal by wandering in and out of forbidden places unnoticed, like a shadow no one really saw. And, of course, having a foreign accent didn't hurt, either. Amazing how many things were said by people who assumed he could not follow their conversation.

He smiled distantly to himself. The accent would not work on Ivan Ragozcy, but those other things might. He had accomplished little else this evening. Perhaps he could learn something of worth from this mock vampire.

In his mind Adrian pictured the great hall of Mandelin Castle, torch-lit with fires crackling in the grates and clusters of lush flowers in full summer bloom, spread generously about the ancient chamber. And in the middle of all this, Rielle, as she was undoubtedly adept at doing, would be plying Fagan and his guests with whatever form of liquor came to hand.

They had flipped a coin on this after dinner. One of them would go ahead to Fagan's castle cocktail party; the other would stay at the manor and search Luke's room. Dangerous to separate but unavoidable if they hoped to best the Phantom. And in their own unscrupulous ways, they were both professionals—or had been once. Taking risks of this sort was nothing new to either of them.

He recalled the incident at the joust, Rielle's fall on the cliff, the music she had heard and later the laughter. Yes, they had to take chances to expose this mad creature, but that didn't mean he had to like it, especially where Rielle was concerned.

Unwilling to consider his reasons for that feeling, Adrian lifted his eyes to the moon. He could see Ivan beside him, a silhouette in black with only the front of his white silk shirt breaking the monotony.

"It is quite beautiful in the Transylvanian Alps at this time of year," he remarked with seeming indifference and not looking at Ivan's pale face. "You must enjoy this festival greatly to travel such a distance when the traditional celebrations of your own country are so numerous."

"You have been to my country?" The inquiry was polite but stiff.

Adrian shrugged. "Many times. In Resita I know people, and this town is near Lupeni, I believe. Perhaps you will tell me what stage productions you are performing in this summer. There is a Grand Prix race in Hungary in August. My friends are rather old and not as active as they once were. They would enjoy an evening out."

Ivan didn't bat an eyelash. Neither did he look sideways, Adrian noticed. His black eyes were fixed on the castle. "I will not be performing in Romania this season," he said slowly. "I have decided to rent a cottage near Castletown on the Isle of Man." Again that polished smile that was more parody than pleasantness. "To study faerie lore in greater depth."

"Is that the kind of lore that interests you?"

Ivan's chuckle came out forced, though he didn't entirely evade the question. "I have many interests, my young friend. I have also what you might call—" He paused and made a searching motion with his gloved hand. "There is a word for my unusual habits, it does not come to me."

The genial curve of Adrian's mouth didn't reach his eyes. "Idiosyncrasies?" he suggested in place of the darker word that sprang to mind.

"Yes. That is the term. My English, as you see, is less than complete."

"We could speak Romanian if you would prefer."

This time Ivan couldn't conceal his astonishment. He stared at Adrian, his black eyes both surprised and calculating. Then his red mouth turned up in a slow smile, and he lifted a heavy brow. "There are many dialects in my country," he returned quite shrewdly, pausing as a costumed Gypsy cut across his path. "I think it is unlikely we would be able to communicate in that language."

Adrian moved an unconcerned shoulder. "Perhaps not," he agreed affably enough.

More Gypsies blocked the path, seven of them, staging one of the old faerie rites. Adrian kept one eye on them, and the other on Ivan, whose white-gloved fingers stroked the yellow flower on his lapel in response to a woman's pantomimed question. Interesting that this man always wore gloves.

"You have no charm, I see," the would-be vampire remarked above the airy threads of flute music that unfurled around them. "This is most dangerous. Without one you run the risk of being lured into Odessa's evil faerie ring, as Sir Arundel was the night he died."

Was that a threat? Adrian wondered, still covertly watching the Gypsies. Skin slick with perspiration, they danced closer for their captive audience of two, forming a sinuous circle about the men.

"'Amelia and her mortal lover will never be united!' This was Odessa's promise," one of the masked women cried. "'I, Odessa, Faerie Queen of the Underworld, will prevent this happy joining!' And so she did. On Midsummer's Eve when the moon was full and her powers were at their evil peak, she concocted her most clever disguise and lured the bold knight to his doom. To her faerie ring. And once inside, he was helpless. Once inside she bestowed upon him that most fatal kiss.

"'You are too late,' she crowed in triumph to Amelia, whose arrival had been delayed by a group of Odessa's faithful followers. 'He has been bitten. He has only one hope now. To save his soul, you who love him best must kill him. Otherwise he is mine.' "

"And so, Amelia did this horrible thing," another masked dancer whispered. "She killed the man she loved. But knowing Odessa's treachery as she did, she did not stop there. Around his neck she hung an amulet, a twig of oak and one of thorn, bound together with a long red thread. This would protect her bold knight in death. Odessa could not spirit him away to her underworld realm while he wore such a charm, and neither could she remove it from him. Sir Arundel's soul would not be stolen by the evil faerie queen. And so Odessa had not won after all."

The first woman swayed closer, taking up the story again. "Fury, this was Odessa's reaction. Faerie rage. No, she could not have Sir Arundel now, but she could have the other Midsummer celebrants. Poor, unsuspecting humans. They had no magic to prevent her from feeding on their blood. She would feast on them. Steal their souls.

"An unspoken plan of malice, but again Amelia foresaw it. And off she flew to gather armfuls of St. John's wort, which she showered down upon the mortals below. And once again Odessa was defeated."

The Gypsy glided nearer still, drawing the circle down, forcing the men into closer proximity. "It is said the good queen rules still in the magical world of Faerie. But it is an unhappy reign. Each year on Midsummer's Eve, she returns to Sir Arundel's home in the hopes that her lover's immortal spirit will be allowed to cross over for one night. But she is not alone and this she knows, too. Odessa rises with the moon, a Metamorph whose red eyes pore over the crowd, watching for her queenly rival and the ghost of a brave medieval knight."

The slender finger that came up to touch Adrian's neck stopped short, then slowly withdrew. "She will feed on unprotected souls," the breathy voice behind the mask warned. "Kill them. But they will not know who has done this evil thing to them—unless they chance to see her cold, red eyes in the moonlight."

Adrian's shoulder brushed against Ivan's chest, but he said nothing, merely waited patiently for the ring of undulating bodies to dissolve.

"So now you understand, my friend," Ivan said softly as the Gypsies, their tale complete, vanished into the crowd. "You must find yourself a wort."

Pushing one hand through his hair and the other into the back pocket of his jeans, Adrian nodded. "I will do that now," he agreed.

He moved away, leaving the other man to continue on to the castle alone. Only when Ivan was gone did he allow himself a tiny smile of satisfaction—and just the briefest moment of regret. It seemed he hadn't lost his touch, after all.

Still smiling faintly, he strolled with seeming indifference, over to one of the flaming columns. Smoke swirled down in gauzy tendrils as he turned his back on the clamorous scene behind him. No one watched or even appeared to notice as he withdrew a black leather wallet from his jeans pocket.

He flipped it open, studying the contents with a thoughtful eye. The numerous credit cards, the Knights of the Round Table Club card, the driver's license that had been issued in London last year—all were made out in the name of the same person.

"Spencer Roe," Adrian murmured, then glanced again at the picture on the Southwark license. There was no mistake.

Flipping the wallet closed, he slid it back into his pocket and slanted a narrowed look at the castle. His companion of moments ago was just mounting the outer steps. A man whose name was not Ivan Ragozcy.

Chapter Ten

Fagan had done magical things with the great hall. Adrian stepped through the doorway and had to stop for a moment to absorb it all.

The chamber was immense, in ruins naturally, with chunks of stone pillars lying in huge heaps on the floor. He saw a ravaged staircase that had once swept upward to an open balcony and cracks the size of his fist zigzagging down the walls. But these things were no more than a backdrop, an ancient sandstone palette on which Fagan had splashed every color in the spectrum.

There were flowers all over, as Adrian had known there would be, great bunches of purple orchids, moonflowers and tiger lilies, as well as cascading trails of honeysuckle, cinnamon vine and creeping fig. There was jasmine and wild thyme, vases filled with red primroses and, of course, plenty of St. John's wort. There were long velvet curtains with tassled cords hung on the walls and draped around cornerstones and pillars, the rich tones of burgundy and midnight blue changeable by torch and candlelight.

Dust and cobwebs had been swept away, and everywhere Adrian looked he saw columns of flames burning brightly. Linen-covered tables ran the length and width of the room, overflowing with trays of fruit and succulent cakes, fresh fish and even a slightly charred leg of lamb.

And of course he saw people, dressed in everything from denim to damask. All of Fagan's guests were present and perhaps a hundred more from the village. Faerie airs played softly in the background, courtesy of a battery-powered stereo system and perfectly placed speakers.

"So, are you suitably impressed, *senhor?*"

Rielle managed to catch him unawares, the second time such a thing had happened that night, but Adrian wasn't concerned. The Phantom wasn't likely to stick a knife between his ribs with a hundred witnesses milling around.

She came up beside him, delectable as always in a peach silk halter dress and matching two-inch-high heels that almost brought her up to his height, handing him a drink, a twin to the one she held.

"Mineral water," she remarked with a delicate shudder. "Fashionable and alcohol-free, but it tastes like wet dirt."

Adrian felt that elusive stab of amusement she alone could evoke and, lifting the glass to his lips, took a moderate sip. "It is not so bad," he told her with a shrug.

Her smile was serene. "You've been spending too much time on the Continent, amigo." Her hand closed about his wrist as she spoke. He felt her surreptitious tug and let himself be drawn over to the wall. "Did you find anything in Luke's room?"

He shook his head, his gaze sweeping the pockets of laughing, chatting, slightly tipsy people before them. "No. But I did run into your vampire on my way up here."

She hid a teasing smile behind her glass. "Did he try to bite you?"

"Nothing quite so drastic, *querida,*" he murmured, then realized what he'd said and squeezed his eyes closed in disbelief.

"Are you sure?" She sounded puzzled now and that, Adrian knew, could lead to trouble. It did. He felt her hand catch his jaw, felt her turn his head until he had no choice but to look into her eyes. "You're not sick or anything, are you?" she demanded. "You didn't eat any weird food at the manor, I hope. At the risk of sounding paranoid, I still don't trust Gretchen. She keeps coming over and offering me the same selection of pressed duck."

"I will make a point of avoiding her."

"Smart man." She patted his cheek, satisfied he hadn't been poisoned, then to Adrian's regret let her hand fall away. He wanted to pull her back, bury his face in her hair. "If you're sure you're okay," she went on, brushing that beautiful hair back, "why don't you tell me what you and Ivan talked about on your way up here."

Adrian leaned against the wall. "He is not who he pretends to be."

"What?" Rielle stared at him in astonishment. "How do you know that?"

He took another sip of his drink. "I lifted his wallet."

Her eyes lit up with delight. "Really? And he didn't feel it? For ten years out of the business, that's pretty impressive."

Adrian inclined his head, unable to hold back a small smile, though he offered no comment on the matter. "According to his personal identification, Ivan Ragozcy of Lupeni, Romania, is really Spencer Roe of Southwark, England."

"So he's a fake, hmm?"

"Right down to his Transylvanian accent."

Rielle regarded the man across the great hall where he stood sipping red wine and staring enrapt at the fair-skinned woman beside him. "I thought he was just some spook who had a fixation with vampires. I guess I should have known he was a phony all the way." She motioned at him, a caricature in black. "He's wearing a St. John's wort on his lapel. It's a symbol of the sun, you know, inconsistent with true vampire nature."

"A subject on which you are an expert."

She grinned. "I told you, I did *Dracula* in my senior year."

"The next Sybil Fawkes," he recalled with a trace of humor. "I remember."

Her expression grew troubled, and she took up a leaning position on the wall next to him. "But Sybil's dead now, and so are a lot of other actresses. And Paul," she added, glancing again at Ivan. "Did you learn anything else about this guy?"

"Not really. He wears gloves most of the time, but then so does Fagan."

"Do you think he might be the Phantom?"

Adrian made an indecisive motion. "There is no way to be sure," he began, then cut himself off as a familiar voice pierced the din around them. Taking Rielle's drink from her hand, he set both glasses down beside a potted banana tree and pulled her back, away from the wall to the burgundy velvet curtain that was elegantly draped around the corner.

"What is it?" she whispered, not fighting him when he drew her into the black shadows behind the curtain. "Did you see something?"

"Heard," he said softly against her cheek, and indicated the area in front of them with his head. "I think Fagan has been drinking much of his own champagne."

On the heels of that remark, their host's delighted chuckle penetrated the curtain, a slurred sound of laughter that preceded his cheerful, "Oh, come now, old friend. You can't tell me you're not the tiniest bit irked at this Phantom fellow. Eight women murdered wearing your costumes—surely that can't be good for business."

"Can't it?" Reuben Bishop didn't sound the least bit disturbed by Fagan's comment, although Adrian knew his own judgment was questionable right now. To have Rielle pressed so tightly against his body for the second time that day did not make for a clear head. Calmly Reuben continued, "I rather think you underestimate the power of publicity, Fagan—good or bad. This will not hurt me, or you, either, for that matter. Many's the time a profit has been turned by an ugly set of circumstances."

"Ugly," Fagan echoed. "Yes, I suppose one could put it that way." A thread of dark humor crept into his tone. "The least ugly circumstance being Sybil's death. The start of it all. They ran a piece on her in tonight's *Times,* you know. She would have opened in *Taming of the Shrew* this weekend." He sighed, the quintessence of mock sorrow. "Such talent that woman had. And such a tongue." His voice grew sly. "She also had a silent investment in your costume company, as I recall."

"The woman was never silent," Reuben stated sourly.

Smoke from his pipe floated behind the velvet drapery. It was hot and close back there, and while he might be imagining it, Adrian thought he detected a faint samba beat in the music that swirled around them. He knew that beat well, and the sensations it stirred in him. But it wasn't the music alone, and he knew that, too. The sensations that shimmered through him now had to do with his own emotional vulnerabilities.

He felt the dampness of his skin, hot in the cramped space. He shouldn't let this happen. And yet, he wondered, was it really so important to be always in control? Did it really matter?

Amazingly he could find no answer to those questions, and with a small shake of his head, he gave up the struggle, willingly for once, turning his face into Rielle's soft hair, letting himself enjoy the silky texture of it against his mouth. He breathed in Eternity perfume and the warm scent that was entirely hers. Maybe he'd been wrong to fight his feelings so hard. Right now he wasn't even sure why he did it.

She relaxed into him, making no sound but not pushing him, either. Warm in the shadows, so delicious and soft she was, and not holding out for the sweet words of seduction he might never feel comfortable saying.

He brushed her hair aside, touching the side of her neck with his lips. Only distantly was he aware that Fagan still talked of Sybil Fawkes. Or, more correctly, of the column about her in the London paper. Nothing important in that. Until he caught Fagan's strangely satisfied...

"Look at it this way, my friend. She's gone. Dead, buried and no longer a problem, thanks to this mysterious Phantom at large." The slyness in his tone deepened. "A toast to the man, whoever he may be, for the great favor he has done so many of us by ridding the world of her annoying presence."

Adrian raised his head for a moment. There was a clink of glass and a tiny sound of disgust from Rielle's throat, though her body remained snugly fitted against his. Too distracting, in ways he could no longer ignore. Easing himself back a bit, he grappled with the darkness and the heat and all the uncontrolled sensations that raced through him. And would have lost it all if Rielle hadn't suddenly stiffened and turned her cheek into his shoulder.

"...A most unpredictable creature was Sybil," Reuben commented, not quite able to master the contemptuous sneer in his voice. "And spiteful. She almost ruined us that time in London. Started talking to those friends of hers at the academy." The enmity faded; his voice lowered. "It was a close-run thing, Fagan. We could have been caught, and all for a mistake in judgment." A long pause followed before he spoke again, as if eager now to be done with the subject. "However, there's no point beating a dead horse, as they say. She *is* gone, and we have our new project to concentrate on." A note of suspicion edged in. "Speaking of which, why didn't you tell me you were down in the city recently?"

Hard to miss the lack of concern in Fagan's smiling response, the almost mirthful quality it contained. "This was a pleasure trip, my friend. A personal matter that left no time for business. You understand."

Did he? Adrian doubted it from the displeased grunt Reuben emitted.

"Adrian, look." In the darkness Rielle grabbed his wrist, twisting herself around in his arms and nodding at a tiny opening in the curtain. "That's Noah behind the banana tree. Look at his face, his body language. He's listening to them. He's eavesdropping on his own father."

Adrian brought his eyes into focus on the man, well concealed from the other two as he strained not to miss a word they said.

"One last toast," Fagan proposed blithely. "To success. To problems that solve themselves as if by magic, and to the Phantom who, for us at least, has made that magic happen."

There was a chink of Waterford crystal and then nothing more. Until Noah in an eerie fluid motion lifted his own glass of champagne and whispered a barely audible "To the

Phantom'' before swallowing the contents in a single smooth gulp.

He didn't leave immediately, but stared at the delicate glass, his grip on it tightening visibly. Adrian heard the tiny snap as the stem finally broke beneath the pressure of the man's slender fingers.

Rielle gave a little jerk against his chest. Nothing to see or hear, but it wouldn't have mattered. Noah's attention was fixed on his own hand—and the blood that slowly trickled from it.

''THAT MAN IS spooky,'' Rielle stated in a disgusted whisper. ''He's enjoying the pain, he really is.''

She'd eased the curtain back a bit; now she let it go and looked at Adrian's shadowy features. That was a mistake. So sexy he seemed in the dark confines of this secluded corner. And he'd come so close to kissing her. Yes, but she shouldn't be thinking about that right now.

She glanced back at the opening. ''He's so strange, Adrian. I bet he dreams about pain.''

''And Ivan dreams of vampires.'' Adrian studied the man, then shook his head. ''We are still guessing, Rielle, about all of their motives. This will get us nowhere.''

Damn. That meant it was time to emerge from this wonderful secret place. At least he could kiss her first. After all, they couldn't really go anywhere until Noah left—which of course he did a second later.

Did Adrian understand the resentful look she aimed at Noah's back. Possibly. A smile played on the corners of his mouth, but he reached around her to draw the curtain aside and made no mention of it.

''You are a distraction, *querida*,'' was all he murmured, his eyes already roaming the room. ''This will get us both into a great deal of trouble if we are not careful.''

Hard to believe he would let that happen, but it was a nice thought. So was the idea of food, she realized with a sudden pang as a hired waiter passed by carrying a tray of hot scones.

Had she eaten any of the roast beef Gretchen had put before her at dinner? No, she'd been watching the other guests,
thinking about that horrible chuckle she'd heard earlier, as
well as what she and Adrian had come to refer to as Fagan's latest scam—which almost certainly he was running on
some unsuspecting soul. And then there were all the bruises
that would undoubtedly appear on her body by tomorrow.

Rielle took one of the proffered scones and a napkin and
started for the far side of the room. So much color, so many
spicy scents. And so much mystery. Who was this horrible
Phantom, and where on earth was Luke? Was he safe? She
hoped so.

She forced her thoughts to change direction. "What did
you make of that conversation between Fagan and Reuben?" she asked Adrian beside her.

"About as much as you did." His shrug was noncommittal, a sensual motion that brought a smile of regret to her
lips. "It was interesting, yes, but such things can be easily
misinterpreted."

"True. And God only knows what Noah was up to, or
why Ivan is masquerading as a Central European vampire." She burned her tongue on a hot raisin and winced.
"We're going about this all wrong, you know that, don't
you? Searching Luke's room, trying to pick up on bits of
conversation and then make sense of them. It's too indi-
rect. Too polite."

Adrian arched a meaningful brow. "*You* are polite,
Rielle," he reminded her. "I have Ivan's wallet in my
pocket."

Yes, he did, but why that thought should send a ripple of
excitement across her skin was beyond her. Still, it did, and
she smiled to herself. "That puts you one up on me," she
said, tearing off another bite of the steaming biscuit and
blowing on it. "Which means I'll have to think of something equally intrusive to catch up."

He halted by a long banquet table, pushing the fingers of
one hand through his hair. "This is not a contest, you
know."

Weary amusement in his tone—and in his face. Suddenly Rielle wanted very much to smooth those tired lines away. To forget about phantoms and plots and death for just a few short hours.

She came so close, she really did. But in the end it was her heightened senses that betrayed her. She picked up on an irritating little noise she might otherwise have missed—the delicate tinkle of cut crystal that could only mean Ava and her occult earrings were in the vicinity—and was momentarily diverted.

The woman sailed past on the other side of the table, looking pale and slinky in a one-shouldered affair that would have worked well on the female spy in a bad movie. Dark red and typically dramatic.

Rielle started to dismiss her as Adrian had already done. But no, there was something else, something in the background. Another person who caught her eye. Jonathan Lynch was following Ava, not in open pursuit the way a normal fan would have gone about it, but rather in stealth, as if he didn't want his actions to be noticed—by Ava or anyone.

Now, that was interesting. He certainly hadn't been this furtive earlier at the tournament. So why the secrecy now?

Rielle watched him closely, took note of his pale, attentive eyes, cool and sharp like those of an Arctic wolf. Not as spooky a man as Noah, but suspicious and definitely keeping close tabs on Ava. Ava the stage actress who, like all of the Phantom's previous female victims, had a connection to the prestigious Brittany Rhodes Academy. Ava, whose qualifications in this sordid game were impeccable.

And who could very well be the Phantom's next target for death.

BENEATH A PAIR of steady fingers, the lock clicked open, a small sound that shot down the second-floor hallway like the snap of a dried twig. No matter, there was no one in the mansion to hear it. Two thorough sweeps of the place had proved that.

It was midafternoon with a high bright overcast, another hot muggy day that even the sea breeze couldn't affect. The woodland clearing beyond Mandelin Castle was once again the center of activity for the festival. Plays today, everything from five-minute mime shows to offbeat operettas and all telling the story of the two faerie queens.

Rielle removed the lock-pick and climbed to her feet. "Piece of cake," she lied, though her inner voice was much less glib. Ten seconds to slip a lock was unconscionable; Luke would be mortified.

If Adrian felt that way, he kept it to himself, as always. But then maybe breaking and entering wasn't his forte. With nothing more than an enigmatic smile, he eased open the door to Jonathan's room, the second to last on their list of places to search.

They'd already done Fagan's private chambers and Gretchen's more Spartan quarters, as well.... "Because I still don't trust her," Rielle had maintained when Adrian would have questioned her motives. Not that it mattered. Both rooms had been immaculate, barren of incriminating clues. If Fagan was in fact running a con—or worse—he wasn't working it from there.

Reuben's sleeping quarters and Noah's next door turned up nothing that could be considered impeachable evidence.

Well, no, she amended, that wasn't quite true. They had found two wrinkled laundry tickets in the pocket of Noah's navy blue blazer. And the address on them was less than a block from the scene of the last Theater Murder, the old Cobdon Theater on Shaftsbury Avenue. Still, as a director Noah often worked in that part of London. Not fair to damn the man for something as indefinite as a pair of laundry tickets.

So now it was Jonathan's room they ransacked, a neat but thorough job for which Rielle had trouble summoning much guilt. And wouldn't Aunt Lavinia dress her down for that failing, she thought, smiling a little as she pulled open the doors of an exquisite Elizabethan armoire.

She noticed the corrective shoes right off. There were five pairs sitting at eye level, all designed to compensate for

Jonathan's disability and polished to a spotless shine, lined up like sentinels on the shelf. "I wonder if the Phantom has a limp?" she mused aloud, examining the thickened right sole of one oxford. "Do you realize nobody even knows that much about this fiend? Not a single physical trait. Not height, weight, age, hair color—nothing."

Adrian was crouched down beside her, going through the dresser drawers. Rielle had the good sense only to glance back quickly at him. No man could have looked better in jeans than he did, and today he was also wearing a deep orange T-shirt that mysteriously intensified the color of his eyes and hair, made them appear even darker than usual.

"He has never shot his victims," Adrian remarked in an obscure tone. A strange comment to make, but Rielle couldn't argue it.

"No, he always strangles them," she agreed, dropping to her knees and feeling around the wardrobe floor. "I suppose that would make him quite strong physically, since he always does it with his hands."

Sitting back on her heels, she pushed the damp hair from her face, hunching her shoulders in a moment of uncharacteristic frustration. It was so hot today. Even cutoffs and a baggy cotton top couldn't keep her cool. And being with Adrian only made matters worse. Her body temperature shot up every damned time he accidentally brushed against her. He got her all hot and bothered with a touch, and yet when she looked at him all she saw was calmness, characteristic and maddening. She wanted to shake him. And to kiss him.

Something appeared suddenly in her peripheral vision, and she jumped slightly. "A gun?" She frowned at the thing. "Where did you find this?"

"In the nightstand." Adrian rested his arm on her shoulder, letting the weapon dangle from his fingers. "It is not loaded but there are bullets, as well."

"And questions," Rielle said softly, not bothering to ask the ones that were already obvious. She pictured Jonathan's gray eyes on Ava last night. "But the Phantom always uses his hands," she murmured.

And felt a chill crawl along her backbone when Adrian added a dark "Yes, but the Phantom is also a madman. And in madness there are no absolutes."

Chapter Eleven

For one brief moment the heat in the room seemed to reach claustrophobic proportions. A cold shiver engulfed her. There were no laws in madness, no rules to be followed, only the madness itself and whatever chaos the mind in its possession chose to create.

Before she realized it, Adrian had taken the weapon out of her sight. "Did you find anything?" he inquired, and she shook her head, disappointed that his arm no longer rested on her shoulder. She liked the weight of it there, the heat from his body that ran along her spine.

"Laundry tickets, and now a gun." Sighing, Rielle got to her feet, once again shoving the hair from her face. She regarded Adrian, who was returning the weapon to the nightstand. "Have we accomplished anything today, really? I mean, yes, we found a few tokens, but not proof positive of any crime. And we already knew these people were strange."

"We also knew the Phantom would not be obvious." He made a quick search of the video library, apparently finding everything in order, then held out his hand to her. A surprising gesture, but Rielle didn't hesitate to accept it. "Something subtle," he said, checking the hallway before pulling her out of the room. "That is what we are searching for. A small detail that could be easily overlooked."

"Or something so big we could miss it simply because it is so very enormous."

"No," Adrian returned slowly. "I do not think so, Rielle. Not in the case of this creature. But even if I am wrong in my thinking, one thing is certain. We will have to be better than he is or we will not survive."

Rielle's smile was wry. "Now, that's a lovely thought. True, I'll grant you, but better left unsaid."

Adrian gave his head a shake as they climbed the stairs to the third floor. "Easier perhaps, but not better. Always a dangerous situation must be considered from every angle."

This from a man who put his life on the line every time he stepped into a race car. "Is that what you do when you're driving?" she challenged. "When you're out there on the track, going for the win, do you consider that you could spin off at any given corner, or worse, get into an accident with someone in another car because he's decided to take a risk that you couldn't possibly have foreseen?"

Adrian arched a dark brow at her, his lips curved slightly. "Of course," he said simply.

And Rielle, startled by the serenity of his response, the utter absoluteness of it, could only stare at him in astonishment. "I really don't know you at all, do I?" she asked, and though he didn't look at her, she saw him shrug.

"I think you do. To even ask me that question, you know much more about me than those who would claim, 'Yes, I can tell you everything about him. Cold, he is very cold—always keep your distance, even when there is no race. No life before or after these three days and nothing more to him than that.'"

They'd reached Ivan's door by now, and Adrian squatted down to work the lock. There was no evidence of bitterness in his voice, or in his features. If anything, Rielle thought he seemed vaguely amused by it all.

She watched him ply the lock with hands that were slightly more skillful than hers. "Don't you ever correct the people who say these things about you?" she couldn't resist asking.

He nudged the door back. "There is no point, Rielle. People believe what they wish to believe, based on what they think they see. Few individuals matter so much to them that they will take the time to look deeper. I am guilty of this myself—I would not condemn someone else for having the same fault."

She kept her expression a mask. "And what if someone wanted to look deeper?"

To her shock he smiled, really smiled, and it was a stunning transformation. More beautiful because he also smiled with his eyes, and he seldom did that. Closing the gap between them, he slid his thumb and finger under her chin, tipping her head back and inclining his own until his lips brushed lightly across hers. Barely a kiss, but one of the most erotic touches Rielle had ever felt.

"I think," he answered, his mouth still very close to hers, "that it would depend on who was doing the looking."

What was he talking about? she wondered, totally lost. Then she remembered, and it was her turn to smile. And to sigh. Bad time for all of this, really. They were standing in Ivan's room.

Thankfully Adrian could reason out the situation as well as she could. His mouth brushed over hers once again, then he stepped away. And Rielle told herself firmly that she was relieved. This thing had to be done before the guests returned to the manor. And speaking of doing things...

"Did you ever give Ivan back his wallet?"

"Last night, as we were leaving the castle." Adrian took the closet this time, leaving Rielle with the dresser and bookshelves. And a faint cloud of depression she quickly shook off. "He seemed not to notice that it was missing."

She smiled now, with distance between them. "Busy staring at someone's neck, was he?"

"And talking about the faeries of Morgate. This subject fascinates him, and yet he acts and dresses as though he were a vampire. I do not see the connection."

Rielle pawed through socks and underwear and neatly folded white shirts. "Odessa drinks the blood of her victims," she said over her shoulder. "She can also be destroyed by sunlight. That's probably the connection right there. Unless—" she paused to push at her unruly hair "—it turns out that Ivan is the Phantom, the expert at disguises. Then he might be fascinated by Odessa's similar ability to change form at will. Her glamour.''

She climbed to her feet, noticed the green light on the VCR that indicated a cassette inside and gave the Eject button a casual poke. Might as well see what kind of movies fake vampires liked to watch.

"Dr. Jekyll and Mr. Hyde," she read out loud from the label. "Seems fitting, doesn't it? Familiar, too," she added, staring at the tape. "I've seen this title recently, Adrian, but I don't remember where."

And in the next second, didn't care. It came, as everything had these past few days, out of the silence itself. There was nothing, no one around, and then suddenly the footsteps were right outside the door.

Hurried steps, light, but moving toward them. She wasn't mistaken about that. Ivan. The imposter was returning unexpectedly to his room.

On reflex Rielle stuffed the cassette back into the VCR, her eyes on Adrian, who was halfway across the carpeted floor. "The closet," she whispered, seeing no alternative, but he shook his head and, grabbing her hand, pulled her in the opposite direction. To the window.

"A vampire's closet is not safe," was all he said before yanking open the sash and practically tossing her up onto the stone ledge. The narrowest, oldest, most decrepit-looking ledge Rielle had ever set foot on. And not her entire foot at that.

She was badly out of practice at this, she realized, uttering a wordless prayer as she forced herself to creep sideways. Her fingernails clawed for any little pit in the wall behind her. Of course, there were none, and really nothing except prayer to cling to.

Breath held, she sidled a few more inches to her left. Don't look down! All her instincts told her that. Screamed it. Beyond the terrace, the sea was down there, wet and wild as always, and the rocks, a huge black jut of coastline just waiting for her to lose her nerve or her balance, to come crashing down onto it. She swallowed hard and tried to shut out the roar of the waves, the fear that made her limbs feel lead-weighted.

Where was Adrian?

She twisted her head to the side, and for an instant the fear for her own safety vanished. But it was all right. He was there, dragging the window shut and stepping away from the glass.

He did look down. Brave man. He stared at the sea below like a kid mesmerized by some intricate scientific process, which in a way this was, though certainly of no consequence right now.

As he moved closer, she managed to ask, "Was it Ivan?"

He nodded and she groaned—and wished with all her heart that she could forget about the twenty-foot drop to the terrace underneath them.

She felt Adrian's arm, his shoulder, pressed against hers. There was a certain illogical reassurance in the contact. She wasn't alone, and how different that made it all seem.

But it didn't lessen the danger or produce a magic stairway for them to descend. And the ledge was so narrow, the waves hitting the rocks below so loudly.

She made herself think. Do something. Keep moving. Sideways. Away from Ivan's window, on to the next one. Yes, of course, that would work. Get to the next window and climb through it.

Her hair blew across Adrian's chest, in her own eyes. They both ignored it.

"Be very careful, *querida*," he cautioned. "Go past the first section, and I will try to push it open."

The windows, like the rest of the mansion, were ancient. Long and thin with lead-rimmed panes shaped like diamonds. The glass under Rielle's fingers felt slippery, smooth, cold despite the heat that was cloying even high above the water. She made it past the center and finally to the far side, still praying, still not looking down.

Not to worry, though; they were almost there. Give the latch a twist and push.

She breathed slowly, fearfully, not moving a muscle now, watching as Adrian reached for the heavy brass handle, as he gave it a sharp downward tug. And then had to fight hard the wave of dread and dizziness that swept over her.

The window was locked!

"WHO ARE YOU?" a German voice boomed in Luke's ear.

He didn't flinch, but thought carefully. Track security; he'd have to be careful.

Hardening his blue eyes, he turned to face the man. Goliath in red coveralls. This was going to be tougher than he'd thought.

"I'm looking for Adrian Da Costa," he snapped back in properly affronted English. "Have you seen him?"

The man snarled. Well, at least he understood the language; that was something. "You have no pass, no authority—you are not permitted here."

Luke sent him a cold look, brows arched. "I'm Adrian's brother-in-law, married to his sister, Lucia. And I suggest you believe that, my friend, because I didn't come to this place—" he indicated the empty track with a wave of his sunglasses "—on a whim."

"*Was ist dies* 'whim,'" the man muttered. Hands planted menacingly on his hips, he barked something to one of his colleagues, then glared at Luke. "We will soon see how much of what you say is true, *mein Herr.*"

Fine, Luke didn't care, as long as he could talk to Adrian. He shook his head. When British cousin couldn't get in touch with South American cousin by telephone, one of those cousins was getting too big for his Brazilian racing boots. And God knew, this was the worst possible time for those media evasion tactics Adrian had become so adept at lately. The Phantom was out there, somewhere, and Rielle wasn't.

He paced behind the barrier, saw a projectile whiz by in a deafening roar but didn't care about that, either. A thousand thoughts converged in his head. They were testing the cars this week, not racing. Adrian should be here, but who knew? Rielle was missing; her partner said she'd gone to Silverstone. With the key, no doubt. Adrian had been at

Silverstone last week—and he knew all about Fagan and Brede Manor.

Luke wanted to shake one of the trees in the pine forest behind him. No longer any point wondering why it mattered, this feeling of desperation that embraced him. It was stupid to deny what must surely be. The Phantom wasn't chasing him. Thanks to Paul, the Phantom knew everything, or at least enough to be in Morgate by now. And Rielle was probably there, too.

Luke tugged at his long hair. He knew he should phone and find out for certain; he should have gone there the moment he'd put it all together, made himself face facts. But what would that accomplish, really? Go to Brede Manor, and the Phantom would have him. And of course he would threaten to kill Rielle if Luke didn't hand over the stolen proof.

Where the hell was Adrian!

He growled in his throat. All he could think about was that night, the murder, the proof—and that other thing. That nagging detail he simply could not pin down.

Talking. Luke remembered that well enough. He heard the silky voice in his head still. What a creepy timbre. And the Phantom's mask for the death scene. Ghastly white with a bright red mouth and eyes outlined in black. Like a skull, only worse, talking, laughing.

"You will die, Sybil," he'd crooned to poor, terrified Charity Green. "Again, again and again. My love for you is hatred now, and I will kill you every time you try to come back."

And so he had, his long, gloved fingers closing about the woman's throat....

Luke cringed inside, remembering. Not real, not possible, he'd told himself then, too stunned to believe let alone react. Paul had agreed. No chance to prevent Charity's death, because they hadn't supposed that any of it was actually happening—not at first. It had to be a private performance, sick, but a fantasy, surely.

A choked scream came from her. She looked so scared. Good acting or...

Another shudder, and then that voice again. Those smooth hideous tones. A phantom's voice. And he had the most lissome way of moving. Slow and hypnotic. And those eyes of his, Luke swore they burned. And then suddenly the light went out of them.

It was over. She was dead. The screams were gone. Only a delicate silence left. And Luke, reeling in the shadows with Paul in shock beside him.

Laughter, soft at first, a silky strand of sound, building gradually to a roar. The laughter of a madman, a murderer. Chimes ringing in the background. Candles flickering all around the Phantom's painted face. And the darkness behind it had a nightmarish quality. It seemed to swirl, and Luke felt so sick.

But the laughter had stopped; the Phantom was looking. He saw. He was coming for them.

Luke's head spun. Do something! Run! Shake Paul, shove him. Cut through the old orchestra pit; don't fall. Don't trip. On what? What was this thing in his path?

He fell hard. Where was Paul? Gone, safe, because the Phantom was after Luke. Scramble up out of the pit, onto the stage. Don't panic, go around the body. And then where?

So many candles burning. Sound of the Phantom breathing behind him. More chimes. And then a blur of sound and motion wrapped in darkness.

No thought for what came next, no recollection. But when he hit the alley, he had something in his hands. Proof of the Phantom's crime!

People rushed past, a montage of startled faces, staring at his streaming blond hair. No Phantom chasing him now. Even a madman knew better. And Luke knew, too. He was in deep trouble.

"...I'm very sorry you've gone to all this trouble, but the fact is Adrian Da Costa's not here this week."

The voice that penetrated Luke's confused thoughts was British, the man standing in front of him polite of expression.

"Do you know where I might find him?"

The head shake was an outright lie. "I'm sorry," the man said again. "I really couldn't tell you."

Yes, he could, and he would. Luke dropped all pretense and blurted out his real name. No time now for caution. "I'm Adrian's cousin," he explained. "And this is important. Really. Your number-one driver could be in a great deal of danger."

"In danger?" The man blinked. "In the north of England?" He smiled. "I don't think so."

The north of England... Yorkshire!

Luke's entire body went cold. Rielle, Adrian, the Phantom, they were all at Brede Manor. And so was the proof that would unmask a murderer. A mad murderer.

Chapter Twelve

One of the people at this dinner table was the Phantom.

That thought along with several others crowded into Rielle's head as Gretchen placed a bowl of hot consommé on the plate in front of her. She stared through an ornate flower-and-candle centerpiece at Ivan, seated directly across from her. Maybe him, maybe not. Right now she tended to think so, but that was probably because she was still thinking about the close call on the ledge three days ago. It felt more like three hours to her still-quaking nerves.

A chill passed through her. Nightmarish, crawling along a five-inch stone ledge. And what a jolt to find their only portal to safety locked tight.

She shuddered deeply. In her mind she was back out on that ledge, like one of Fagan's stone statues. Only not nearly so well anchored...

...She was a prisoner of the air. She could not force herself to move. Hair flying about her face. Palms glued to the window behind her. Wind swirling about her trembling limbs.

Yes, the wind...

Why did she get the feeling that each gust grabbed at her, that like all the other elements, this one too was in league with the Phantom?

She gritted her teeth. No time for such idiotic thoughts. Get rid of them. Concentrate. Be calm like Adrian. Go on to the next window.

Huge waves hammered the rocks below. Wet blasts of wind clawed at her hair and clothes. She forced herself to look sideways and immediately felt her palms go clammy.

No more windows! Only stones and the corner of the manor.

"Adrian," she managed to croak. "There's nowhere else to go."

"Yes, I see this."

She wanted to scream at him. How could he sound so matter-of-fact when it was all she could do to find her voice? Be human, panic, she longed to shout, if only to ease a portion of the tension that had stretched her nerves to the breaking point.

But no, she wouldn't break. She wouldn't look down.

What could they do? Think. Forget the sharp spears of pain that shot along her spine to her shoulders and up the back of her neck. Strain caused this. Relax and concentrate.

They couldn't return to Ivan's room. He'd be hanging in the closet like any good Transylvanian bat. Never mind that it was all for show, that the man only pretended to be a monster. Or did the monster pretend to be a man? One way or another he'd surely be there. So retreat was out. And there was no advance, was there? Only the wind that seemed to have developed nasty hands and the tightly bolted window behind them.

"How thick is the glass, Adrian?" she whispered suddenly. "Can it be broken?"

He crouched down. Rielle winced. How did he do that? Her wet palms were plastered to the window, and nothing short of the ledge giving out from under her was likely to change the situation.

"Maybe we can break one of the panes," Adrian agreed, then the wind seemed to catch him and he almost lost his balance.

Rielle's hands came automatically off the glass. She grabbed for his arm, missed, felt her fingers wrap themselves instead around the sleeve of his T-shirt.

The yank she gave the material must have been enough. Either that or Adrian was part mountain goat. In any event he didn't fall—and she didn't want to be out here for another second.

But how could you smash a window when you had nothing hard to break it with? Her eyes widened. Adrian was pulling the T-shirt over his head. She was out here with a crazy person.

It took her a moment to realize he intended to wrap the shirt around his hand and break the glass with his fist. And she would brace him while he did it, because as terrified as she was for her own safety, she was at least that frightened for his. Maybe more.

She pressed her palms down hard on his tanned shoulders, her weight into his body. "Close your eyes," he told her, and she did that, too. And prayed.

Oh, what a blessed thing, the sound of shattering glass. And the wind didn't even blow any of it back at them.

He pulled the sharper pieces from the pane, and Rielle slipped her smaller hand inside. A click, a twist and the window swung inward. All they had to do was fall through, into an empty room, probably the no-show Fortesqueue's, but right then Rielle wouldn't have cared if they'd burst into someone's bath.

She tumbled to the floor, landing hard on Adrian's chest. "Are we alive?" she murmured, her face buried in the hot skin of his neck, the dark silk of his hair.

"Yes, *querida*," he murmured, his breath warm against her cheek. With gentle fingers he stroked her tangled hair. His mouth brushed her temple. "Very much alive."

So tempting to let herself be carried away by sensations made infinitely finer in the aftermath of danger. Seductive. But there was exhaustion tugging at her, too, and countless other emotions. They all pressed in as one, it seemed, and Rielle had trouble thinking let alone separating her feelings. Maybe if she just stayed in Adrian's arms a while longer, everything would come clear to her...

"FAERIES INDEED!" Noah's scornful tones intruded roughly on Rielle's memories. Rielle shook her thoughts aside. Back to reality—more or less.

Three uneventful days had passed with no new clues and thankfully no more close calls. It was Friday night; only two days until the big Midsummer's Eve costume party. The Festival beyond the thick walls of the manor house was a riot of shouts and cries and lyrical chants, while inside, Fagan talked with great enthusiasm about Odessa's misdeeds. Her faerie "glamour."

"Glamour is really nothing more than camouflage," he explained from his place at the head of the table. "To a degree, all faeries have the ability to disguise themselves, but Odessa, ah, she was truly unrivaled in this capacity. She could pass for mortal, and few other faeries could ever hope to do that. And oh, what nasty tricks she would play on people. She set neighbor against neighbor, wife against husband, father against son. And for no reason, really, other than she loved to cause trouble."

Noah, seated next to Ava, grunted. "I've known a goodly number of performers like that. A bothersome lot who refuse to stay in their place."

He didn't look at the woman beside him, but then he didn't have to. His contempt for her and indeed for the rest of the performing world was clear. In a way it was spooky, too, Rielle thought, still not sure what to make of this man. Why would someone who so obviously despised stage players, actresses in particular, choose to make his living directing them?

Evidently Fagan didn't care. He merely smiled and lifted his wineglass. "To all the 'glamour' that manages to live on in the modern world," he offered pleasantly. "May it exist forever. A mystery no mere mortal can ever explain."

An odd toast, but no one really seemed to notice. Or if they did, they kept their mouths discreetly shut. Which was pretty much the way it had been at every meal. Very dull. Unrevealing. Rielle looked around the table. Maybe it was time to shake things up a bit.

She glanced over at Adrian, probably the worst offender when it came to mealtime chatter. Noah threw in the occasional grumble, and even Jonathan managed a quiet remark or two when he wasn't staring at Ava. But Adrian tended not to utter a single word once he came into the dining room. Not if he could possibly avoid it. He sat down, he ate, he nodded politely or smiled a little if someone spoke to him. Yet he never really talked.

Must be something left over from his childhood, she decided, dragging her eyes away before she could get too sidetracked by him.

She waited only until the word "glamour" came up again, which it did just as the main course of steamed halibut was being set in front of them, before venturing a completely fictitious, "I heard once that Sybil Fawkes was rather *glamor*ous, herself, if the term in that sense can be applied to a human." She cut into the tender fish, not looking at anyone in particular. "A woman of many masks, the critics claimed. It's really quite tragic that she had to die at such a young age."

Rielle's sigh was as false as her statements, but it produced the desired effect. Everyone there, including Gretchen, who stood stiffly by the sideboard, reacted instantly to the mention of Sybil's name. Curled lips mostly, except for Fagan, who merely chuckled and Adrian, who leaned back in his chair, hiding a small smile behind his water glass.

It was Jonathan who spoke first, giving his head a solemn shake. "Sad, perhaps, in that she was young and talented, but her death could scarcely be called tragic in any other way. Sybil Fawkes was not a nice human being. Even her most ardent fans understood that."

"Her fans and her lovers," Noah added with a sneer. "From what I heard and saw that summer I worked with her out of Brittany Rhodes, I'd say the latter outnumbered the former by a considerable amount."

Ava gave her short bob a disdainful flip with her fingernails. "Sybil Fawkes was a tramp," she stated coldly. "After he directed her in *Marionette,* Paulo Scholotti swore he'd never have her in his pictures again. She was poison, and he knew it."

Reuben made a pretense of studying his wine. "Pure poison," he echoed, seeming lost in thought. "How unfortunate that those other women who were—oh, how shall I put it—"

"Murdered?" Fagan inserted with a wicked grin that brought from his old friend nothing more than a shrug.

"An indelicate term but apt, I suppose." Reuben bared his pointy teeth in a smile that didn't quite ring true. "As I was saying, how unfortunate that those other women who were murdered should all have been associated with the Brittany Rhodes Academy, on whose board of regents Sybil Fawkes just happened to hold a seat. Coincidence perhaps that the Phantom's victims all knew Sybil, worked with her in fact through the academy."

Ava's pale features whitened even more, but only for an instant. Then she lifted her chin in a gesture of defiance. "There were hundreds of us who worked with Sybil over the years," she announced tightly. "More likely thousands. And out of those, a dozen have been murdered. As for Brittany Rhodes, the academy has limbs that extend across the Continent to Asia and into both the Americas. You're stretching a very thin connection, Reuben. And if you're trying to frighten me with all this talk of coincidence and death, let me assure you, your scare tactics fall entirely flat. Unlike those other foolish women, I have no intention of hopping cheerfully into costume and greasepaint and letting some lunatic Phantom get his hands on my throat."

"Perhaps not," Reuben said again, his wolfish smile intact. "Still, one never can tell about these things. All else aside, the fact remains that this Phantom fellow is a lunatic. Not likely to wait for his victims to hop into anything of their own accord." The smile widened disarmingly as one fine gray brow rose in her direction. "Food for thought, don't you agree?"

Before Ava could respond, or lose every last scrap of color in her cheeks, Ivan rushed to snatch up his wine. "Perhaps another toast," he suggested, looking to Fagan for support.

And Fagan, being the perfect host, nodded his head, motioning for Gretchen to refill his glass.

And that was a curious thing, too, Rielle, having listened in rapt silence to the conversation, noticed. Gretchen, usually so stony-faced and grim, seemed put out, almost angry if the rigid set of her jaw was any indication. But angry at whom? Fagan, because he'd asked for more wine? No, that made no sense. Yet neither did the housekeeper's black expression. Maybe, Rielle mused, she and Adrian should consider taking another look through this woman's room.

Fagan's voice called her back to the present. "I give you Sybil Fawkes," he said, his tone an odd blend of solemnity and humor. "May she rest in peace."

REST IN PEACE...

Such a simple toast.

But the Phantom, recalling all that had been, all that was yet to come, knew this was something Sybil would never do.

AN INTRIGUING "Murder by Death" dinner and now a mystical faerie-tale play under the theater of the stars. Rielle stared at the costumed Gypsies on the tiny stage before her without really seeing their nimble antics. How could she lose herself in magic after everything that had happened these past few days?

It absorbed her, this puzzle. So many rich textures it contained, so many possibilities, of intricate webs being spun and half-painted pictures that could, as things stood now, lead to a dozen different ends. Rielle's head was positively crammed with thoughts, none of which she could finish. But of course she didn't have to. That kind of reasoning was more Adrian's area of expertise.

"Take each thought to its logical conclusion," he'd told her as they'd approached the festivities in the forest clearing. "You will see then that the Phantom could still be anyone. All of Fagan's guests behave suspiciously in some way. So too does Fagan. Then there is Jonathan, who talks little about himself. He says he has played the Cobdon Theater when we know this is not possible and follows Ava around as if obsessed by her. Ivan is not the person he pretends to be and perhaps, beyond this preternatural charade, not even a performer. Fagan and Reuben as a pair speak in riddles of Sybil Fawkes, the woman we know to be the Phantom's first victim. And I hear how they taunt each other, as well, as if neither completely trusts the other. And then there is Noah, who is in many ways the greatest mystery of all. Not a nice man, I think, but perhaps not a Phantom, either. This we will have to determine.''

Yes, but not tonight, it appeared. Reuben, who thought his son drank too much as it was, had been less than silent when Gretchen informed him that Noah would not be attending the festival that evening. He'd taken the footpath to the Boar's Head Inn, she said, a cozy little thatch-roofed pub situated in a small glen between Brede Manor and the village. And you couldn't spy on a man who wasn't around.

Had Ava followed him? Rielle let her eyes roam the audience in front of the stage. No, there she was, looking bored as only she could, with Jonathan directly behind her, his silvery gaze fixed on the back of her head. Creepy, but there was really nothing that could be done about that, either.

Pushing up the sleeves of the loose black sweater she'd thrown over her black silk jumpsuit, she glanced at Adrian. He was sprawled in his chair with his head resting on the back, apparently watching Odessa dance across the stage. No point looking at a fake faerie when there was a fake vampire less than thirty feet away and making notes in a little black book.

"He's probably cataloguing his victims," Rielle said in a low voice. "Why don't you pick his pocket again when he puts the book away? Maybe it'll give us the proof we need to nail him."

Adrian didn't move, just lounged there in his chair in that deep orange T-shirt she was beginning to love on him, and sent her a mildly humorous look out of the corner of his eye. "You are reverting quite badly, you know. Pick this one's pocket, break into that one's room. Perhaps we should have come here in a wagon, posing as Gypsies. Then you could really have enjoyed yourself."

"Don't be petty," she replied, not the least bit upset. "Luke needs our help. I won't let him down. This is an important thing we're doing here, Adrian. And if you think for one minute that I get some weird thrill out of crawling along high stone ledges, you can think that one through again." Arms folded across her chest, she leaned back in her chair and regarded the colorful stage. "I'm legitimate now, and happy to be so. And don't you dare misinterpret that statement," she said, shooting him a level look of warning.

His lips curved into a lazy smile. He'd slumped down in his seat, and she felt his shoulder rub against her arm. She shivered lightly. His skin was so warm, even through the bulky wool of her sweater. And she was so tired of thinking about the Phantom. All she had to do was press a little closer, and...

"Fagan." She blurted out the name as her eyes landed unexpectedly on their host. He was scurrying along the path between Mandelin Castle and Brede Manor, evidently heading toward the unlit mansion. But he wasn't supposed to be here tonight, she recalled, thinking back to dessert and the announcement he'd made less than two hours ago.

"You'll want to attend the faerie plays this evening," he'd said to his guests. "I promise, you won't be disappointed. I only wish that I could join you, but I'm afraid I have some business to take care of with the village butcher. A little matter of the solstice feast the day after tomorrow, you understand."

Well, the village butcher certainly didn't conduct his business out of Mandelin Castle. And there was no question that Fagan had just come from there. He'd lied about his plans for the evening. Surprising? Not really, but it did make his covert little trip down the footpath extremely suspicious.

"You know, I'd appreciate it if a couple of these people would eliminate themselves from our Phantom suspect list,"

Rielle murmured moments later as she and Adrian crept along the path behind Fagan.

Adrian kept his fingers firmly wrapped around hers. "This might be possible if we could come right out and ask them for explanations. It is because we slip from shadow to shadow spying on them that the answers come so slowly."

"What answers?" she muttered, then swallowed a cry of pain when she accidentally turned her ankle on the grass. She should never have worn high heels to an outdoor festival.

She concentrated on Fagan instead, squinting into the darkness. "Where's he going? That's not the front door. That's not any door, is it?"

"It is the cellar," Adrian said quietly. "A small entrance, seldom used, I think. Reuben pointed it out to me yesterday."

Rielle held tight to Adrian's hand as Fagan's wiry silhouette disappeared through the low entrance. Was he meeting Reuben in there? She couldn't recall seeing the elder Bishop in the clearing tonight.

Of course that idea only complicated matters more, at least in terms of the Phantom. There couldn't be two murderous fiends, could there?

Sticky little leaves plastered themselves to her cheeks as Rielle followed Adrian down five stone steps to the tiny door. Thank God she couldn't actually see the cobwebs that also got caught on her face and hair. And what was that horrible fetid smell that hit her the moment Adrian shoved the door back? Please, not human skeletons, she prayed. Don't let this be an old crypt.

More steps awaited them, though how Adrian knew that was beyond her. She couldn't see a thing.

Her eyes began to adjust about halfway down the narrow stairs. She almost wished they hadn't.

"Crates!" she whispered, staying as close as possible to Adrian's back. "Long wooden crates. Dracu—" She caught herself in time, forcing a hasty smile when he turned his head to stare at her. "Never mind. Where's Fagan?"

"There is another door on the far side of the room,"
Adrian said, his amusement evident if restrained. "And a
light showing at the bottom of it. He must be there."

That would be the dungeon, no doubt. An old torture
chamber, if manor houses contained such things. And
wouldn't Gretchen make a splendid executioner? Or Noah.

The ground beneath her felt like stone, worn but uneven,
covered with a fine layer of dirt. The air was nonexistent,
really, the smell of decay much stronger now. Best not to try
to figure out the source. Just stay close to Adrian, walk
softly and don't trip.

The silence was thick this far below ground. Rielle heard
each breath she took, the sound of her heart beating in her
ears. And she saw those crates everywhere she looked. Cof-
fin-sized wooden boxes that made keeping her imagination
under control doubly difficult.

She was still struggling with visions of native soil, black
capes and bony white fingers when her shin banged hard
into a sharp corner. A bolt of pain shot up her leg, and she
had to set her teeth to keep from crying out. She grabbed
Adrian's arm for balance; his hands had come up automatically to steady her.

She glared at the offending crate. "Stupid box," she
muttered, and gave the side of it a childish but satisfying
kick. Or more specifically, a sound wallop. Although she
hadn't intended to dislodge the lid, that's exactly what happened. And it wasn't any moldy old count she saw lying inside.

Something white, though. She peered at the neat rows,
then glanced uncertainly at Adrian. "Jars?" she said.
"Crates filled with glass jars?"

Adrian crouched down. "Porcelain," he corrected, picking one up and studying it. "No labels."

"Crates filled with unlabeled porcelain jars." Rielle went
down on her knees beside him. "In Fagan's cellar." She
twisted off one of the lids. "It smells a bit like St. John's
wort, and a few other flowers and spices."

"Herbs, perhaps."

"Maybe." Rielle sniffed the thick cream again. "Whatever it is, I can't imagine what it's doing down here."

Or could she?

The answer came with Adrian's slow grin. Of course. Fagan's con. His and Reuben's new "project." The cloth pouches, too. Possibly Gypsy herbs to be used in these jars of cream.

"Facial cream, you think?"

Adrian shrugged. "It could be anything. Perhaps it is not even the scam we assume it to be."

"Right, and Fagan might have acquired all his wealth legitimately." Rielle capped the jar and returned it to the crate. "Nice try, Adrian, but he's doing something underhanded with this stuff. The question is, does it in any way relate to the Phantom?"

Adrian pulled the lid of the crate back in place. "There is no way we can be sure at this point. I think you are correct. Fagan and Reuben are up to something, and if one of them is in fact the Phantom, then possibly this something is merely a new way for them to secure another victim. You did say that Fagan spoke to someone regarding three actresses he wished to hire. And the Phantom did use a con to set up his last murder."

"A con—and Luke." Rielle squared her shoulders in determination. "We've got to figure this out, Adrian. Luke won't be safe until the Phantom's behind bars. And we're close, I know we are. I'm positive that he's right here at the manor. The Phantom, I mean, not Luke."

Adrian climbed to his feet, bringing Rielle with him. "Perhaps he is even closer than we think." He motioned to his left, to the sliver of light still visible near the floor, drawing her forward as he did so.

A faint shiver passed through Rielle's body. Yes, very close indeed. Much too close if Fagan turned out to be the Phantom.

"This door opens in," Adrian said now, his mouth close to her ear. "It will be difficult to see what we are walking into."

Cautiously Rielle pressed the side of her head to the heavy oak door. "I don't hear anything," she whispered finally, stepping away. "Maybe Fagan's moved on to another room. Unless for some reason this isn't a complete cellar, it should be enormous."

Her fingers closed briefly about Adrian's arm, holding him back. At his questioning look, however, she gave herself a little shake. No cowardice, she thought firmly, regaining her composure with a decisive effort. "All right, do it," she said, and braced herself for whatever might await them on the other side.

It was anticlimactic, really. There was nothing but a wide corridor in front of them, lit with converted gas lamps, not nearly as gloomy as what they'd left behind. In fact, it was charming, all the dark wood and soft round stones that lined the passage. Silent, and maybe a bit daunting for that reason, but at least no one sprang at them from the shadows or any of the arched doorways that came into sight.

But where was Fagan? Rielle glanced at Adrian, who merely shrugged and slipped soundlessly across the threshold. Stepping out of her shoes, she followed him through, careful to leave the door open.

Once inside, she paused next to Adrian, her brow knit. Strange. Though she couldn't pin it down, something felt wrong. Too quiet in here. Where was the festival music? And where did all these dark doors lead?

She didn't dare ask Adrian any of her questions. Better to leave the silence alone.

By unspoken consent they moved along the passage, slowly, noiselessly, listening for that first telltale sound, any small shuffle or scrape that would give them direction.

Adrian's fingers tightened around hers, and for a moment Rielle was able to ignore the icy sensation that had begun to crawl over her skin. She hadn't noticed it at first, but it was stronger now, inexplicable, yet almost a tangible thing.

Fear, she decided, nothing more than than, and clenching her teeth fought the chills running through her. Think of something else. Adrian. Yes, he was very much alive, warm and so real. Listen to him breathe.

She relaxed a little, aware that the shadows had grown murkier, longer. Not her imagination. The lamps had dimmed faintly. Ah, but that sort of thing happened often in the old manor house. The wiring was outdated, the power a fickle thing. There was no cause for alarm.

As if they'd read her thoughts, the lamps flared then faded again, three times in quick succession, finally settling down to a lustrous glow. Soft yet eerie, the electric wicks burned with a peculiar radiance, like spirits trapped in opaque glass cages.

Rielle heard it then, behind her, a tiny almost imperceptible break in the silence. It could have been a rat—but she knew that wasn't it. So did her pounding heart, and Adrian, whose body went suddenly taut against hers.

The Phantom!

Eyes wide, she spun around and knew that Adrian had done the same. But it was too late, and they were too far from the door to keep it from swinging shut—like the inexorable lowering of a coffin's lid, Rielle's frantic mind offered as her own body went rigid. And the person who'd lowered it stood there, completely recognizable even if he was partly trapped in shadow.

Fagan, of course, smiling as he always did in that sly cryptic way of his. Glimmer of something in his blue eyes, half-gloved fingers splayed against the oak door.

No sound again once the horrible echo died away. Nothing except the three of them in the poorly lit passage.

But what did Fagan hold in his other hand? A dark object with a long barrel. And he was lifting it, pointing it at them!

His smile widened. The object came higher.

And then the lights went out.

Chapter Thirteen

"Oh, bother."

Fagan's sigh drifted through the darkness as clearly as any gunshot. Rielle heard a sharp click and instinctively pressed her hand to her chest, checking for blood. But, no, that hadn't been the sound of a weapon firing, and anyway Adrian had pulled her aside the second the power failed. It would truly have been a lucky shot in the dark for Fagan to have hit either of them.

Another click, another sigh. "Rotten luck," Fagan muttered with obvious regret. "Ah well, I guess we do this the old-fashioned way."

The Phantom always strangled his victims....

Rielle choked, then pushed the thought aside and got hold of herself. Fagan couldn't take on two adversaries at once. He probably wouldn't even be able to find them with the lights out.

Something flared in the darkness, blue-white, then orange. A match. The flame rose, leaving a thin trail of yellow in its wake, then was suddenly transformed to a blaze.

"There, much better." Chuckling, Fagan settled an old torch back into its wall sconce and picked up the barreled object he'd set on the floor.

"A bottle of wine!" Rielle breathed, her body sagging. Relief and laughter swept through her. She pressed her forehead against Adrian's shoulder. "I don't believe it."

"Believe it, my child," Fagan assured with a smile of oblivious delight. "Côtes du Rhone Rodet, 1986." He kissed the dusty label. *"Magnifique."*

It was no explanation, really, and it certainly didn't account for those jars of cream, but those things didn't matter to Rielle just then. Fagan had been holding a bottle of purple wine, not a deadly weapon. And she'd been checking herself for gunshot wounds.

Lifting her head from Adrian's shoulder, she tried not to look at the little man. It didn't work. Neither did reminding herself that he could still be the Phantom. The whole thing just seemed so ridiculous in retrospect. So utterly absurd.

And shaking her head, she dissolved into a helpless fit of laughter.

"THIS IS THE WINE CELLAR. As you might imagine, it's my pride and joy." With the torch Fagan indicated a deep, black chamber, honeycombed with row upon row of floor-to-ceiling shelves. "And just along here is the costume room. From my old theater days," he added with a wink that suggested not everything inside had been obtained in a legal fashion.

He was waiting for a response from his unexpected guests, and since Rielle was still struggling to control her laughter, Adrian was left to murmur a polite, "Very impressive, Fagan, as are all of your collections."

His impassive gaze touched on the colorful racks, on the delicate silks and satins, the ribbons and dyed feathers, the tunics and the soft rawhide vests with their feudal crests painted on the front. Faded by time and wear, they were, but still quite beautiful. Rielle would look like a medieval princess in any of the gowns, ravishing even in the plain brown wool one that hung sleeveless and straight to the floor.

Fagan scuttled farther down the hall. "Over here is what I call the junk room, where I keep my less valuable collectibles—copies of Grecian urns, carpets from Damascus and Khartoum, bad Italian busts, that sort of thing. And across the hall is the film library. Quite well equipped, as you can see.'' He gestured with the torch to a vast array of machinery, some of it new, some of it ancient, all laid out on a table by the far wall. ''There hasn't been a movie made that I can't put on video. Many I've already done. Scholotti's work, for example, and Carl Dreyer's—Hitchcock in the early days, some Murnau and no less than twenty obscure silent pictures, most of which were made in Germany. I've even spliced together a number of old prewar shorts. Copies of those you'll find in your rooms.''

Rielle surveyed the gleaming silver cannisters that in torchlight seemed to go on forever, then turned to their host with her most captivating smile. Trouble, Adrian thought, but held back the smile that played on his own lips and let her continue.

''We thought you might be a prowler,'' she lied with flawless credibility. ''That's why we followed you down here. I mean, we didn't think it could be you because you said you'd be tied up in the village tonight—with the butcher.''

Whatever Fagan's reaction might have been, it was concealed by the darkness. However, his head did move, a slow nod punctuated by a regretful ''Yes, that was the plan, but I'm afraid something else came up—for the butcher.'' A hand waved dismissively. ''No matter. We shall simply talk tomorrow instead.''

A good enough explanation, ambiguous yet difficult to challenge. ''I see,'' was all she said, and really all she had to say. Fagan's fingers tightened momentarily on the neck of the bottle, but only for a second. Then he was chuckling again and offering no answers whatsoever.

''I think, all things considered, that we should probably abandon our tour and return to the Festival, don't you? Mustn't miss the final act of whichever play you choose to watch. Either the faerie island will rise or it won't.''

''The what?'' Rielle asked, though Adrian knew she was far from being diverted by the little con man's charm.

''The faerie island,'' Fagan repeated. He led the way back down the corridor. ''Legend has it that if Sir Arundel does manage to cross over and Amelia can get to him before

Odessa does, the two lovers will ride the mists to their own magic island, a woodland realm with sweet blossoms and fruit and gentle twilight skies. For one brief moment at the solstice it will be visible to human eyes. Then back into the depths of the ocean it will sink. And there, in that lovely shimmering middle world, Amelia and her mortal lover will reside throughout eternity.''

''And if Odessa can prevent this?'' Rielle asked. ''What happens then?''

They'd reached the crate-filled chamber, which seemed even more repellent by the flickering light of the torch. Fagan moved easily across the dirty stones. No guilt in his casual shrug. ''Very little, I'm afraid.'' His eyes sparkled with mischief. ''Which is why I've arranged to hold a fireworks display each evening from now until the end of the Festival. Three nights in all. You see, faeries, lovely air-creatures that they are, have a tendency to be quite unreliable. If the faerie island fails to rise, I must provide an alternate form of entertainment, something to keep the visitors from demanding their gate fee back. Can't be doling out refunds simply because an old ghost and a couple of precarious faeries choose not to cooperate.''

''You are a shrewd businessman, Fagan,'' Adrian noted, reaching around Rielle to hold open the door at the top of the stairs.

More mischief danced in their host's blue eyes. ''Many would say opportunistic, some even worse things. But then I've never been one to worry about what people say. At least not on a personal level. Professionally, now that's a different matter. I've always found it, oh, shall we say satisfying, to turn a profit. That's why I left the London stage, you know.''

Rielle regarded him curiously as he extinguished the torch in the dirt of a weed-infested flower bed. ''You were a stage actor in London, Fagan? I didn't know that.''

Fagan continued to roll the torch as if lost now in some distant, private thought. ''A character actor,'' he said finally, his voice soft, inscrutable. ''A good one, I felt, but those who mattered never could see my talent. Because I had none, as a few of them so bluntly put it. But I showed them, I did—though they never really knew it." His smile had become vaguely mysterious, and his voice. "No, there were no curtain calls for the performances I gave. I think—I hope—there never will be."

Both his expression and tone sharpened then, the dreamer suddenly awakening to the real world. He tucked the wine bottle under one arm and grinned. "At any rate, those days of powder and paint are for me but a memory. Now off you go. Enjoy the merriment around you. And don't forget to find yourselves a couple of worts."

"Protection against evil," Rielle murmured, her back pressed firmly into Adrian's chest. A cold sense of dread passed through him, although why he couldn't say. Not until...

Fagan's teeth gleamed in the pale glow of moonlight. "Protection against faerie evil, my lovely," he corrected softly and again in that odd mystical tone. "Remember that. Only against faerie evil."

"'FAIR IS FOUL, and foul is fair. Hover through the fog and filthy air.' *MacBeth,* Act One, Scene one."

Rielle shoved aside a bowl of leftover potatoes in the refrigerator and pulled out a plate of two-day-old roast chicken. Too bad if Gretchen or her kitchen assistant didn't like having their territory invaded. They hadn't been on the receiving end of Percy Fagan's disturbing soliloquy tonight.

With a shiver she handed the plate to Adrian, who'd managed to find a bottle of milk on one of the top shelves. "It's just like the witches chanted on that Scottish heath. Nothing is as it appears." Standing, she glanced out the kitchen window. She wished the power would come back on, wished at least that the Gypsy music floating along on the warm night breeze would lose the eerie thread of melancholy that seemed to be weaving itself right into the fabric of her fear. Irrational fear perhaps—Fagan hadn't actually threatened them in any way or confessed to being the Phantom—but the seeds were definitely there. And they frightened her.

But he was gone now, she recalled. Back to Mandelin Castle, she felt certain, with his bottle of wine, a loaf of French bread and a block of cheddar cheese. Those last two things they'd watched him take from the kitchen after he thought they'd returned to the celebration.

Should they have followed him? Rielle wondered. Probably, but it was hard to always act nerveless. And the castle was so old. So dark. And Fagan knew it so well.

Adrian pushed the refrigerator door closed with his foot, then placed a firm hand on Rielle's spine, startling her out of her morbid thoughts. "Come, *querida*. Let's do what we have to do, and perhaps we can still watch the fireworks."

She hunched her shoulders, more to bank down the hot little shiver his touch called up than to challenge his suggestion. Although really, how many times had they searched Luke's room already? Two? Three? And always with the same results. Whatever his proof, it was either too obscure for them to see or too well hidden for them to find. Still, a late-night picnic in his room might be nice. And fireworks. Who knew, they might blunder into something after all.

Like each other in the dark? Rielle smiled to herself, conscious of a slight tear in the fear that gripped her. Adrian's doing, she knew. Silly maybe, but somehow nothing ever seemed as bad when he was with her, even Fagan's disarming last words.

Fagan. Yes, a true puzzle, that man.

Flashlight and chicken platter in hand, Rielle looked at Adrian next to her in the third-floor hallway. "As strange and confusing as it all seems, I just don't see how Fagan could be the Phantom, do you? What I mean is, assuming as we have that Luke's proof will expose this Phantom, why would he come to Brede Manor, Fagan's home, to hide it, if Fagan was in fact that Phantom?"

Even in shadow there was no mistaking the smile that touched the corners of Adrian's mouth. "You make a good point, Rielle," he agreed. "But do not forget that we are also assuming Luke hid his proof here. Mailing you a key, reserving this room under an alias, all of it might be for show. An elaborate plan to throw the Phantom off the trail.''

Rielle thought about that for a moment. ''No, I don't think so,'' she said as he unlocked the door. ''Luke's not that devious. Good at hiding, yes, but he was scared that night he came to my flat. Too scared to be plotting double deceptions.''

Shrugging, Adrian went into the room and opened the heavy curtains. Moonbeams and distant firelight immediately poured in, bathing the shadows with their soft rays. ''You are probably right.'' He scanned the lawn below, then turned back to her, taking the platter and flashlight from her hands and setting them on the dresser next to the flashing digital clock. Obviously the power had come back on. Keeping his expression veiled, he brushed a thumb lightly across her cheek. ''Come, let us stop guessing and make this search, and while we do it you can tell me all about your life of larceny and why you do not now live in New Orleans with a husband and three babies and a collection of Anne Rice and Bram Stoker novels.''

Lifting her head in defiance—or was it self-denial—Rielle met his dark gaze. ''It's Baton Rouge. My new career takes up a great deal of time and energy, and I do have a wide collection of Gothic horror books. As for my life of larceny—'' she stepped quickly away from the hand that continued to stroke her cheek ''—that's a very long, very involved story. Sometimes I look back and can't believe all the things I've done.''

Adrian made no attempt to follow her as she shoved up the sleeves of her sweater and yanked open the armoire door. Of course he wouldn't, she realized, annoyed with her rash withdrawal and the tiny glimmer of panic that had, for a second, gotten the better of her.

Forget reason, she wanted this man. But she'd blown it now, hadn't she?

''Idiot,'' she muttered under her breath, unaware that she'd spoken out loud until she heard Adrian's quietly amused reply.

"Do you refer to all these things you say you have done that you cannot sometimes believe?"

Rielle pushed the hair from her face and stood, staring blindly into the empty cabinet. "Among other things," she answered. "While we're on the subject, why don't you tell me about your past. Who taught you to pick pockets?"

For once his response was unguarded, almost reminiscent, as if the memory she'd accidentally evoked was pleasurable to him in some way. "It was Emile who taught me," he said, and in his voice Rielle detected a slow smile, maybe a tug of affection. "Because I had natural ability, he claimed, but in this I think he exaggerated. I called him my uncle, though he was really no relation to me. Just a man we knew who lived as we did and thought to live better at the expense of those who carried enough money to feed an entire family was not such a terrible crime as starving."

There was a certain logic in that line of reasoning. Rielle took the boxed parlor games to the bed and dumped them out while Adrian examined the bookshelves. "Where is your Uncle Emile now?" she asked.

"In Rio, still," Adrian said, his humor evident, "promoting kart races. A fitting choice, I suppose, since this is how my career began. My present career," he amended as he scanned the pages of *A Midsummer Night's Dream*.

The light was faint but adequate for the purposes of their search. Except that Rielle was suddenly tired of searching, tired of avoiding feelings a wiser person would probably bury or at least store away until the timing was more appropriate. She wanted something else tonight, and it had nothing to do with searching this room.

She stared at the mess around her. Sorry Luke, but a break right now was an absolute must.

She slid her gaze to Adrian, to his dark curling hair and beautiful slender body. So much lovely darkness around them, and soon the fireworks would start. They could talk some more. They could watch the jeweled starbursts cascade through the night sky. Bits of glistening color breaking above the oak and lime trees and the castle that had once belonged to Sir Arundel. And then . . .

"There is nothing here." Adrian's quiet statement pulled her out of her fantasy. He returned the books to their proper shelves, then pushed his fingers through his hair and regarded the entertainment center consideringly.

Nothing extraordinary there, Rielle knew. Only a handful of compact discs and record albums and a selection of videocassettes.

She paused on that and wandered over to the polished wood cabinet. Maybe they should watch a movie. Something fantastical like Disney's *Peter Pan* or Scholotti's *Marionette*.

No. The last one was too maudlin. Sybil Fawkes had starred in it. She'd also been the Phantom's first victim. And despite period costumes and stunning visual effects, the subject matter had a decidedly macabre air about it. Not especially conducive to romance.

She would have moved on then to a more pleasant movie, but something held her in place, kept her staring at the long row of VHS tapes. Something wasn't right about them.

Her eyes landed on *Dr. Jekyll and Mr. Hyde*. A copy of this tape had been in Ivan's machine. Was that what had made her hesitate? No, too trivial. The one next to it, then: *Dial M for Murder*. No, nothing unusual about a Hitchcock classic—or *Marionette*, either, for that matter. Or was there?

Her mind spun. What was it she'd noticed that first night? Something about these three tapes.

Not in alphabetical order!

The realization hit her with unexpected force. That was it. The tapes were out of order.

Her mind pounced on the possibilities. She called Adrian over from the dresser and asked him point-blank what he thought.

"Play the tapes and see," was his practical response, and Rielle had to smile as she pushed the first cassette in the machine.

In crackling back-and-white, the credits for the first movie appeared. Not what she'd wanted to see, but she let it go.

More black-and-white scenery, more credits and then the movie itself. Interesting, but no help.

"Try Hitchcock," Adrian suggested from close behind her. His breath on her neck was warm, and that, Rielle thought with an inner tremor, was no help, either.

She shoved the tape in. Credits again, and then the opening scene. Damn. That left only *Marionette,* and something told Rielle she wasn't going to find anything unusual there, either.

"Sybil Fawkes," she murmured in disappointment, reading the cast list aloud from the flickering screen. "Angelo Diamonti, Francesca Pirrone, Claudette de Bertrand, Reuben Bishop, Roberto Tomasini..." Her eyes widened suddenly. What had she just said?

"Run it back," Adrian instructed, then reached around her and did it himself, pausing the tape on the appropriate name.

"Reuben Bishop!" Rielle stared at the screen in disbelief, although she had no idea why this discovery should shock her so much. Was it such a big deal for Reuben to have acted in a movie?

In her mind she heard him humming the song that had drawn her to the cliffs her first morning here. She heard his conversation with Fagan at the castle cocktail party and his taunting remarks to Ava at the dinner table tonight. Yes, perhaps a very big deal indeed.

She felt herself bump against Adrian's chest. So solid and strong. "Reuben was an actor, too." She said it out loud in the vain hope that it would sound reasonable. All it did was deepen her confusion. "He never told us about this. But his name's right here where anyone watching the movie could see it, so it can't be a deep dark secret he's trying to keep, can it?"

Adrian's head moved against hers, and his warm breath grazed her cheek, sending shivers down her spine. "I would say no. And yet you are correct—he did not mention that he had acted with Sybil, either when he talked to Fagan alone at the castle or tonight at dinner. I find this interesting."

Rielle leaned into him, hard, not caring how he viewed the action. "I find this whole thing frightening," she said with a shudder that came from deep inside her. "The Phantom's watching us, Adrian, I can feel it, I really can. He knows who we are, and he has a plan. And the horrible thing is, I don't think he intends for either of us to be alive once it's been carried out."

HE STOOD beneath the ancient oak, staring at the darkened manor house, thinking, wondering, plotting. Smiling to himself in that eerie, crazy way he never smiled at others. The whispers were with him tonight, silent for the moment, but tucked away in his mind where Sybil could not steal them.

Where were Rielle and Adrian right now? And Luke? Did he realize that his friends were here? Would he care?

Faerie music danced on the breeze, swirling about the Phantom's head. A sprightly sound, prelude to the fireworks and something more. Sybil's death, perhaps? Ah, luscious thought, that, but likely premature at this stage.

He looked at his long thin fingers. How alive they seemed to him, beyond the control of his mind. Hungry for the kill.

He clenched them slowly, tightly, so hard that little bolts of pain shot up his arms. And then as the music behind him reached a frenzied crescendo, he threw back his head and laughed.

Chapter Fourteen

Adrian's mouth closed hungrily on Rielle's. His breath came into her, warm and wet and wanting.

"Tu estás linda, querida."

Mmm, intoxicating, that declaration, that quiet murmur she felt rather than heard. The words came into her, as well, but it wasn't enough. Words never would be. She wanted more, so much more.

His skin beneath her hands felt sleek and firm and smooth, like satin. Hair on his chest and arms, just the right amount, dark curls against her face—so perfect he seemed to her. And the taste of him, exciting. Hot. And now his hands touched her, too, though she couldn't have said where exactly. There were so many other sensations racing through her: his tongue, exploring with delicious intimacy her lips and mouth, the heat of his body, of hers, the hardness of him and her own instinctive reaction to that.

Faerie music rose behind her, spinning through the night air, embracing them both with its lyrical magic. She heard it, felt it, used it as she used the darkness and the soft lavender mists that had floated in. Not a natural phenomenon, her brain warned, but she wouldn't listen, wouldn't lose this moment to a bout of practicality.

Adrian's mouth left hers briefly; his dark eyes stared down at her; his hand brushed the hair from her cheeks and forehead. "Love you, *querida*," he said softly.

Another strong caution from her brain, then more mist. And there were other discrepancies as well: faeries gliding through the night sky, beautiful beings with transparent wings that reminded her of pastel-colored cobwebs. They formed graceful rings around the tree limbs, these creatures, and sang their haunting tunes. Then suddenly they looked down as one and stopped the dance.

"Odessa!" cried the smallest of the group, and pointed to a similar yet infinitely darker being below.

Wrapped in layers of brown wool, even to the lower half of her face, she stood at the base of the oak, her red eyes shining with undisguised menace. The vampire faerie queen, the Metamorph, looking for victims, seeking to prevent a lover's union.

Red eyes, lavender mist, faeries—Rielle's heart sank. Not real, any of it, a voice in her head whispered. You're dreaming, Rielle. You've made all of this up in your mind.

The whisper faded out, and she was alone. But she shouldn't be alone. Where had her dream-conjured Adrian gone?

Desperately she looked around the—what? Room? No, she was down in the cellar now, and there were people circling her. Fagan and all his guests. She knew that, and yet she couldn't see their faces. She could only see that someone was missing from the circle.

"Run, Rielle."

Adrian's voice came to her through the mist. What was he doing? Who was he struggling with, the person in shadow whose face was that of a skull and whose limbs were covered in black. The Phantom!

"Take the proof and run, *querida*," Adrian said, and threw something into her hands.

But she couldn't run, couldn't see the thing she held or even Adrian any longer. The human circle around her was closing ranks, pressing in on her, shoes knocking against the stone floor, heels tapping a dull, methodical rhythm, moving closer, tapping . . .

...She awoke in a cold sweat, heart pounding, breath coming in short jerky gasps. She was sitting up in bed and she could hear the roar of the sea beyond the manor.

A nightmare, she thought numbly as her fear slowly began to fade. Only a nightmare. But why could she still hear that dreadful tapping?

Across the room the door suddenly swung back and a light slanted in, a flickering orange flame that gave the face behind it an even more austere look than usual. It was Gretchen, wearing a high-necked cotton nightgown and drab flannel robe, her gray hair hanging in a long braid down her back.

"There's a phone call for you, miss," the housekeeper announced stiffly and without preamble. "You can take it in the sitting room at the end of the hall."

A phone call, at—Rielle glanced at the bedside clock—2:00 a.m. How bizarre. She reached for her robe.

"Power's out again, miss," Gretchen stated, her slate gray eyes anything but friendly. "Here's another candle. Telephone's in the niche by the window. Watch your step in the dark. There's things about that can be knocked over. Dangerous things."

"Thank you," Rielle began, then realized she was talking to the shadows. Gretchen had shoved a candle between her fingers and vanished into the blackness. How Phantomesque of her.

If she hadn't been so convinced that said Phantom was a man, Rielle might have pursued that thought. For the present, however, she would content herself with finding the phone.

Pulling the belt of her white terry robe snugly about her waist, she started down the hall. By candlelight it seemed positively unearthly, like something out of a bad medieval dream. To her right stood a chain-mail hauberk and next to it a glass case filled with weapons. A full suit of plate armor loomed to her left and of course in its gauntleted hand it held what Fagan called a halberd—a cross between an ax and a lance. An impressive sight in broad daylight, granted, but terrifying in the dead of night.

Her bare feet made no sound on the carpet. In fact, with the exception of the old grandfather clock downstairs, there was no sound that she could hear anywhere in the mansion. Just the sea outside and the soft whisper of her robe.

She should resent Gretchen for deserting her, Rielle knew, but her curiosity was far too strong right now to permit such a petty sentiment.

She felt her way carefully through the door of the sitting room, her mind only now starting to function properly. The obvious questions came to her. Who could possibly be phoning her at two in the morning? And who even knew she was here?

The obvious answer to both followed. Luke!

She bit down on her lower lip and with that small gesture forced her enthusiasm down, as well. She would be calm about this, shrewd, and above all, careful. No doing or saying anything that Phantom ears might overhear—assuming the caller was even Luke.

She'd made it past the Elizabethan sofa, around the mahogany end tables and Italian floor lamps, to the niche by the window. She could see the telephone, touch it if she wanted to. But did she want to? Had Luke learned that she'd come to Brede Manor? Or was the Phantom trying to scare her? Possibly trap her?

With a telephone? Somehow that didn't seem likely, at least the part about trapping her. And as for being scared, she'd passed that stage long ago.

Taking a deep breath, Rielle closed her eyes and in a swift, decisive movement snatched up the receiver. "Hello."

"Rielle, is that you?"

"Lisa." She sank into an armchair beside the table and breathed a huge sigh of relief that changed almost instantly to a suspicion-laced "Why are you calling? Who told you I was in Yorkshire?" And then a more indignant "Do you know what time it is?"

Her designing partner's short grunt went a long way toward answering Rielle's questions. Lisa was one of those rare individuals who'd been born with aristocratic poise. She didn't grunt or even raise her voice unless she'd been truly provoked, and that, Rielle knew from experience, was something that seldom happened. Something was wrong.

In a more guarded tone, she inquired, "Everything's all right, isn't it, Lisa? Has that old yellow tomcat I used to feed shown up again? He's not hurt or anything, is he?"

Thankfully Lisa was very sharp. She also knew a great deal about Rielle's past. "Not hurt at all, and he showed up ten minutes ago," she confirmed with a sigh. Lisa and Luke didn't get along. "Mangy creature, all wet and demanding. He's been howling at me ever since he showed up at the window. I think he's looking for you, and since you so thoughtfully gave me this phone number before you left the city—" sweet stab of sarcasm in that remark "—I decided to call and see what you want me to do with him."

Rielle breathed easier. Thank God. Luke was alive and unharmed. "Okay," she said slowly. "Give him—" She heard a soft click on the line and stopped quickly. "Lisa? Are you there?"

Nothing. Dead silence. Dead phone line, too, Rielle was certain, but she ordered herself to remain calm. She'd heard talk during dinner of a summer storm moving northward from London, and Lisa had said that Luke had appeared ten minutes ago "... all wet and demanding..." This could be a coincidence, horribly timed, but nothing to worry about.

Or the Phantom might have been listening in on her conversation, might have cut the outside wire. He might even have cut it right here in this room!

Rielle cringed inside. Not a good thing to think with only a single candle standing between light and darkness and who knew how much distance stretching between herself and her room. And when she got right down to it, how safe was her room?

Safer than this place, she decided, sliding quickly from the chair. With her hand she cupped the dancing flame, forcing her eyes to comb the shadows. Nothing to see, but what did that prove? The Phantom wouldn't be a phantom if he allowed himself to be sighted indiscriminately.

It took an eternity for her to get back across the room. Shadows everywhere, it seemed, and each piece of furniture she passed now looked to have taken on grotesque human form. Claws and limbs to grab her, eyes to watch her struggle.

She swallowed the terror that crept into her throat. Her legs felt wobbly; her skin was ice-cold. Listen to the sea, she told herself. Forget the darkness. Keep walking. There's no one here. You're making up phantoms in your mind.

The flame popped a little as it caught on a drop of melted wax clinging to the wick. Naturally her pounding heart did the same. She pressed her lips together. This was awful, worse than her nightmare. But she'd made it to the door, at least. That was something.

Turn right, her brain instructed once she'd looked both directions down the hall. Now walk back the way you came. Back to your room.

No, wait, not there. Go to Adrian's room. Two together is safer than two separated, even with bolted doors.

Her palms were damp, cold and clammy as she was. She could crawl into the middle of a roaring fire and not be warm right now. Although she would rather crawl into Adrian's arms.

She clenched her teeth. Not now. Dream later. You have to watch, listen. Keep moving!

The weapons cabinet materialized in front of her, and the heavy armor. For an instant her eyes locked on the metal suit, a daunting black obelisk by candlelight. A hollow shell, she prayed as she drew closer.

But it looked real, or more correctly, occupied, especially around the head and hands. She shivered. She'd seen too many horror movies. Murderers didn't dress up like knights.

The tension in her muscles eased slightly. Adrian was right; logic was good. And his room was only a few yards away now. Once she got past the armor and the hauberk, the mace and the flail, she'd be safe. Should be simple enough to do.

She never really could say what happened next, or even how it happened. All she heard was the faintest creak—her only warning of danger—and the perpetual roar of the sea as it crashed against the rocky cliffs. The candle's flame fluttered and danced, then in a sudden whoosh of air was extinguished completely. Darkness again and a deepening of the silence in the corridor.

And then another creak.

Rielle froze. One of the doors? No, the sound had been beside her. And wasn't she standing next to the knight's armor? Or had she in her shock spun to face the thing?

She dropped the candle and sprang backward. No conscious thought in the action, just a spontaneous motion that sent her stumbling into the paneled wall behind her.

Her breath came in short terrified gasps. There was a presence in the darkness. Evil! She felt it in every part of her body. An apparition created by her frightened mind? No! This thing lived. It breathed. She heard that sound now, too, beneath the pounding of blood and fear in her ears. Darkness and breathing and a creak, all of it hitting her at the same dreadful instant.

Her heart raced out of control. What was real here? She couldn't tell. Maybe it was all a bad dream. But then something flew past her face, slashing the air in a vertical direction, and she knew it was nothing of the sort.

She felt the thing glance across her skin. Narrow, sharp, embedding itself in the carpet with a crisp whack. And directly above it, a screech of jointed metal.

The ax held in the knight's gauntlet had dropped, the deadly blade missing her by only a fraction of an inch!

She couldn't choke back the scream that was as much astonishment as fright. Not possible, any of this. Her mind was a whirl of sight and sound and motion. Definite burst of motion in the blackness. Someone hurried away. Or did the person come toward her?

Rielle didn't stop to think. She launched herself from the wall with all her strength. At least she started to. Something bright flared suddenly, breaking the gloom. A candle being lit. And the person who'd done it blocked the path to her room.

She pulled up short, unsure, conscious of the halberd at her feet, wondering obscurely if she could wedge it free and use it on...

Her eyes adjusted to the flame, fastening on the features behind it, on the smile that didn't belong on such a severe face. Gretchen, staring at her from the top of the stairs, smile hardening as she lowered her gaze to the fallen halberd.

"You didn't listen to me, miss," she said in a voice so empty of emotion that it was, in a macabre sort of way, fascinating. Her eyes came up to meet Rielle's. Fascination turned instantly to dread. Pure acid in those eyes. The housekeeper's smile grew colder, harder. "I told you there was danger about." Her voice roughened. "Next time you might not be so lucky."

A HUSHED STILLNESS had crept over the old English manor house. Beyond the walls the sea smashed against the coastal rocks, an eerie underscore to the black vacuum inside.

Adrian liked the distant roar, the contrast of silence and sound. He remembered it, though he wasn't quite sure why. Maybe it reminded him of his first trip to the British Isles, his first meeting with the people who would ultimately shape his racing career. His first meeting, too, with Luke's curious assortment of friends.

No, not those memories again, he decided. He'd had enough of them.

Resting his head on his arms, he stared up at the frescoed ceiling. Faeries painted on the plaster and in his mind. And Rielle, of course. Yes, she was always in his thoughts these days, as he wanted her to be. Yet he held back still, fought his feelings still. What made him so afraid that he couldn't let go?

No answers came, and he was tired of the search. Maybe if he stopped trying so hard...

The night shifted around him; clouds in silhouette drifted across the face of the moon. His mind wandered back in time, and he made no attempt to stop it.

It wandered back to another place, another lifetime. He was in Brazil now, seventeen years old and sitting cross-legged on an overgrown hill. Yes, a whole different world this. Leafy green trees cut off his view of Rio, which was just as well since the view from this particular hill consisted mostly of cardboard shacks. Besides, he wanted to be alone, and this spot with its high brush, long grass and fresh breezes offered as much solitude as he was likely to find anywhere in the city.

And his mother was buried here.

He slid his dark gaze to the cracked headstone that he and Emile had dragged up here so long ago. Mary Alexandre Da Costa. No epitaph, just the usual dates and a bouquet of dried flowers from Adrian's last visit.

Curling strands of hair blew across his eyes. The breeze had stiffened. It washed now across his warm skin. Storm coming, he could feel it, but this did not matter, really. In two days he would take off for England, to test a new car for a man he had met this past week in Rio. And so it would begin...

Rustle of leaves to his left. Adrian lifted his head and found himself staring straight into Luke Prentice's bright blue eyes. This could only mean trouble.

"Afternoon, cousin," Luke greeted, dropping to a careless cross-legged position on the grass and plunking down a brown paper bag between them. "I need a favor."

"This is nothing new," Adrian murmured. "You have been in Brazil for two months now, and every second day you need a favor."

Luke was unabashed. "I know. I need another one today." He patted the bag in front of him. "I have to get to São Paulo, and you have to drive me."

Tipping his face toward the cloudy sky, Adrian closed his eyes. "I thought you were conning the owner of a catering company here in Rio."

Luke waved him off. "Old news, *meu primo*. A caterer isn't worth anything compared to the clients whose parties he caters. I wangled myself a position as function overseer. For the past week I've been casing estates you'd have to see to believe.'' Placing a handkerchief on the grass, he dumped out the contents of the bag. Triumph in his eyes as he observed his latest haul. ''This is what I came away with.''

Adrian regarded the pile of fat, brown sausages before him, managing somehow not to smile. ''And you think to fence a bag of sausages you must go all the way to São Paulo?''

''Don't be smart.'' Luke picked up and surveyed one of the links. ''Any con man worth his salt knows you have to look beyond the surface to find the truth. Sure, at first glance you see sausages, but these little beauties aren't exactly stuffed with meat.''

''So I assumed.''

''And you'll take me to my fence?''

With a noncommittal shrug Adrian picked up a link, as well. ''You are inventive, Luke, I will give you that.''

''Inventive enough to want to unload this stuff and get out of the country,'' Luke told him. Then he grinned. ''Don't look so solemn, Adrian. No one's going to figure it out. Unless of course we get pulled over by a hungry cop on the way to São Paulo...''

...In his mind Adrian saw Luke's smile. So confident. And that scheme, at least, had worked.

The scene dissolved, leaving Adrian to stare at the swirled plaster ceiling above his bed. Memories wouldn't help him. What he wanted he could not have. As close as Rielle's room was to his, he could not bring himself to act on his urges. Then why did he pull away so fiercely, resist his emotions with such force? What did he really fear?

The answer was there, inside him. But so, in the next instant, was something else. A scream that jerked him back to reality faster than anything else could have.

Rielle!

He was out of bed before he realized it, fear and something much stronger slicing through him.

As Adrian grabbed his jeans, he realized in some dim, seldom-used corner of his mind that the past with all its open wounds, its bruises and complex emotional consequences didn't matter anymore. Maybe it never really had.

Chapter Fifteen

Shadows shifting in the hallway. Flicker of candles. And then a woman's voice. Gretchen!

Did she threaten Rielle? Adrian missed the words, but her expression was clear enough even by candlelight. Malice in those flinty gray eyes of hers.

And an ax blade buried in the carpet!

Adrian's jaw clenched when he saw that. He emerged out of the darkness to reach for Rielle. And she came to him willingly, relief and terror showing plainly in her eyes. Not usual for her, but then who knew what had happened here.

He said nothing to the housekeeper, just cradled Rielle in his arms.

"If you'll excuse me," was all she offered. Then she nodded stiffly, looking one last time at Rielle and disappeared into the shadows.

Gruesome creature, that one. Callous and cold, perhaps not as unsparing as she seemed, but exactly what form the feelings she buried might take Adrian could not guess. And did not at this moment care.

In his arms Rielle trembled. Not with cold but with fear. He stroked his fingers through her long hair, saw again the ax beside them, and wanted suddenly to gather together everyone at the manor, put them in a line in a small room and walk back and forth in front of them holding the weapon.

"If this could be done," he murmured obscurely, his mouth moving against Rielle's hair.

She lifted her head from his shoulder. Maybe she understood his thoughts. At any rate she didn't question his odd remark, merely stared at him, and though he could no longer see her eyes, her body felt slightly less rigid to him.

"The Phantom was here, Adrian," she said in a shaky whisper. "Right here in this corridor. I swear I heard him, felt him go past me. Felt—I don't know how to put it exactly—the evil that he is. Like an obscene black cloud going by. Then the ax dropped, and when I turned to run, Gretchen was standing there."

This was not all of it, Adrian realized. For the moment, however, the details didn't matter. They would come. Right now he wanted only to hold Rielle, to tell her that everything would be all right. To lie through his teeth if there was even a remote chance that such a thing would make her feel better. Likely it wouldn't.

He ran his fingers along her slender spine. So delicious, this woman. Rielle knew how to love. Strongly. She loved Luke. She would go through this nightmare for him, and it wouldn't occur to her to wonder why she did it.

Adrian sighed into her hair. Strong love—did he know this feeling, too? Had Rielle given back to him his ability to care?

He shook his head, not certain of anything just now. Sliding his hands to her shoulders, he reluctantly put her away from him, massaging her collarbone with his thumbs and staring down into her eyes.

"Somehow I do not think that either of us will get much sleep tonight, *querida*," he said softly. "Come with me to my room, and we will lock the door and talk and you can tell me why you're here in this corridor in the middle of the night."

A tiny smile curved her lips. Touch of wickedness in it, but that was Rielle, wasn't it? To be bold and not wait for him to do what his emotional barriers might never permit.

"To your room, huh?" she echoed. Then her gaze landed on the ax, and she shivered, pressing against him once again.

He let his arms close about her warm body. And might even have enjoyed the sensations that slid through him had it not been for the icy chill that crawled over his skin when his bare foot accidentally made contact with the steel of the ax's very cold, very deadly blade.

"HOW ON EARTH could such a thing have happened?" Fagan's thin face was a mask, a perfect blend of outrage, bewilderment and apology. He thumped the handle of his knife on the lunch table. "The halberd fell, you say, just like that, at your feet?"

"Just like that," Rielle confirmed. "And no, I didn't knock against it in the dark." She glanced at Gretchen, who was serving plates of spiced mutton to the guests. Nothing to see in the woman's face, but last night...

A chill slid down Rielle's spine. What more might the woman have said if Adrian hadn't suddenly appeared behind her in the corridor? Eyes laced with poison, what might she have done?

No! she would not become mired in this. Rielle reined in her morbid thoughts. Adrian had come, Gretchen had drifted off and the moment had passed.

Concern in his dark eyes, she remembered that, and in the arms that held her. They'd gone back to his room, too. They'd sat across from each other on the window seat, eaten the basket of complimentary figs and chocolates that Fagan provided for his guests, along with a bottle of Bordeaux. And they'd talked. About auto racing, fashion design, old movies, North America, South America, even Grimms' fairy tales.

And of course they'd talked about Luke, and Lisa's phone call. And the dead phone line, which had conveniently been repaired by the time morning rolled around.

Ava's voice cut in, stilling Rielle's thought. "You're certainly braver than I am, Rielle. I wouldn't walk down a pitch-black hallway to talk to anyone, even my husband." She sighed then, as if burdened by some nagging problem. "Speaking of Gilbert, I really should call his office and find out when he's due back in London. Is there dessert today, Fagan?''

"Gooseberry tarts with dairy cream," he answered. "If your call can wait for a few minutes." He looked around the table, then out the window at the dark clouds blowing up from the south. "It would appear we're in for a bit of a storm, but there will still be plenty of Midsummer festivities taking place at the castle. Plays and such. An archery tournament if the rain holds off."

Noah grunted behind his wineglass. "And the pub, what time does it open?"

"The Boar's Head?" It was Jonathan who responded, although Rielle noticed that his gaze remained on Ava. "I believe the sign on the door said 10:00 a.m."

"Good enough." Noah finished his drink in a single, satisfied swallow. "That's all the entertainment I'll be needing this afternoon."

Reuben lit his pipe as Gretchen began clearing away the lunch plates. "Why don't you give the pub a miss today, my boy," he said gently. "Take in the performance up at the castle."

Noah's finely shaped brows went up. "Is that what you plan to do, Father? Take in a play with your old school chum Fagan?"

"Absolutely," Fagan rushed to answer. His eyes flicked to Reuben, then back to Noah's cynical features. "Right after I have that postponed chat of mine with the village butcher. Tomorrow is the solstice, you know. The feast must be prepared."

"You could come with me, Noah," Ivan suggested, patting his red lips with his napkin. "I know much about Odessa and her followers, more even than her Gypsy disciples."

"He would," Ava said in an undertone to Rielle and Adrian. Her tart arrived, and picking up her fork, she aimed the prongs across the table at Jonathan. "Why don't you join them, Mr. Lynch? Go off and stare at the faerie folk for a few hours. You do enjoy staring, I've noticed, and these Gypsy performers so love to be gawked at."

"I . . ." Jonathan seemed ill-prepared for her sudden attack. Lowering his eyes to the table, he nodded. "Perhaps I should," he agreed in a lame voice.

"Wonderful." Ava ate her tart swiftly, blotted her mouth and stood, licking a dab of juice from her thumb. "Now, if you'll all excuse me, I'll go upstairs and make my call to London."

Fascinating exchange, full of undercurrents. Rielle shifted her gaze to Jonathan's flushed face. But it wasn't the color in his cheeks that caught her attention; it was the expression she glimpsed briefly in his eyes. Something cold and quite black, difficult to describe. Possibly the way a cobra might look if it were to take on human form. . . .

Rielle ate her tart slowly, counting the seconds that positively crawled by. Forty, sixty, eighty. Jonathan didn't move, didn't do anything except stare at his water glass. Around them the table talk continued, a light banter with Fagan relating a story about Sir Arundel and even Noah looking mildly interested for a change.

Adrian had long since removed himself from the parley. Like Rielle he now watched Jonathan. And waited.

She counted to ninety. A minute and a half since Ava had left the room. Finally Jonathan's eyes came up. Slowly. He didn't move his head, only those pale, silvery eyes of his that suddenly seemed so—what? Cold? Soulless. Like twin mirrors that held no reflections.

Rielle swallowed the last bite of her pastry. Frissons of fear slid down her back.

Now he stared at the doors through which Ava had passed, mumbled a quiet "Excuse me" to anyone who might care, rose with an awkward kind of grace to his feet. And left the room.

Did a smile pull at the corners of his mouth? Some faint twisting of his lips that didn't involve his eyes? Rielle wasn't sure, and now he was limping off. Through the doors, toward the central staircase, the fingers of his right hand clenching and unclenching at his side . . .

RIELLE HUNG OVER Adrian's shoulder. She couldn't see anything except towels, bed sheets and shadows inside the stuffy storage closet. "What's he doing now?" she demanded in an anxious whisper.

Adrian shook his head. "He is still at the end of the hall, listening to Ava."

One hardly had to lurk outside the sitting-room door to do that, Rielle thought, falling back a little and brushing damp strands of hair from her forehead. Ava's voice carried extremely well, better than usual in fact because of her rising agitation.

"What do you mean, you don't know when my husband is coming home?" she snapped. "You're his secretary, for heaven's sake. He must have left you a copy of his itinerary." Silence for several seconds, then an indignant "Of course he did, but you surely can't expect me to remember dates and times and flight numbers. That's your job, Mrs. Prewitt, not mine. Now, go back and check your calendar again. I'll hold."

Adrian pulled away from the slightly open closet door, his body digging into Rielle's. She caught her breath. This she didn't need, not in such a confined space. "Stay back," he said quietly. "He is coming this way."

Curiosity momentarily overcame discomfort. Pushing Adrian's dark hair aside, she peered around his head. "And going that way," she finished as Jonathan crept stealthily past. Then she frowned, "Is it my imagination or does he look awfully pleased with himself?"

"It is not your imagination." Easing the door open a bit more, Adrian glanced out. "He has stopped in front of Ava's room," he relayed over his shoulder. "He is taking a look around. And now he is going in."

Rielle couldn't resist running her fingers through the curling ends of Adrian's hair. So soft. Sexy, as he was. Maybe this cramped little closet wasn't so bad after all. "How is our mysterious Mr. Lynch at picking locks?"

"Quite good." Adrian sent her a knowing look. "Better even than Luke."

That was good, all right, Rielle conceded as he wrapped his fingers around hers and drew her out of the storage area. Ava's irritated tones continued to drift along the corridor.

"Twelve o'clock, what?" she demanded, presumably of her husband's secretary. "Noon or midnight? And flight 319 tells me nothing unless there's an airline to go with it...."

Not important, this one-sided conversation. Rielle dismissed it and turned her mind instead to Jonathan. Why would he want to break in to Ava's room? To catch her off guard when she entered? Did he intend to knock her out? To drag her off somewhere, dress her up and kill her?

A shiver of revulsion passed through Rielle's body, a reaction that must have made itself known to Adrian, for he turned his head to stare at her.

"It's nothing," she whispered, motioning him forward. "Just a horrible picture my mind conjured up."

No heavy silence filled the mansion this dark afternoon, although the eerie overtones managed to persist. Church bells tolled ominously in the distance, a warning perhaps to the freighters and smaller fishing vessels of the approaching storm.

They'd reached Ava's room. Rielle curled the fingers of her free hand around Adrian's arm. If any sound came from inside, she couldn't distinguish it, though Ava's voice could still be heard quite plainly. Pity the unfortunate woman on whom she was venting her anger. Pity more, Rielle thought with a grimace, those unfortunate souls who might be about to confront a Phantom.

She stared at the closed door, then at Adrian. "What now?" she asked, her question barely audible above the roar of wind and sea and bells.

He pressed his ear to the paneled door. "I can hear him," he said at length. "He is going through her dresser drawers, I think."

"Pervert," Rielle muttered, then stiffened as Adrian tested the polished doorknob.

It turned without creak or rasp. Nothing to alert the man inside—unless he happened to be looking in this direction.

She held her breath and prayed, poising herself to respond to whatever might come.

Her fingers dug into the soft fleece of Adrian's red sweatshirt, into the skin and wiry muscle of the arm beneath it. Small sounds only from the bedchamber: a clack of brass and wood, a light tap, a scrape. Then movement, faint but discernible. Her eyes refocused. Shadow on the carpet, long, slightly bent. Wind in the background, a weird howl beyond the mansion's walls. Another subdued scrape. And finally Jonathan himself, back turned to them, thin fingers skimming the pages of a small book.

Rielle hesitated, uncertain. Not what she'd expected, to find the man she'd more or less convinced herself must be the Phantom going through Ava's belongings, specifically through her diary.

She stepped cautiously across the threshold, sticking close to Adrian, still clutching his arm. Jonathan seemed not to notice.

Would the Phantom be so imperceptive?

Wind lashed the diamond panes in violent gusts. Jonathan's head came up. Slowly. As if he'd sensed something. Rielle saw a muscle twitch in his shoulder, the fingers of his left hand curl into a fist. And suddenly he spun to face them.

Perhaps not so imperceptive after all, she decided, catching back a startled breath even as his seemed to hiss out of him.

Adrian's body was rigid, his muscles taut. So were Jonathan's. But what was it that Rielle glimpsed in his eyes? A peculiar light that spoke more of alarm than aggression? They'd taken him by surprise obviously, so why wasn't he reacting like a mad creature? Launching himself away from the bed, going for the door? For their throats?

No movement, no answers to her questions. Jonathan merely stood there, staring at them, his features inscrutable now except for the glimmer of doubt that invaded his pale eyes.

"What are you doing here?" he asked.

No real accusation in it. Thankfully no hint of madness.

He held Ava's journal in his hand. An intruder caught in the act. Rielle looked first at that, then at his face. The reddening of his cheeks told her he got the message. He returned the book to the drawer and straightened his narrow shoulders.

No surrender, really, in his stance, but no belligerence, either. Rielle didn't know what to make of this. Apparently neither did Adrian. In the end he simply arched a dark brow and gave the man a truthful enough reply.

"We saw you break in."

Faint irritation, perhaps self-directed, entered Jonathan's expression. "I see." A rueful smile pulled at his thin lips. "Bloody sloppy of me, I must say. I thought the corridor was empty, and I knew Ava would be tied up on the phone for quite some time. 'Here's your chance,' I said to myself. 'You can get in and out, and no one will ever know.'"

Rielle eyed him distrustfully. "No one will ever know what? Who are you?"

Jonathan started to sigh, but the sound was interrupted by a small clatter, or more correctly, a delicate tinkle of crystal—from Ava's signature earrings.

She didn't come into the room, but lounged, arms folded, in the open doorway. "Yes, Mr. Lynch," she drawled with exaggerated sarcasm. "Do tell us who you really are. I'm sure we'd all like to hear this story." One burgundy brow arched in faint mockery. "Or would you rather I guessed. I'm very good at that—especially when it applies to the games played by my dear, devoted husband. Off in New Orleans and all alone. How sad. Oh, but he wouldn't think of bringing Ava along. Send her to Morgate instead. Such a remote place, and everyone there at this time of year will be immersed in faerie lore.

"Gilbert knows this from personal experience," she continued in an aside to Rielle and Adrian. "He motored here several years ago with his first wife. Didn't like it much—too many weirdos wandering around for his tastes—but Aggie, his ex, adored it. Maybe he thought I'd love it, too." She directed a wintry smile at Jonathan. "Is that what he thought, Mr. Lynch? Do tell me. Are you a friend of his? A business associate? One of his polo club teammates? Or maybe cricket's your game.''

"It's polo," he answered quietly.

"How lovely. So you are Gilbert's friend. And you just happened to be in Morgate at the same time as his wife." She sauntered closer. Her hostility was beginning to show. "Very convenient, Mr. Lynch."

He didn't deny a thing; nor did he defend himself. He simply held his ground, meeting her cold glare with a cool one of his own—although a hint of regret did reveal itself around the corners of his mouth.

Rielle took in everything. So did Adrian beside her. Two spectators trapped in a very strange arena. But then without warning, a tremor passed through her, something cold and clammy and entirely foreign to her. More than fear, but in what way and for what reason she couldn't say.

Her eyes darted covertly about the room. Nothing here. No one that she could see lurking in the doorway. And yet she'd sensed—something.

The feeling vanished then, as suddenly as it had appeared, leaving her confused, doubting her senses. She gave herself a shake.

She looked from Ava to Jonathan and back again, waiting. Of course there was more to this than coincidence or friendly favors. They all understood that, even if the actual words had yet to be spoken. Jealous husbands seldom ask members of their polo club to spy on their wives. Not unless . . .

Reaching into his pants' pocket, Jonathan pulled out a leather case. "Your husband asked me to watch you, Ms. Giordano," he revealed without inflection. "We do play polo together, it's true. That's how we met. And why he hired me." He extended the case to her. "I'm a private detective."

Chapter Sixteen

The calm before the storm...

Adrian smiled to himself. He'd heard those words many times in his life, but only in metaphor, never in the literal sense. Until this afternoon.

Absolute stillness on the wooded road to the village. No birds sang, no leaves rustled, no wildlife scampered around in the underbrush.

"It's wonderful, isn't it?" Rielle said softly as they walked along the dirt track. "I love days like this. Dark and magical, with all the black clouds hanging over the treetops just waiting to unleash their fury."

A smile played on Adrian's mouth. "And we will be caught in the middle of this fury. You have an unusual sense of what is wonderful, Rielle."

"Not really." She shoved her hands into the pockets of her brown aviator jacket. "I just think that anything, even a trip to the local inn, is a good idea right now. The storm brewing out here is nothing compared to the one we left behind." She grinned and hunched her shoulders beneath the worn jacket. "You know Ava's going to crucify him, don't you? If Jonathan were smart, he'd head straight for the village depot and hop on the first available train, regardless of its destination."

Tipping his head back, Adrian regarded the lowering skies. Very ominous, the atmosphere in these woods. He liked it. There was a strong sense of menace in the air, of nature and forces beyond his control, of things about to happen. It intensified his emotions, deepened them, brought them closer in a way that was as hard to ignore as it was to understand.

So many surprises he'd faced these past few days, he reflected, sliding his amused gaze to Rielle's face. Most of them involved this woman, although he had to admit there were a few others, as well. This last one, for instance. He had not expected Jonathan Lynch to be a private detective.

He paused on that, frowning a little. "Was a very strange situation," he murmured, then hesitated, choosing his words with care. "Something did not feel right in that room. It was as if we were being watched."

Rielle's head came up, and she nodded. "I know. I felt it, too, though I couldn't tell you what 'it' was. Maybe a presence of some sort, it's hard to say. I'm not really big on ESP."

"It is an old house," Adrian mused, staring off into a stand of gnarled oaks ahead of them.

"Full of secret passageways?" Shrugging, Rielle rubbed her temples, as if she'd been running this over in her mind several times. "Maybe you're right. Maybe someone was watching us from behind a wall panel. Or maybe we're both overreacting. I mean, when you get right down to it, almost everything has a peculiar feel to it lately. Even this." She waved a hand at the hushed forest that crowded in on the sides of the road. "First there's wind, then suddenly it disappears. Like a ghost. It was the same thing this afternoon. We see Jonathan watching Ava, see him break into her room and think we've figured out who the Phantom is, only to discover that he's a private investigator. A great bit of deductive reasoning reduced to ashes. Before that, we follow Fagan into the cellar, find that he keeps unlabeled jars of cream down there. Why, we're not sure, but facial cream doesn't make him a murderer. I'm certain that Noah's going to push me over the edge of a cliff, but instead he helps me get back to the top. And then of course there's Gretchen, Ivan and Reuben and a dozen other weird occurrences I could mention involving the three of them."

No argument there, Adrian acknowledged in silence. And yet something was not right. He knew this, felt it. And so did Rielle, despite her statements to the contrary.

They'd come to a bend in the narrow road, the leather boots they'd both worn scarcely making enough noise to disturb the unnatural calm. The inn stood to their left, a cozy-looking building with a thatched roof and a wooden sign hanging absolutely still beneath the eaves. Thin trails of smoke rose from two of the seven chimneys, flower-patterned curtains hung at the second-floor windows, and in the garden, just visible behind the side wall, a white rabbit hopped on soundless paws through a carrot patch.

"Peter Cottontail," Rielle said, smiling. "Sometimes I swear we've accidentally stumbled into a child's nursery rhyme. And then I remember the Phantom and amend that to a Gothic horror story." She ran lightly up the steps to the porch. "One thing I'm sure of—it's good that we got out of the manor, away from everyone for a while. They'll all so odd and, with the possible exception of Fagan, so creepy. It's like we're staying in a hotel full of ghouls."

Adrian pulled open the door, smiling every so slightly. "Whereas we are perfectly normal."

She grinned. "Don't be cheeky. At least we don't look or act like gruesome things. I mean Gretchen with that stone-cold expression of hers makes my skin crawl, and Ivan, well, he's just plain..."

"Unearthly?"

"Purposely frightening anyway," she allowed. "And a phony to boot." She shuddered. "As for Noah Bishop, he's..."

"Sitting in the dark corner on the far side of the room," Adrian put in with a nod of his head. "It seems we did not get away from everyone after all."

"Yes, we did." Taking firm hold of his wrist, Rielle steered him to the opposite wall, on the other side of the oak bar. "I don't feel like making small talk with a woman hater, or actress hater, or whoever it is he really hates."

"Perhaps it *is* actresses he hates," Adrian suggested, draping his leather jacket over the back of a hard chair and glancing around the room. Dark and close with polished-timber walls, beamed ceilings and crude furnishings that looked to have been fashioned during the Crusades. He brought his gaze back to Rielle's face. "Maybe Noah Bishop is the Phantom."

She leaned forward on the table, her long hair spilling over her shoulders. "So why didn't he shove me over the cliff when he had the chance?"

Adrian shrugged, vaguely fascinated by the dark lashes that surrounded her eyes. Long enough to cast shadows on her cheekbones. She was so beautiful in that simple, elegant way of hers. A look he had come to like very much. Possibly even more than that.

What would she do if he said this to her? Told her of his thoughts, his feelings? And yet—how could he tell her things he still did not understand himself?

Raking the hair from his face with faintly impatient fingers, he sat back in his chair. What had she asked him? Something about Noah.

His eyes flicked to the man across the room. Caught between shadow and firelight, he sat hunched over a glass of dark whiskey, staring at the scarred tabletop. Yes, a ghoul, Adrian thought, recalling the broken wineglass at Mandelin Castle and the blood that had trickled from between Noah's fingers.

But if he was the Phantom, why *hadn't* he shoved Rielle from the cliff? Because that was not the Phantom's way? Because he liked to watch his victims die, enjoyed the feel of their flesh beneath his fingers?

A shudder ran through Adrian's body, chilling him in a way no other thought could. He would not think about such things.

"Good afternoon," a voice next to Adrian's left shoulder greeted. "I had not thought to find anyone except perhaps young Mr. Bishop here today."

It was Ivan—or whoever the hell he really was—wearing a black rain cape that hung to his knees. A wet cape, Adrian noted absently. So much for the calm before the storm.

"It is raining heavily," Ivan said unnecessarily, his red lips stretching into a ghastly smile. A trick of the dim light. Adrian ignored it. "I suspect," the would-be vampire continued, "that we will find it extremely difficult to return to Brede Manor. Already the winds are bending the trees."

Ever polite, Rielle summoned a pleasant smile. "In that case we'll have to spend the night here. I'm sure the innkeeper has some rooms available upstairs. In fact—" she slid smoothly from her chair "—I think I'll go talk to him right now."

"Ask him if he will serve us dinner upstairs, as well," Adrian suggested, willing for the moment to go along with her on this. Dangerous, though, such a move. Possibly a mistake for which his emotions would pay heavily.

Or possibly the smartest thing he would ever do.

Soon enough he would know. In the meantime he would be civil to Ivan, who had shed his wet cape and, uninvited, pulled another chair up to the table.

"Still you wear no wort," the man remarked in his false accent, touching with one pale hand Adrian's white T-shirt. A brief contact, but Adrian's immediate instinct was to jerk away in revulsion.

He managed not to. "A flower in the sun," he said instead, nodding as a large man using a dish towel for an apron set three pints of lager in front of them. "You do not seem the type, Ivan, to wear such a symbol."

The ghastly smile widened. "You have done your research, I see. You are also most observant."

"He drives high-speed Grand Prix cars," a man's slurred voice inserted. Noah, weaving slightly as he halted beside Ivan's chair. "Life on the edge and all that. This is a very observant man, Mr. Ragozcy. And he has a most delicious *amiga*."

"*Namorada*." Adrian made the distinction calmly, unperturbed by Noah's lewd tone. "Soon to be a *minha noiva*."

My girlfriend, soon to be my fiancée...

A smile grazed Adrian's lips. Had he really said this? He turned the words over in his mind. How lovely the spell they wove around him. He could get lost in it so easily.

But no, this was madness, surely. He shook his head to clear it. He had made the remark without thinking—and because he did not like the look in Noah's eyes. Lust, yes, he had seen that, but it was the glimmer of cruelty lurking beneath the surface that had disturbed him more. Not mentally sound, such a look. Not unlike the Phantom.

Sitting back, Adrian sipped his beer while Noah pulled up yet another chair and mumbled a bleary order for a bottle of Cutty Sark.

"Faerie lore," he was grunting now under his breath. "Red eyes, Metamorphs, glamour. Maybe the faerie queens will return—maybe we'll even see them. Don't hold your breath, though, chaps. Chances are Fagan's talents don't extend that far. And what does he care, anyway? Stuff a few of your hard-earned quid in his coffers and watch the Gypsies do all the work. In the meantime he'll set his crooked sights on an altogether different project. And what would that be, you ask? Who knows, I reply, but I suspect something *glamor*ous. Yes, our Fagan knows all about deception. Or thinks he does, at any rate."

Noah's chuckle went beyond cold, into an area that bordered on savage. So much malice in the sound, but for what reason, Adrian wondered. Because Noah knew he was a better deceiver than Fagan?

He said nothing, just kept his eyes on the man's face, noting that Ivan too appeared enthralled by this bitter monologue.

Something not right in that, Adrian decided, but then the tiny building seemed to quiver around him, and he shifted his gaze to the window.

Broken fury had erupted beyond the thick panes. The sky was black and angry, the air a whirl of electricity. Rain streamed down in wind-whipped sheets, the sound of it pelting the walls drowned out by yet another ground-shaking rumble of thunder. A long tongue of forked lightning sliced through the gloom, turning everything it touched an eerie shade of blue.

"Looks like we're well and truly stuck," Noah noted, and raised his glass to the window. "What a shame we'll have to miss the faerie fun tonight. Wonder if my dear old pater will even notice. Probably not." He took a long drink of whiskey. "Did you know he was a crook once? He and Fagan and all the other theater folk he ever dragged through our front door. The Pied Piper couldn't have done it better."

More thunder shook the inn, a fitted underscore to the bitterness that blackened Noah's features.

He should pursue this, Adrian knew, but to what end? Already Noah had clamped his mouth shut, and that cruel light was back in his eyes. The Phantom would give nothing away, so if Noah Bishop was in fact the Theater Murderer, no amount of prodding would make him reveal this information. And surely he would pass out long before the alcohol could loosen his tongue.

Adrian closed his eyes for a moment. Excuses, all of this, but suddenly he didn't care. He was tired of phantoms, of analyzing all that he saw and heard and not knowing in the end whether he was right or simply misinterpreting everything.

And now he wanted to be with Rielle. To hold her, to touch her, to feel her mouth on his, her hands and lips exploring his body. To let loose all those things he had kept locked away for so many long years.

"We got the last room."

Adrian hadn't seen her return, couldn't see her even after he opened his eyes. She was behind him, her forearms resting on his shoulders, her mouth close to his ear.

"The proprietor's a fan of yours," she continued. He could hear the smile in her voice. "For an autograph, we get dinner brought up to us. He offers his apologies, wishes the fare could be fancier, roast pheasant or something equally fussy, but I told him plain would be fine."

"You did all this in five minutes," Adrian asked, then had to clench his teeth as she murmured a soft affirmation in his ear.

Beside him Ivan stirred. "It was the last room, you say?" he inquired, sounding dismayed.

"That's what the man said."

Rielle combed her fingers through Adrian's hair, as she had done earlier in the storage closet. Back then he had managed not to react; now to hide the response of his body no longer seemed important. Also, it would be impossible, he thought, concealing a rueful smile behind his beer glass.

"I'm sure you can work something out, though," she went on, giving Adrian a nudge to get him on his feet. "That's the proprietor over by the bar, if you want to talk to him."

"Maybe we could bunk down together," Noah suggested, his eyes settling on Rielle's soft green T-shirt.

Adrian felt the revolted shiver that ran through her, and standing, sent the man a serene look. "No," he said with impeccable politeness. "We could not."

Yet even as he retrieved their jackets and took Rielle by the hand, he did not miss the reaction of the two men before him. Minor changes in mien that should not have been significant, but were: the subtle stretching of Ivan's lips that seemed to ossify his already hideous smile. And the relentless way Noah's fingers tightened about the base of his empty glass.

SHE WOULD NOT THINK about the two ghouls downstairs, Rielle promised herself for the tenth time in as many minutes. Red lips, white fingers—yes, maybe one of them was the Phantom, but she couldn't believe that determination would be made in a pub. Nothing was ever that easy.

Thunder rattled the tiny windows of the second-floor room. Such an exciting sound. She fixed her attention on that, shivering slightly as the proprietor set a platter of thick beef stew, cheddar cheese, jam and heavy bread on a crudely crafted table, smaller, but of the same medieval vintage as those one flight below. A real wood fire burned in the grate, its glow on the sloped ceiling reflecting the rain that continued to stream down in wind-driven torrents beyond the windows.

Sweet wine and dates joined the food on the table. More wood for the fire. Then with a smile and one last thank-you to Adrian for the now-autographed racing program he held, the proprietor dissolved into the darkness of the narrow corridor.

Rielle glanced out at the storm. Nature in a whirling electrical rage, while inside all was dry and warm—a moment beyond reach of the Phantom.

We could share, Noah had suggested with just the hint of a leer. But Adrian had scotched that idea fast enough. Maybe not for the reasons Rielle was hoping, but she wasn't going to make that determination downstairs, either.

Certainly she did not want to return Brede Manor just yet. What she wanted was Adrian and total inaccessibility. And she couldn't count on getting the last part in a mansion where locks were nothing more than a minor annoyance. No, here was better, even with Noah and Ivan on the premises.

She slid her gaze to Adrian's face. He was leaning against the window frame, watching the lightning that shot through the sky at irregular intervals. Faintest hint of a smile on his lips. Well, of course he knew, didn't he?

Or maybe the ending would be hers to write. Maybe she would lose her nerve and nothing would be resolved at all.

Rielle considered that idea for a long moment, then rejected it. She had more than her share of nerve and a store of feelings for this man that had the power to astound her. Better to take the risk and possibly learn things she would rather not than to go on blindly slogging through this tangled emotional bog in which she was caught.

"More people have arrived," Adrian said now, breaking in on her thoughts. "Soon the pub will be full. You were wise to do this."

Rielle settled herself against the table. "A good con artist always keeps one step ahead of the crowd. Would you have preferred to stay downstairs?"

He looked at her, his dark eyes unreadable in the pale amber light. "If I had, I would be down there now," he said softly, and in a tone that was as difficult to interpret as his expression. Didn't he ever give anything away?

She shook her head, pushing herself from the table. "You know, don't you, that you're an impossible man to reach?"

The smile on his lips widened a bit. "Not impossible, Rielle. Private. Careful. Maybe other things, as well. I am not always sure of what I feel."

His eyes darkened, and he turned away from the window, shutting out the elements. He still leaned against the frame, but Rielle sensed it was only to maintain his distance. His attention was now focused entirely on her.

The air around her felt suddenly alive, charged with little particles of energy. A pleasant paradox. The unfamiliar wrapped up in the familiar, the atmosphere tinged with wood smoke and the rich smell of stew. She was moving toward him, slowly and with no conscious thought for what she might be starting. It didn't matter to her, this reversal of roles. But would it matter to him?

For all his Latin-American attitudes, she didn't think so. Whether he wanted to or not, he would not approach her. Not yet. And so she would be the one to do it; she would take the first step.

She stopped mere inches in front of him and looked up. Something in his face, in the set of his features, shadowed by the fire and the streak of blue-white lightning that split the blackened skies. Something she didn't understand.

"You don't always have to be sure of what you feel, Adrian," she said gently, and thought that she saw a shudder pass through his body. "Not everything hurts, or turns out in disaster if it isn't taken apart and analyzed first. Race cars are technical—emotions aren't. Don't you know that by now?"

They weren't touching, and yet she could feel every part of him. The heat that radiated from his slender body, the tension in his muscles. And most of all his response to her, the one scrap of physical proof he could not hide away.

Lashes lowered, he stared down at her, his eyes wonderfully compelling and perhaps a little melancholy. "It is not so easy for me, *querida*," he murmured. "For twenty years

I have let myself care deeply for no one. Not in the way you want." His shoulders moved in a dismissive gesture. "There is Emile, but this is a different thing. I have known him all my life."

Reaching up, Rielle touched his cheek, his temple, pushing the hair aside, certain that he shivered again. "You don't have any other family?"

"Brothers and sisters in Brazil." A flicker of remembered pain crossed his face. He closed his eyes, swaying slightly on his feet. "I do not know them. They were taken away when our mother died."

She understood then, some of it anyway. And she hesitated, unsure now what to do. Was it fair to push him?

His words of a moment ago came back to her. If he didn't want to be here, he wouldn't. So simple, yet in other ways so very, very complicated. And yet, wasn't it everything?

Only one lamp burned in the cozy chamber. Outside, rain continued to drum against the sloped roof, a lovely, wet sound, so much a part of English summers. Behind them the fire crackled in the grate and all around was comfort and warmth . . .

. . . Until the next clap of thunder that shook the floor beneath their feet and shattered whatever sense of tranquility might have been about to settle in.

Anticipation stirred Rielle's blood. Pure violence in that sound, the essence of nature in turmoil, responding to the very turbulence it had created. Balance by reciprocation, the same thing she now wanted. And possibly she could have it, but not through cowardice.

Sliding her fingers through Adrian's silky hair, she stared up at him. "You need to care about people," she told him softly, simply. "Twenty years is much too long to bury your feelings."

And having said that, she took the final step and pulled his beautiful mouth down onto hers.

Chapter Seventeen

Ecstasy. . . .

Adrian didn't consciously think the word; rather he felt it the moment, the instant, his mouth opened on Rielle's. And what, he wondered hazily, could be so wrong about that or anything else that could make him feel so good. So cared for.

Delicious, the sweet, warm taste of her, the feel of her body against his. One hand slid about her waist while the fingers of the other gently cupped her head.

He wanted her so badly. Perhaps too badly, a tiny, terrified part of his brain put in. His mind was a blur, his lips and tongue devouring, his need for her a thing beyond his control. His body was hot and hard where he pulled her closest, his breath warm against her face, the tremor that ran through him a reaction he could not contain.

Did the urgency of his kiss, his touch, frighten her? Could he stop what had begun even if it did? All of this went through his mind in an instant, an insignificant jumble of thoughts he could sort out later. Already his mouth was back on hers, wet and hot and wanting. Demanding what he now knew she would not be afraid to give.

Another tremor passed through him. He felt the fear in it, the faint edge of terror. So many feelings he had stored up over the years and all of them were now in danger of being ripped out of him.

Even so, he did not pull back, did not attempt to set Rielle away from him. Too late for caution, his body insisted, at odds with the mounting apprehension in his brain.

He murmured something under his breath—and pulled her closer, crushing her against him, his hands tugging at the hem of her cotton T-shirt, eager to discover the silky skin beneath it. Her body came alive at his touch, as his thumbs slid up her rib cage to the soft lace of her bra. He felt her tremble and marveled distantly at his ability to excite her.

This could never be wrong; he knew that now. Possibly it was not even dangerous, although of that he was not so certain.

Shutting this out, he lifted his mouth from hers once more, not out of fear this time but because he wanted to see her expression. Did it please her, the touch of his hands on her breasts, the hard feel of him pressed against her thighs? Did she want him as desperately as he wanted her?

"Yes," she whispered, longing and something more, something he did not immediately understand, making her voice a raw thread of sound in the smoky air.

He caught her mouth again, his tongue thrusting deeply between her lips, proof of his own need, his hunger for her.

She made a sound deep in her throat, and to his surprise—though her mouth still clung to his, her kiss if anything became even more demanding—she detached herself from him slightly.

He knew a moment's confusion and then, quite unexpectedly, he knew nothing at all. His mind and body both gave a convulsive jerk, the breath was torn from his lungs and he almost cried out loud.

Through a shocked haze he realized that she had not moved away from him at all. Now it was her hands that explored. And discovered with exquisitely painful accuracy the heart of his bodily need.

She smiled; he felt her lips curve against his as her fingers stroked him, arousing him to a dangerous level through the worn denim of his jeans. If she spoke as well, he didn't hear the words, couldn't make himself care about anything except her touch. Nothing she could say would make this moment better.

The room seemed to move around them. More thunder in the background. And then he was hauling her back into his arms, and it wasn't the room that moved but the two of them. Across the floor to the high double bed.

"Life on the edge," he murmured, drawing Rielle onto the mattress beside him, then raising his body above her. No attempt made to hide his arousal. He stared down into her beautiful blue eyes and pushed her hair from her cheeks. "I think, *querida,* that this is the biggest risk I have ever taken."

Her eyes were wide, enchanting. He thought she would say something then, about all things in life being a gamble or never knowing for sure what the future might hold. But she didn't. She simply gave her head a little shake and reached for him. And Adrian made no move to stop her.

NO PERSON, NO CON, no situation alone or in combination would ever be as exciting as the man she loved. Rielle remembered that thought drifting through her mind at some point in the night. The very long, very exhausting, very revealing night.

A pleasant ache ran through her muscles. Restrained in his lovemaking, Adrian was not. She'd felt the raw edges of his sexual hunger, the casting aside of control as the blood of his Latin ancestors took hold—of him and of her, she thought with a smile. She'd never been through such a night before.

She stretched in the cozy bed. Ashes glowing in the grate, trace of wood smoke and wine in the air and darkness still embracing the storm-swept coast; she could stay in this wonderful place forever. No Phantom lurked in the shadows of this room—maybe a ghost or two, but no mad thing bent on murder.

And of course Adrian was here, beside her, his body sleek and warm and currently relaxed in sleep. Skin like satin, hair long and silky, maybe a little damp with perspiration, muscles smooth and lean—yes, to her this man was perfection.

Rielle sighed, a happy sound. To make love to Adrian, that's what she'd wanted, though in all honesty she hadn't really gone beyond that thought at the time. Would it have mattered even if she had? Surely nothing could have prepared her for all that had taken place in this little wooden room.

Magic? Well, yes, some might call it that, but Rielle was more earth-rooted in matters of the heart. The reality, the wet pelt of rain on the roof, the streaks of lightning that slashed through the sky, the thunder and the wind and the fire that embraced her—that was her vision of magic. And she'd known she loved Adrian long before that intoxicating moment when he'd actually entered her, the best magic of all.

"Beautiful, *querida,*" he'd whispered, his voice a sensual caress, his lips brushing lightly against her feverish skin. *"Dizer-me o que deseja."* Show me what you want.

And she had, in detail.

His mouth had closed hotly on one hardened nipple, his hand moving across her stomach to her hips and finally between her legs. She could still feel the shock, the jolt of pure delight that had gone through her then, bringing a strangled cry to her throat even as her body arched up into his.

It made no difference really where he touched her, only that he did. With his hands, his mouth, his skin, his hair. The heat of his body, his breath in her ear, words he'd whispered in Portuguese that had required no translation— she remembered it all. And then her response, yes, that she remembered, too, relived it even as she lay beside him now in the ancient feather bed.

Mmm, so lovely those recollections. Exciting. She should wake him up, make him do this wonderful thing to her all over again.

Of course, she thought, snuggling closer beneath the soft eider quilt, there might be an even better way to coax him out of his slumber.

Rielle shifted against him now. Smiling softly to herself, she let her gaze travel to the window. Darkness lingered out there still, the remnants of night tinged with streaks of violet and gray. It would be dawn soon. Midsummer's Eve. The rain had stopped an hour ago, though the residue still dripped from the thatched roof, hitting the mossy earth below in tiny wet plops. Beside her, Adrian made a sound in his throat and flipped over onto his stomach, his right arm hooking itself about her waist as if it belonged there.

Twisting herself around until she was on her side, Rielle lifted the dark curls that fell over his neck, letting them fall back against his smooth skin. "How long have you been awake?"

He didn't open his eyes. *"Só um minuto,"* he murmured in sleepy Portuguese and right into the pillow. "Is it morning?"

"More or less."

"Are you very tired?"

"Not especially."

His lips curved against the cotton casing. "Then I must not have lived up to the reputation of my Latin-American countrymen."

Bending her head to his, she kissed his ear. "Or maybe it just isn't possible for me to get tired of you."

"I like this idea," he agreed, inching open one eye. The arm about her waist tightened. She felt him shift slightly as he drew her closer. His mouth caught hers, and he turned a little more, his hands pulling her onto his fully aroused body. And she'd thought he was asleep.

A shiver of delight ran through her. This night was not over yet.

SUMMER SOLSTICE, midmorning, and the village of Morgate was going about its business as usual. Fishermen still took their boats out to sea, vegetable vendors still marketed their wares, the bakery truck still made its daily rounds. And all of this was done under a canopy of nasty black clouds. But that was the British way, wasn't it? Come rain or shine, life goes on. This much at least would never change.

He sat in the smallest, dingiest café he could find and sipped the worst tea he'd ever tasted. Through the grimy window he saw the beginnings of the forest; nothing more than that, but he knew to the tenth of a mile the distance from this place to Brede Manor.

Tonight, he promised himself, closing his eyes and breathing deeply the salty air. The proof would be in his hands no later than tonight. He had to make this thing happen, had to make his plan work.

A faintly cynical smile pulled at his lips. No real triumph in any of this. He was a desperate man whose time was fast running out. The noise and color of the Midsummer Festival would be his cover, and it would work, he vowed, directing a cold look deep into the forest. No matter what it took, the proof would be back in his hands.

Tonight.

IT WAS GOING TO BE a wild party, whether the rain held off or not. Adrian strolled across the crowded grounds between Brede Manor and Mandelin Castle and watched with distant amusement the preparations being made by Gypsies and villagers alike.

Huge columned firepots dotted the lawns with several of the more traditional wood pyres interspersed between them. As always, there were people dressed in Odessa's brown robes and Amelia's flimsier air-gowns, but tonight there was also a variety of other costumes to be seen. Tights and tunics and feather caps for the men, and everything from peasant skirts and floral wreaths to the simpler gowns and scarved hats popular during the Crusades for the women.

Color, yes, there was certainly plenty of that, Adrian had to admit. And music and noise and a general feeling of anticipation that was not dampened at all by the blackness of the night sky. Rain was a definite threat and perhaps more thunder and lightning, as well. There would be no stars shining down on this Midsummer Festival, although the moon did become visible at times, a pale orb that broke through the cloud cover just long enough to announce that it was full.

Shoving his hands into the pockets of his leather jacket, Adrian continued on to the manor. He had needed to walk for a time, to be alone, to think. About Rielle mostly and his feelings for her.

He closed his eyes briefly, a faint smile touching his lips. Confusion in his mind, certainly this still existed, but one thing had come clear to him: what he felt for Rielle was remarkably strong. Overwhelming in many ways. Perhaps he loved her, though this word even now had the power to terrify him, to make him tremble inside.

He didn't like it. To fear anything or anyone was completely foreign to his nature. He did not feel afraid when he drove race cars at excessive speeds; he had never thought twice about such things. So why should one beautiful ex-con-artist with long dark hair and exquisite blue eyes scare him half to death?

No, that was not correct, he amended swiftly. Rielle didn't frighten him; it was all the emotions he could not control when he was with her that brought about this sensation, this confusion he could not seem to sort out no matter how hard he tried.

Perhaps, then, the answer was to stop trying.

Fighting a weary sigh, he forced his mind to another place, into a much darker arena.

The Phantom. A black mystery, insoluble through thought. And yet there should be something in all this man had done that would provide a clue to his identity.

Adrian's troubled gaze was drawn to one of the pyres. Ivan stood there cloaked in his usual black garments and wearing his St. John's wort. He stared in seeming fascination at the roaring flames, the shadows that flickered against his face giving him the look of a true vampire.

Noah was around somewhere, as well. Adrian had seen him a few minutes ago chatting with Ava. Smiling at her with that ever-cruel gleam in his eyes. Worth noting, but little more. Ava Giordano seldom strayed from the limelight. If Noah was indeed the Phantom and on the prowl for another victim, he would be hard-pressed to trick that one into anything.

"Hello, Adrian."

Reuben approached from the right, detaching himself from a circle of dancing Gypsies. He was dressed as a twelfth-century peasant, a tinker, in brown tights and ankle boots, feather cap and cape. Quite a sight. Adrian politely hid a smile as the older man lit his pipe.

"You haven't seen Fagan, have you?" he inquired, his question barely audible above the music and noise—and the distant rumble of thunder that rolled through the night sky. "I'm having a devil of a time finding anyone in all this commotion."

"It will be worse soon," Adrian said, his eyes roaming the crowded lawns. He returned his gaze to Reuben's thin face. "And, no, I have not seen Fagan since this afternoon."

"Did you say Fagan?" Jonathan limped up from the other side, still wearing his linen pants and shirt. He pointed to a ring of robed faeries near the manor house. "I believe that's him over there. I've been up at the castle," he explained, mopping his damp forehead with a handkerchief. "There's enough food in the great hall to feed a small army. If the rain holds off, they'll be bringing it down here shortly. It should be quite a celebration. At any rate I left the hall just after Fagan did. But of course—" he rubbed his injured left knee "—with the damp weather and all, our nimble host soon left me in the dust, as it were."

"Yes, one does have to be in good shape to keep up with Fagan." Drawing consideringly on his pipe, Reuben scanned the faerie ring, smiled and lifted his hand. "I'll be off, then," he said. "Best get into your costumes, both of you. The merriment begins in earnest at 10:00 p.m. That's less than an hour from now."

"Costumes." Jonathan sighed, staring after the departing man. "I suppose if we must we must, although I have a hard time seeing myself dressed up as Robin Hood."

Hands still stuffed in his jacket pockets, Adrian started again for the manor, at a more decorous pace this time. "I had thought you might decide to leave after Ava discovered who you were," he said, watching as Reuben approached Fagan's circle. "She was quite angry."

''She was livid.'' Jonathan tucked away his handkerchief and grimaced. ''What could I do, though? Gilbert hired me to watch her as long as she was here in Morgate. Maybe he suspected a tryst of some sort—he never actually said. In any event I did agree to take the job.'' He chuckled. ''Admittedly I'll have to do it from a distance now, but Ava's rage aside, it really isn't so bad.''

Not yet, it wasn't, Adrian agreed in silence, his eyes once more locating Noah, who appeared to have dropped Ava in favor of a young Gypsy woman, one of the performers from the outdoor plays, if Adrian wasn't mistaken.

So where was Ava?

He followed Jonathan's gaze to the brightly lit manor house. And he found her. She was dressed for the feast already in a simple Norman gown that looked like ivory sackcloth with long sleeves and a rope belt. Not her usual dramatic style. Maybe that explained why she was talking to Fagan near the porch, tapping an irritated foot and not looking particularly happy.

But where then was Reuben? He seemed to have vanished, yet he'd said he was looking for Fagan. This could, Adrian thought tiredly, prove to be a very long night.

''I should probably duck in the back way,'' Jonathan spoke up, his voice glum. ''Ms. Giordano appears to be in a temper, and it's a certainty that I can't outrun her.''

Adrian glanced sideways. ''How did you injure yourself?'' he inquired politely.

''Chasing down a lead in Scotland a few years ago. In the end I was the one who got chased down. Twenty feet down and into a stoney loch.'' He patted his thigh. ''The doctors had to take a full inch of bone out of my left leg. Not a pretty sight at all—'' He stopped suddenly and frowned. ''What's—what's she doing? Where's she going?''

Lifting his head from the path, Adrian saw Ava accompanying Fagan around the side of the mansion. ''To the cellar, perhaps.'' He moved an unconcerned shoulder. ''There is an outer door that leads to the wine cellar and wardrobe room. Possibly she wishes to choose a different costume for the Festival.''

"I hope so." Jonathan sounded despondent. "I suppose I can't get around this costume business. Oh, good evening, Rielle," he inserted with a somewhat awkward smile—and much to Adrian's surprise. He hadn't seen her coming. And he realized why the instant he looked at her.

She was in costume already, and such a costume it was. Soft peasant skirts billowed over layers of white petticoat. She wore a simple white blouse, threaded with ribbon at the neck and a vest with crisscross lacing on the bodice. Her hair was loose and wavy about her shoulders, and on her head sat a coronet of pink and white and yellow roses. Always she was beautiful, but now she was transformed—a medieval vision.

"Good evening, Jonathan," she greeted even as she took Adrian firmly by the wrist and tugged. "Excuse us, please. Senhor Da Costa here has a rawhide tunic waiting for him in Fagan's cellar wardrobe room."

Adrian let her pull him away. "I have a what waiting for me?" he asked, arching a humorous brow.

"A tunic, and don't argue with me—I'm in a bad mood. I just went through Luke's room. Again."

"And no doubt came up empty. Again."

"Empty, frustrated and worried."

She was dragging him toward the cellar door, and while a rawhide tunic was not what Adrian planned to wear tonight, he offered no resistance. Perhaps this would be the case always with Rielle; he still did not know.

"I have a funny feeling about the Festival," she went on, her expression thoughtful. "A bad one, actually. There's a sort of inevitability about it."

"You think something will happen?"

She stared up at him, her eyes very blue in the firelight. "I think it makes sense, don't you? I mean, the Phantom must want to get his hands on Luke's proof, and while I could be wrong, I suspect he hasn't been successful in doing that yet."

Adrian regarded the manor house. "Yes, this is my feeling, as well," he said slowly. "Luke knows how to hide things. I think the Phantom has learned this, although as you say, we could be wrong. But why do you feel something must happen tonight? The proof will not walk away at the conclusion of the Festival.''

"No, but most of Fagan's guests will. Assume the Phantom knows that we know he's here. And why. Once the Midsummer Festival is over, the celebrants will go back to their homes, leaving only you and me and the Phantom. So much for anonymity.''

Adrian's lips twitched. "Perhaps," he agreed. "But it does not have to be this way. The Phantom could make a pretense of going home, too. He does not have to stay at the manor—and in fact it would be wiser for him not to—in order to watch us. If," he added, "watching us is all that he is doing.''

They'd reached the cellar door now, and with a shake of her head Rielle descended the cracked stone steps, her skirts ruffling in the sticky breeze. "Conjecture," she said flatly. "All of it. The best thing we can do right now is keep watching the guests, because I'm telling you, Adrian, I can't find anything in that room upstairs. And I did everything tonight except strip the paneling.'' She pushed the door open, drawing back a little as the fetid air flowed over them. "I really hate this place.''

"Dracula's dungeon," Adrian said with a small smile for her hesitation. It was not like her, though he could understand why she would find such a place distasteful. He took her hand and started down the staircase. "Come, *querida*, we will do this quickly, and it will not be so bad.''

Could not possibly be bad when done in her company, his mind added, and again he felt a slight stab of amusement pass through him—and then something more, an emotion that went much deeper. A ripple of terror. But not for himself. No, this had to do with Rielle. It went deeper even than fear, was much more complex. And he had no idea what it entailed beyond the startlingly simple fact that he did not want to lose her. Not to a madman, not to anyone. Not ever.

They'd made it to the far side of the room. "I think," he began, then stopped as a loud crash broke the stillness around them. An echoing clang of metal and a string of colorful curses that could only have come from Fagan's throat.

Adrian shoved the door back and stepped into the passage. Shadowy again, but power was available. Rielle had hold of his jacket—curious, he knew, yet experienced enough not to rush into the darkened passageway beyond.

"Right you are, my beauty," Fagan hissed in a menacing tone. "It's the graveyard for you and long past time, I must say."

Another crash was followed by an evil chuckle. And then silence filled the cellar once more.

Chapter Eighteen

Movement on the old stone floor, yet not a whisper of sound to be heard. The oddest sensation rippled across Rielle's chilled skin. Dark shapes, formless or deformed, shifted against the stonework, an eerie distortion that made her blood run cold.

Ava had come down here with Fagan; Adrian had told her that a moment ago, his low voice making no impression on the dead air.

Dead air... Rielle squeezed her eyes closed. What a horrible thought. Would they find a dead actress, too?

She shuddered deeply, her eyes opening, fastening themselves on the shadows, her fingers clutching Adrian's leather jacket. They had to do something, her brain insisted. Now. But already Adrian was creeping forward, a wraith in his own right, his boots noiseless even to Rielle's keen ears.

She stayed with him, glued to his side. Because she would not lose him to a lunatic, she swore fiercely to herself. Because she loved him, and he couldn't have kept her back in any event.

They crept closer to one of the chambers, the only one that was lit. A satiny rustle floated out from inside. Blue-white light spilled across the threshold. Rielle tried hard to remember their torchlight tour of the other night. Not the wine cellar, this place—the film room. An endless tract of shelves and silver cannisters and machinery. And Fagan in there with Ava...

Something clanged again. More rustling and scraping and really no longer any attempt being made to keep things quiet. And that seemed a rather unlikely development to her.

Adrian slowed, pressing a cautionary hand against her stomach. "Something is not right," he said so softly that she had to read his lips to understand.

She didn't question him but merely nodded and braced herself. Whatever horrors awaited them down here, she would be prepared to face them.

"What is this!"

Fagan's hoarse roar was filled with outrage. Rielle couldn't imagine why, suspected she didn't want to know. Still, she forced herself to take a deep breath. Then, glancing at Adrian to see that he was ready, she peered around the edge of the door frame.

She couldn't believe what she saw. Certainly she couldn't assimilate it right away.

Fagan stood in a metal trash bin, alone, covered with bits of film and cardboard. Beside him and upside down sat a broken Louis XVI chair. Around his neck and caught in his beard and hair were dozens of yards of black videotape, all twisted and tangled and reminding her of the elastic inside an old golf ball she'd unwrapped once.

He stared at the shiny mass, then at them. No madness in his blue eyes, though clearly he was mad. Angry, indignant—not at all his usual cheerful self.

"Who could have done this?" he bellowed, climbing at once from the bin and holding up the ruined tape. "My guests are at liberty to select movies from this room, but no one is allowed to tamper with the equipment."

Rielle gave her head a little shake. "Fagan, what are you talking about?" she demanded with a frown. "Where's Ava?"

He flapped an unconcerned hand toward the ceiling. "Upstairs, I should think. She only wanted to augment her costume." He began hunting for something, bending and stretching and peering into every cupboard he passed, muttering things to himself. "This is intolerable, an abomination, willful destruction." He slapped an empty videocassette down on the bench, pulled the tape from around his neck and began winding it onto the spools. "Well, we'll just see what damage has been done here. Destroy one of my videos, indeed. I'll not stand for it, let me tell you. Someone will answer for this."

Rielle was lost. Totally. She looked up at Adrian, paused, then looked again. He was watching Fagan, and he didn't seem lost or confused or even unsure. Did he see something here that she was missing?

"The sausages," he murmured obscurely as Fagan continued to load the VHS spools. "You have to look beyond the surface to see what is really there."

Sausages, surface? Rielle said nothing, tried to consider everything as a whole, waiting for some part of it to click. She drifted closer to the bench, her mind a jumble of thoughts. Her eyes made a covert sweep of the floor. No sign of a body. No blood. No indication of a struggle. Fagan must have fallen off the broken chair and into the trash bin. Probably the "graveyard" he'd referred to was in fact a junkyard. Logical enough, but she was still missing something very big here.

Adrian was close behind her; she could feel the heat of his body through her costume. Distracting. But then Fagan slapped the casing back on the cassette and shoved it into one of the three available VCRs, and her attention was immediately diverted.

"Now we shall see what damage this anonymous vandal has done." He gave the Play button a stab with one thin finger. "Oh, to know who would commit such a crime. Butchering one of my good tapes—"

He was cut off midsentence by a woman's scream. An onscreen shriek that came from the terrified mouth of Sybil Fawkes.

Rielle recognized both the actress and the movie instantly. *Marionette.* But they weren't watching the beginning of the movie. This particular scene took place somewhere around the middle of the film. So where then was the first half of the videotape? In the trash bin? She looked. Nothing there. And Fagan was muttering the same question himself, so clearly he didn't have the answer.

"Adrian, what . . . ?" she started, then almost choked as it finally did click. Maybe. She didn't want to be hasty about this. And of course her brain was racing ahead of itself now, collecting momentum so rapidly that her mind had trouble keeping up.

Marionette. First half of the film missing, second half found in the garbage. Luke's mysterious proof. Not a fingerprint. Something videotaped. Most damning, especially if that video happened to contain a real-life murder.

Three VHS tapes had been out of order in Luke's room. Nothing unusual about them at first glance, but she hadn't watched them all the way through.

And the first half of *Marionette*—this movie that was now playing—was missing! Could it be upstairs in Luke's room? With something else spliced onto the end?

She looked sharply at Adrian. Yes, he was thinking the same thing as she was. He must be. He'd taken her hand and was drawing her away from the bench and a still-muttering Fagan.

"Luke once hid jewels he stole inside sausages," he told her briefly. "He has used this same trick again, I am sure of it."

Rielle had no idea what sausages he was talking about, but it didn't matter. "He hid his proof on a videocassette," she whispered, stunned. Excited. "He left the first part of the movie intact, took out the last part and replaced it with something else. Something the Phantom wants very, very badly." A shudder of undisguised horror went through her; her tone became one of urgency. "Adrian, we have to get to that tape before the Phantom does."

AVA WALKED quietly up the stairs in her ballet slippers and sackcloth gown, a long-sleeved robe of brown wool draped over one arm. She *would* outshine those second-rate Gypsies tonight. Performers—pah! What did they know of portraying a character?

A smug smile flitted across her painted lips. Her version of Odessa would put all others to shame, and put those pathetic players nicely in their place.

Key at the ready, she started down the dim second-floor hallway for her own room. But a creak on the staircase distracted her. She caught a glimpse of someone dressed all in black, creeping stealthily up toward the third floor.

She frowned. Not Ivan, this furtive figure in black. The vampire-man didn't wear ski masks and black turtleneck sweaters. And really, what reason would anyone, except perhaps Jonathan Lynch, exposed PI—she chuckled darkly at that one—have for sneaking around Brede Manor?

She made her decision swiftly, slipping her arms into the wool robe and heading for the stairs. Her steps were quiet, aided by the wild music beyond the mansion's walls. Thunder in the distance—she could hear it, and no doubt about it, a man moving smoothly along the corridor ahead of her.

She hung back in the shadows, watching. An intruder breaking in to an empty room. Interesting switch.

She tiptoed along the carpet, gown and robe swirling about her ankles, earrings tinkling delicately as she moved. Whoever he was, she felt confident he wouldn't hear her. The sea was an untamed roar on this level, the thunder beginning to draw closer, the Gypsy music growing ever more frenzied.

He'd left the door open a crack. Sloppy for an intruder, but it made things easier for her. She peeked inside. Darkness mostly greeted her, black shapes and outlines. He was over by the entertainment center, running the beam of a tiny flashlight over the videocassette library. She saw him stop the beam, heard him let out a strangled sound that could have been anything from a chuckle to a growl and watched his gloved hands snatch up one of the VHS cassettes.

Had she accidentally leaned against the door? She didn't think so, but it swung in a notch regardless, hinges squeaking all the way.

He spun around before she could react. And of course spotted her right off.

Fear clogged her throat. Her mind whirled. Did he have a gun? How fast was he? *Who* was he? Would he hurt her?

And why in God's name was she still standing here!

The last was no question; it was a command for her frozen muscles to move.

She backed away from the door. Get out, her brain shouted. Get help! Jonathan was always close by. One scream from her and he'd be here.

A hand grabbed her before she could turn and run. A hand that yanked her into the bedroom. A booted foot shoved the door closed. Fingers slammed down hard across her mouth. She couldn't scream!

Struggle! Kick! Bite his hand!

But his grip was unrelenting. Even twisting her head from side to side didn't help.

She must have done something, though, because his body suddenly went rigid against her. A low hiss sounded in her ear. Recognition in the growled words.

And then nothing more. Only the rasp of his breath, a clap of broken thunder and the ominous click of the door as he gave it a shove with one foot, shutting them inside the empty room, together. Alone.

THE DULL THUD that penetrated the closed door of Luke's room stilled Rielle's hand on the knob. This room was supposed to be empty.

She snatched her hand away. Or Adrian did it for her. Hard to say who reacted first; all that mattered was that they both knew there was someone inside.

Someone—and the tape.

"What do we do?" she whispered, listening closely to the odd noises on the other side.

Part of a woman's scream escaped, answering that question fast enough.

With a flat "Do not do anything foolish" to Rielle, which was about the best anyone could hope for from her, Adrian kicked the door open and vanished across the blackened threshold.

Light, dim but disruptive, streamed in, illuminating two people: a man in dark clothes and a ski mask and a woman with short bobbed hair. A clink of crystal underscored the struggle, followed by another cut-off scream. It was Ava! And the Phantom had her in his grasp!

Not for long, though. Adrian was right there, the fingers of one hand wrapping themselves around the Phantom's wool-encased throat. Adrian was deceptively strong, as Rielle well knew. As the Phantom quickly discovered.

The arms holding Ava disengaged themselves from her panicky form, gloved hands going out of necessity for Adrian's neck.

"No!"

The cry came from Rielle's horrified lips. She rushed into the room, almost colliding with Ava, who was scrambling on hands and knees across the carpet to get out.

"Are you crazy!" the other woman shrieked, clutching at her ankles. "He's mad. There's nothing you or I can do. We've got to get out of here!"

Rielle ignored the desperate warning. She wished she could avoid Ava's clawing hands as easily, get to the light switch at least. Maybe the Phantom would run. Maybe they could unmask him at last. Right now either one would be acceptable to her.

But don't hurt Adrian, she prayed silently, unable to see much of what was happening. Two figures struggling in that darkness, banging into the furniture, and Ava, on her feet, terrified fingers glued to Rielle's arms, forcing her back toward the door. Not where she wanted to be, but in hysteria the woman possessed uncommon strength. And Rielle really didn't want to hit her, not after the trauma she'd just endured.

She worked one arm free with extreme difficulty. "Let go of me, Ava," she snapped.

"He'll kill us," she panted. "He will. We've got to run. Get help."

"*We* can help. Let go of me!"

It was like trying to talk sense to a crazed cat. Ava would not stop clawing at her, moaning that they had to get away while they still could. And so Rielle hit her, hard, a re-sounding whack across the cheek that brought a glimmer of furious indignation to the woman's dark eyes.

"How dare you!" she challenged, her panic subsiding enough that Rielle could finally shake her loose.

Unfortunately, in doing that, she pushed Ava the wrong way. Off balance, the spluttering actress fell against the door, and the room was plunged into total darkness.

Where was the damned light switch? Rielle's own room was set up differently; nothing was in the same place. And something had just slammed into her arm. Someone, actually.

"Adrian!" His name came out in a hoarse whisper, though he wouldn't have heard it. Thunder was rolling through the skies once more; Ava was yelling in her ear and right back to plucking frantically at her clothes, and the grunts of the two struggling men were punctuated only by the sound of things breaking all around.

In the darkness Rielle heard Adrian swear. Thank God. Somehow, despite Ava's attempts to haul her away, she managed to locate a floor lamp. Amazingly it worked. A quick flick of her wrist, and the room was flooded with light. And the Phantom didn't like that one little bit.

Ski mask intact, he whirled and bolted for the window, throwing back the curtains and twisting open the latch. He was out on the ledge so fast that Rielle caught no more than a fleeting glimpse of his body, really nothing of his build. And a second later, didn't care about either one.

"Adrian, no!" she shouted, ripping Ava's clawlike fingers from her arms one last time. "Let him go!"

But it was too late. Adrian was long gone, as well. Through the window onto the ledge...

...And down the drainpipe, her appalled brain informed her when she ran across the room to look out. Oh, Lord, this was going from bad to worse.

Rielle straightened from the sill, gritting her teeth, her mind a tangle of uncertainties. What should she do? What *could* she do? Not follow them down this way. Besides, that wouldn't help Adrian—if he really needed helping, she thought with an absurd stab of humor, which was instantly wiped out as Ava's fingers closed on her sash, jerking her away from the open pane.

"He attacked me," she declared, hysteria still tingeing her voice. "He was going to kill me, I could tell. He went for my throat."

Who cares, Rielle wanted to snarl, but didn't. She thought quickly. She had to call the police, contact that constable from the village, get him up here now.

Yes, but that would take time.

She stuck her head out the window again, squinting into the night. No sign of movement. Agitated, she tapped the frame with her fists. Where had they gone?

Firelight in the distance, past the oak trees to her right, but below all was bathed in darkness. Wet, silent darkness. It was beginning to rain. Nothing heavy, just a light mist at this point, but it didn't make her feel any better. Everyone would head for the castle if this continued, and Adrian would still be out there, chasing down a mad Phantom.

She shoved the ugly images away, and with them all her doubts and fears and the panicky shivers that sliced through her body. "The police," she said out loud, making her icy limbs move, swatting at Ava's hands as she spun around. This time it was Rielle who did the grabbing, her fingers digging painfully into the other woman's arms. "We have to call the police." She shook her. "Can you do that, Ava? Can you phone the police and tell them to come?"

"Yes," Ava whispered, nodding. Then, in a stronger voice, she said again, "Yes, I can. I will. But what are you going to do?"

"I don't know. Something." Rielle's eyes made a hasty surveillance of the room. "The tape," she murmured, remembering suddenly.

She left Ava to ransack the video library. No *Marionette*. She checked the floor. Nothing.

Damn! The Phantom had the tape!

Chapter Nineteen

"There they are." Ava's abnormally shrill voice came from the window. One finger stabbed at the black air beyond. "Back of those trees. I'm sure it was them—I think."

Rielle almost fell out the window in her rush to see Adrian. "Where?" she demanded.

"Heading up the hill toward the castle. On the other side. Away from the fires."

"I don't see them."

Ava sighed. Her hand dropped. "Neither do I, now. But they were running, and it looked like two men." She grimaced. "One man, I should say. And one nut."

Rielle didn't care to argue semantics. She whipped Ava around in a circle and pushed her in the direction of the door. "Go," she ordered roughly. "Call the constable. Don't give him the details. Just tell him to get up here, that maybe he'll be able to catch the Phantom."

Ava stared at her openmouthed. "What?"

"Do it, and I'll explain later," Rielle said, dragging her into the hall.

"But where are you—"

"I'm not sure. It doesn't matter. Make the phone call, then lock yourself in your room. You'll be safe enough there."

"But—"

Ava's protest, whatever it might have been, never reached Rielle's ears. She was on the stairs and she still didn't know where she was going, what she would do.

No, not true. She knew exactly what she would do. She would take the shortcut through the forest to the castle. Not wise, but necessary. She only wished she had a gun.

Jonathan had a gun, she recalled distantly. But it was too late to turn back. Find Adrian, make sure he was all right—that was the most important thing. Ava would phone the police.

Would she send them up to the castle?

Damn, Rielle swore again as she ran for the trees. She should have mentioned that. But maybe Ava would think of it on her own. Yes, of course she would. She'd seen the two figures running toward Mandelin Castle, and while she might be scared, she was certainly not stupid.

No mist penetrated the leafy boughs of the oaks. It was dark and shadowy, the dream of a faerie-tale forest turned into a witch's nightmare. Ugly, twisted shapes rose up on all sides of her, everything black and out of proportion. The air was sticky and warm, heavy with the threat of yet another storm. Lightning split the cloudy skies, preceding by only a few short seconds a low peal of thunder.

The wind had picked up, too, she noticed. It clawed at her hair, whipping long strands across her cheeks and eyes. But she kept going, running, until at last she reached the forest's edge.

She saw the ruined castle before her, a huge, black monolith in silhouette against a bank of ghostly clouds. A most intimidating sight, and for a moment Rielle faltered. Assuming she even found him, what could she do to help Adrian? She had no weapons at her disposal, no training in the martial arts. But she knew how to defend herself—all good con artists did.

Far ahead something stirred in the gloom. She twisted her head around. Where was she? Not at the front of the castle. Off to the side, perhaps, closer to the rear.

Weak strains of music reached her, lute and tambourine, faintly audible one moment, blown away the next by a weird gust of wind that seemed to emanate from the maw of the ancient castle.

Rielle hunched her shoulders, not liking this yet determined not to turn back. Again that odd stirring near the old stone entranceway. Her eyes locked on the movement. Was it Adrian?

She wanted to call out but knew better. Take care, her brain cautioned, and she listened for once, creeping forward slowly, warily, feeling her way through the rotted gate, over clumps of earth and stone and weed until she was swallowed up in the vast shadows of the outer wall.

More wind caught her hair, swirling in great eerie circles around her. Her fear had reached feverish proportions, so strong now that she felt more numb than afraid. Not good, but she refused to retreat.

What was that over by the arched doorway? A person, surely, but who? She risked a soft "Adrian?" and heard a moaned response. Indistinct yet unmistakable.

The darkness shifted, a black shadow falling across the man's form, enfolding it. She crept closer, breath held, dirt crunching under her feet. The wind howled down from the turrets. No sound now but that. Through the murk the form began to take on a shape. And a very strange shape at that.

She jerked back, startled, staring. Frightened. Not a man, this thing. Not even human.

Then why be scared? she wondered, swallowing hard. A rock and a bush, that's all it was. The bush had moved in the breeze. Surely no cause for alarm.

Her heart continued to pound; she couldn't make it stop. She took another backward step. Terror swept through her in great dizzying waves. Something was very wrong here. But what?

Bushes didn't moan!

It hit her suddenly, bringing an audible gasp to her lips. Yes! Someone had moaned in the darkness—that she hadn't imagined. Not Adrian, her instincts told her. Which left only one person.

In a blind panic she whirled around. Above her, lightning flashed. The wind rose. Her hair blew across her eyes.

But even so, she saw enough to understand that she was no longer alone. A figure in black stood directly behind her, a silent specter whose face was obscured by shadows. Rielle glimpsed an upraised arm, heard a low chuckle, saw the lightning flash again—and then the features it illuminated for one brief horrifying instant.

She'd seen the Phantom unmasked, she realized in that split second before his arm came down. A sense of inevitability washed over her. She should have known. Of course it would be him.

Thunder crashed in the distance. No time at all to react, or even fight. She closed her eyes. Something sharp exploded in her head. Pain shot through her limbs.

As both the Phantom and the night dissolved into the shimmering world of unconsciousness.

ADRIAN WAS very well trained, in shape to run for many miles even when the distance took him through a darkened forest. Branches of gnarled oaks, exposed roots and blackness pressed in on him, but he could shut these things out. He had to. The Phantom was fast, and he knew these paths well.

Still, he was not as agile as his pursuer, Adrian realized as they broke out of the sheltered woods and started up the hill behind the castle. And he had not trained in the rarified atmosphere of the Brazilian mountains. Fast or not, the creature in black was beginning to tire.

But only a little. At such a rate this chase could take them through the village before it ended, and that, Adrian knew, would not be good. He would lose the Phantom there almost certainly. Perhaps he would even lose him in the castle, and that would be no better.

As he did in auto racing, Adrian swiftly calculated his advantages. He was still several yards behind the other man, too far to lunge at him. But if he could shorten that distance by half, it would be a different story.

A streak of yellow lightning shot through the sky, distracting the Phantom. Hesitation in his stride, and a yard of space between them vanished.

The climb also was difficult. Holes appeared out of nowhere, the dirt was loose in spots and damp from the light rain that had begun to fall. Adrian ignored it all, didn't even look at the ground beneath him, a risk the Phantom seemed unwilling to take. More space was eaten up.

But his luck would not hold forever; Adrian knew this from experience. He had to go for the man now, before he put a foot down incorrectly and ended things that way.

He didn't think about it, really, any more than he thought about his driving. At least there was no conscious plan involved. Rather he let his instincts take over, let them assume control of his body, direct his muscles, tell him what to do and when.

The Phantom was not traveling in a straight line. This complicated matters, though no more so than to pass another car in a race. He had only to stretch out with his senses, to feel for the right moment.

He'd done it before and did it now, with relentless accuracy and perhaps a trifle more force than was required. He also landed right on top of the man, and that must have caused some pain, or at least knocked the wind from the Phantom's lungs.

To pin his captive on the muddy ground was not a problem. To turn him over while holding him there was a little more difficult. Still, this too could be accomplished, and several seconds later, amid a barrage of grunts and growls and furious twists of his trapped body, the Phantom lay on his back.

Blue eyes stared out from behind the woolen ski mask. Bright blue, extremely recognizable, and for an instant Adrian was too startled to react. This could not be what it seemed.

The struggling stopped instantly; so did the menacing growls. Only the thunder continued and the lightning, and those things meant nothing to either man.

At a very tender age Adrian had learned to swear, better than any sailor he had ever known. He did so now in Portuguese, releasing a string of curses that even his friends in Brazil would not have heard.

This man understood, though, this person beneath him who no longer fought to escape. The one who had probably given him a black eye during their scuffle at the manor.

For one irrational second Adrian considered returning the favor. But he controlled the petty urge. And reaching down, instead yanked the mask away. . . .

"Luke!"

The name came out in an angry snarl, and Adrian could get angry. Luke knew that better than anyone. He also knew better than to breathe until his cousin removed the fingers that were currently wrapped around his throat. Lightly for the moment, but that could change, given the absolute fury in Adrian's dark eyes.

"If you strangle me, you might never learn the identity of the Phantom," Luke said in as calm a voice as he could manage.

The hand on his throat let up ever so lightly, but the eyes regarding him were still narrowed, angry. Mistrustful—though not in any deluded sense. Adrian knew he wasn't the Phantom. What he didn't know was whether to hit him or give him a chance to explain.

Luke took a deep breath. "We don't have time for this, cousin," he said softly. "Either choke me or let me up."

Nothing changed, not Adrian's hold on him or his implacable expression. "Who is the Phantom?" he demanded in a dangerously restrained tone.

Straight to the point, as always. And damn how Luke wished he had an answer. But the best he could do was shake his head. "I don't know."

The fingers tightened again, but Luke could tell that both the moment and the danger had passed. "I swear, Adrian," he repeated firmly. "I don't know. At least I don't know how you know him. Paul and I called him Gustav. He was in his sixties, we thought. He also had gray hair and a beard, if that helps, which I doubt it does. But those things aren't important right now. I've got to get back and find that . . ."

Luke was in the process of pushing his cousin's hand away when something suddenly clicked in his head, something he'd heard at the manor, that he'd been too busy doing battle with Adrian to stop and recognize.

"Rielle!" He whispered her name in horror. His eyes found Adrian's in the darkness. The lightning was going crazy around them, charging the air, making it crackle with electricity. But Luke scarcely noticed the blue-white bolts. He tore free of his cousin's grasp and struggled to sit up. "Adrian, she was there in the room, wasn't she? My God, we have to get to her. She's in danger."

"The Phantom," Adrian murmured, diverted. "He is still out there." On his feet in one fluid motion, he turned his gaze toward the manor. And probably would have taken off like one of his own Grand Prix cars·if Luke hadn't grabbed his arm with both hands.

"Wait!" He had to shout now above the thunder and the rising wind. "There's more you need to know."

Adrian pulled away but didn't leave. "What more can there be?" he demanded, clearly impatient. And even more concerned. "You said you could not identify the Phantom."

"I can't." Luke forced back the icy claws of terror that wanted to close about his vocal cords. "Listen to me, Adrian, I remembered something when I was in hiding. Something about my proof."

"Proof that you have on videotape."

"Yes—good, you figured that out. But it's not the film itself I'm talking about here. It's something else I remembered." A chill that had nothing to do with the wind crawled along his spine. Shuddering, he found Adrian's eyes. "There's more to this than the actual murders. And more to the Phantom than anyone realizes."

Chapter Twenty

Yes, it had started three weeks ago in London, with Luke on the run and a Phantom on the loose. And somehow Rielle had gotten caught between them....

The memories dissolved. Reality returned. Everything came together in Rielle's mind, an eerie blend of elements: the electrical storm outside, the castle dungeon where she was trapped, the sight of the Phantom's face, the sound of the Phantom's voice, the touch of his mad fingers on her hair....

A shudder so deep it made her teeth chatter ripped through her bound body. She would have cried; she wanted to more than anything, but tears wouldn't help. She refused to give this crazy killer the satisfaction. Let him torment her; let him play his twisted game and retreat like a bug to the shadows. Let him leer at her and wear that ghastly stage makeup and whisper old lines and pretend whatever he wanted to; she would not respond to any of it.

There was so much confusion in her mind. So many questions. Where was Adrian? Was he hurt? Did he know the identity of the Phantom? What exactly had happened tonight at Brede Manor? Did the Phantom have the video-tape, the one that must surely contain the proof of his crimes?

Well, yes, of course he had it. He'd grabbed it and gone out the window, hadn't he? Adrian must have lost him in the darkness. And so, for whatever reason, the Phantom had come here, to Mandelin Castle. Maybe Adrian had gone back then to the manor. Maybe he really was safe and unharmed. Maybe he would come and help her. And bring the police!

Rielle squeezed her eyes closed as yet another bolt of lightning snaked through the dusty chamber. A thousand maybes pounding in her brain and a madman lurking somewhere close by. This was a nightmare pure and simple. The worst she'd ever had.

She released an unsteady breath. A madman. Yes, the Phantom was that, but he'd conned her easily enough, hadn't he? Damn, why hadn't she seen through his scam?

She pictured his face again. Not really recognizable now, but the eyes were the same. Like those of the evil faerie queen, Odessa, the eyes gave him away. He could have masked them, she knew, but why bother? He didn't intend to let her leave this dreadful place. This—oh, Lord, what had he called it—this stage.

"Sybil, my darling, you are a clever creature, aren't you?"

The whispery voice in her ear shocked Rielle so badly that she couldn't keep the gasp to herself. Maybe the sound was swallowed up by the thunder; it no longer seemed important.

Don't let him see the fear, her mind ordered. Don't look at his face. Don't look into his eyes. Those shining, un*glamor*ous eyes.

His pale fingers grazed her cheekbone. "So beautiful," he crooned, his breath stirring her hair. "They were wrong this time, my voices. They told me you weren't Sybil, that our mission here had nothing to do with Sybil. But I knew they were wrong. I knew you would sneak back somehow and try to fool me." He sighed. "But those voices of mine— all they cared about was getting back what Luke had stolen from us."

Voices? Sybil? Us? Rielle felt as though she'd been hit by a tidal wave of nonsense. But was it really gibberish?

Again the silky finger stroked her cheek. Disgusting. She couldn't concentrate. More lightning came, and a damp gust of wind to make the torches dance. Thunder directly over-head. And far, far in the distance, Gypsy music. Strings and wind instruments and then a wild cantata of voices, celebrating the summer solstice.

Rielle managed not to jerk away from the thing beside her, this horrible creature that was breathing on her, touching her....

No! She wouldn't think about that. What had he just said? Something about voices, and he'd called her Sybil. Did he mean Sybil Fawkes, his first victim? Were all his victims Sybil to him?

Rielle fought her revulsion, her panic. She had to think. This was important. It might even be the focal point of the Theater Murders. But she wasn't an actress. Didn't he realize that? Hadn't his voices, whatever they were, told him?

She took a very deep, very shaky breath. "I think you should listen to your...voices," she said, her own wobbly and uncertain. "I don't know anything about acting, really I don't."

His chuckle told her he didn't believe that. His raspy words confirmed it. "You're a true demon, my darling. Good, but never quite as good as me."

His tone grew dreamy. His red lips brushed Rielle's ear, and she shuddered visibly.

"My love," he breathed. "And I did love you, you know, more than any of those other men you played with and threw away. I even loved you when you laughed at me. No talent, you said, and laughed until you almost cried. Yes, I could even love you then, Sybil. You were jealous of my ability, I understood that. I accepted it. But when you told me that it was over between us, that you never wanted to see me again—well, I knew then what you really were. Not a woman—no. The devil incarnate. You had to die, and it was my job to do the killing. But first I had to show you how much talent I really did possess.

"Ah, Sybil, my sweet," he purred, "you try so very hard to match my performances. But always I'm the one who takes the bows. You die, and I go on. You come back, and I wait for you. You disguise yourself, and I see through it. I disguise myself, and you die. Such a vicious circle we've created. And don't you see? Even when you cheat, I win."

She was going to be sick, Rielle thought in desperation. Either that or go mad herself. He was stroking the side of her neck now with his satiny fingertips, and his touch was making her crazy.

Please, God, she prayed. Let Ava have phoned the police. Let them be on their way up here.

The Phantom's breath came into her ear again, hot and moist and so revolting she had to grind her teeth together to keep from screaming. "I have the voices on my side, Sybil," he whispered seductively. "You always forget that, and it's always your undoing. Give it up, my darling, please. Let this be our final performance. You can't take the voices from me, and you have none of your own to guide you. So just let go this time. Take your cruel laughter and your cruel taunts and your cruel heart back to the other side and stay there. It's what we all want deep down. You and me and, yes, even my voices."

"Your voices want the killing to end?" Rielle managed to croak. She had no idea what she was asking or even what she hoped to accomplish. To stall him, perhaps. Or maybe it was his constant references to his "voices" that hit an instinctive nerve. Was there a chance that she could talk to the voices directly, instead of to the Phantom?

She stopped on that thought, her hope draining slowly away. No, if the Phantom was mad, then any voices he conjured up in his head were bound to be similarly affected.

He moved around in front of her, studying her face, his own a mask of near-childlike wonder. "Of course my voices want the killing to end." He sounded puzzled. "It's you, Sybil, you who won't give up. You keep coming back."

Again Rielle uttered a silent prayer that the police would show up, that Ava had called, that Adrian would come with them. She didn't know what to say to this monster, didn't know how long he could be put off.

He touched her now, lightly, running the tip of his index finger across her chin. A streak of lightning created shadows on his features, and she saw his mouth curve into a slow jester's smile.

"Shall we begin, my dear?" he questioned softly.

Rielle swallowed the lump in her throat. "No!" She searched her mind. "I—I don't know my lines."

How could he smile that hideous jester's smile and still talk? "You have no lines, Sybil," he said, doing it somehow. Then he sighed and made a theatrical gesture around the ruined dungeon. "Look at this place. We're not even on a real stage. It's all makeshift this time." He leaned closer, whispering conspiratorially. "Because, you see, my voices didn't believe me about you. They said you were here to help your friend, Luke."

"But that is why I'm here."

Smile intact, he curled a strand of her hair around one long finger and gave it a nasty tug. "Don't lie to me, Sybil," he warned, his tone hardening despite the maniacal smile. "The voices were wrong. Admit it."

Another sharp tug, another clap of thunder to shake the stone column behind her. Rielle bit her lip, fought back tears of frustration and fear and looked frantically at the stone staircase. Where was Adrian? Where were the police? Why didn't someone come?

"Police?" The Phantom arched a surprised brow, drawing back a little. "Did you say police, Sybil?"

Had she? Rielle lifted her chin, a small gesture of defiance that bolstered her courage. "Yes, I did. The constable and his men will be here any time now." If Ava had her wits about her, she added silently, and that too was a prayer.

The last prayer she might ever have a chance to offer, she realized as the Phantom withdrew from her, and she saw...

The horror of it hit her like a blow to the stomach. For a moment she actually couldn't breathe, couldn't blink.

Not one person smiling at her now, her shocked brain informed her, but two. Two people. The man who was the Phantom...and another. One who reached out a pale hand to stroke his hair, to murmur in the gentlest of tones, "You've done well, my Phantom, very well. I'm pleased. And like the others before her, she is yours."

"She is Sybil," the Phantom insisted. "I told you she was, but you wouldn't listen."

The second pair of eyes stared at Rielle's stunned face. "Call her what you will. She's a problem, nothing more."

Thunder crashed. Wind roared down the staircase. The torches flickered. One dark brow rose in judgment. One red-tipped finger came up to point at Rielle's throat. And the delicate tinkle of crystal hung in the damp air.

"Kill her!"

"You were right."

The statement was no more than a thread of sound in the darkness, a low growl that Adrian could not suppress. Luke was behind him, crouched down as he was, in the shadows that half covered the dungeon stairs.

There was more to the Phantom than anyone knew, his cousin had said outside, and explained in quick fragmented sentences:

"Heard the sound the night of the murder. Knew the tape would tell me what my mind couldn't. Then I came to Brede Manor—and saw a woman at the bedroom door. Didn't recognize her. But the sound, Adrian, the clink of crystal. I heard it when we struggled, and thought, Yes! I know this sound. This woman was in the theater when the Phantom strangled Charity Green! Maybe she controls him...."

Did she? Possibly. It appeared that way to Adrian, anyway. Controlled him and videotaped his deadly "performances." A very sick person, this woman.

Adrian's first rash thought when he saw Rielle was to go for the creature's throat. But they had arrived too late. The Phantom stood very close to where Rielle was tied. He could snap her neck long before Adrian could get to him.

"Gustav," Luke whispered, hanging over Adrian's shoulder in the enveloping staircase shadows. "I presume."

He sounded puzzled, and Adrian could only assume that the Phantom now wore a different mask than the one his cousin had known. He squinted through smoke and dust and flashes of forked lightning to the thing that stood in front of Rielle. Slender build, medium height, rather bland features, even in full stage makeup. Brown hair streaked with gray, eyes the color of powdered silver—and no limp.

It was him, all right. And Gustav, and probably a hundred other people. Jonathan Lynch—actor turned Phantom, Phantom masquerading as a private detective, masquerading as an actor. Killer and con artist, as well. And all of this apparently under one woman's control. Complicated, bizarre and—Adrian had no delusions in this area—very, very dangerous.

His muscles tightened to the point of pain, but he didn't move, didn't remove his gaze from the group below. Ava also had a look of triumph on her face, a glow that did not come from the torches about her head or the lightning that shot through the sky beyond the high windows.

The cruelest of smiles pulled at her lips. The gentle tone she'd used on Jonathan vanished. A finger was raised slowly, deliberately, and pointed at Rielle's throat.

"Kill her," she ordered the Phantom, her voice choked with malice and something akin to exultation. "Kill her as you did all the pretenders before her."

Chapter Twenty-One

The sound of Ava's voice faded away. For one long, unnatural moment the dungeon was silent, deathly still, as the wind and the thunder and even the crackling torches seemed to stop and consider the chilling pronouncement.

Rielle didn't have to consider it. She had to think. Fast. Had to stall, at least.

Talk, her frantic brain instructed. Question her. Keep the fingers that are clenching and unclenching at Jonathan's sides from wrapping themselves around your throat.

She steadied her breathing. No panic on her face, only in her mind and every other part of her body. "You're the Phantom's 'voices,' aren't you?" she blurted out in a composed tone that surprised her a little.

Surprised Ava, too, obviously, for the woman's triumphant smile became sly. "Cool head, Rielle. Most impressive, considering your situation. But then I'm letting myself forget, aren't I? You're not an actress, not really. You're a crook."

"Was a crook," Rielle corrected, then could have bitten out her tongue. She was arguing with the puller of a homicidal maniac's strings.

Ava didn't seem upset. In fact, she laughed. "As you wish." She came closer, gloating. "Yes, to answer your question, I am what my Phantom calls his 'voices.' He's quite a fascinating person, as you might have guessed. Completely insane, yet he listens to me. Has ever since the night I chanced to see him strangling Sybil. He loved her, you know.''

"Yes, I gathered that.''

"Myself, I hated her. A Brittany Rhodes graduate. 'Queenie,' the instructors called her. I had a different name for her.'' Ava's lips took an ugly downward turn. "In time, I had names for all of them. Sybil, Ingrid, Janine, Elizabeth—every one of them, right down to sweet Charity Green.'' Her voice changed timbre. "'See them act, up there on the stage. They have talent, Ava. Watch and learn.' That's what those fools at the academy told me. 'Study them—they're going to get the starring roles. They have that special something.... Well now really, Ava, there's no need to get angry. Ava, they're not laughing at you. No one's laughing at you. Ava! What are you doing? You are dismissed, do you hear me! You will leave the academy immediately!' ''

Now it was Ava who stood close to Rielle. Ava, whose features were twisted with rage. "It was one of the instructors who said those horrible things to me. And, oh, how I wanted to kill her. Maybe she knew it. Poor deluded soul. She was eighty-two, you know. A little push down the stairs, and no one would have been the wiser. But as it turned out, I didn't have to do a thing. Two days later the old goose had a seizure of some sort and died. Not before she gave me my walking papers, though, and told Sybil—of all the people to tell—that I had no talent. And you know Sybil Fawkes just thrived on slander. 'You don't have Ingrid's passion or Elizabeth's timing or Annabelle's poise,' she said in that mean-mouthed way of hers. 'And you certainly have none of my presence.' ''

As she spoke, Ava circled the stone pillar, and to Rielle's astonishment began loosening the ropes on her wrists and ankles. But only to a point. Then she reappeared, set the videocassette she must have taken from Luke's room on a slab of stone and withdrew the gun that Adrian had found in Jonathan's room from the pocket of her brown wool robe costume, handing it to the Phantom.

"I suggest a complete lack of movement while I finish untying you," she said, tapping Rielle's cheek as she once again circled the pillar. "My Phantom has rather twitchy fingers. Would you like to hear the rest of my tragic tale before you die?"

Jonathan's head bobbed. "Say yes," he prompted, his lips once again stretching into that horrible jester's smile. "My voices tell wonderful faerie tales. Better than the faerie lore you'll hear around this place."

Before she died . . . Rielle was too dazed to do more than nod. But she probably should hear Ava out. At least she'd have a few extra minutes to think.

"I used to fantasize about killing them," Ava went on from behind the column. "For years, actually. But, you know, it's hard to take that first step, it really is. So I left the academy, quietly, and took what roles I could get. And I watched that wretched Sybil Fawkes and the rest of that no-talent lot rise to the top. Like pond scum," she added with a brittle laugh. "And I dreamed, night after night, of getting rid of them, of butchering all the women who had laughed at me. And make no mistake, they did laugh, just like Sybil laughed at my Phantom. But we got even in the end, didn't we?"

The ropes fell away. Slowly Rielle's circulation returned. The gun was aimed directly at her chest. She rubbed her bruised wrists but wisely didn't move.

"Did Jonathan mur—Uh, dispose of Sybil on his own?" she asked in a cautious tone.

Ava strolled back around the pillar, swinging the ropes like a billy club. "Oh, yes. Much as I'd like to, I can't take credit for that one. All three of us were doing *Dr. Jekyll and Mr. Hyde*—Sybil was the star, of course, we were mere players—and for some reason she decided to have a fling. Jonathan, here, was her choice. Or victim, if you prefer."

Rielle moistened her dry lips. "But if he was involved with Sybil at the time, didn't that make him a rather obvious suspect when she turned up dead?"

Ava sent her a brief, smug smile. "It was a discreet affair, Rielle. Sybil take up with an underling? Unthinkable.

And naturally I gave him an alibi." She shrugged. "There was no reason for Scotland Yard not to believe me, and heaven knows it was the least I could do. You see, everything came so clear to me after that night. As I told you, I saw him do it. Maybe I realized he was crazy, I'm not really sure. At any rate once he'd strangled Sybil, I had no trouble convincing him that a woman as cunning and devious as her would never simply die. No, she'd be back in another form soon enough, and he'd have to kill her all over again." Ava's smile grew positively triumphant. Frightening. "And don't you see, that's precisely what he did. He killed Sybil as Ingrid, as Janine, as Elizabeth and Annabelle and Charity. Sybil as whomever I selected." She spread wide her long fingers. "A perfect alliance."

"Perfect," Rielle echoed weakly.

Another bolt of lightning shot through the gloom. With a toss of her short bob, Ava perched herself on a broken stone and gave the VHS tape beside her a pat. "My weakness," she said, looking rather proud of herself. "I like to record the deaths. For posterity, and, I admit it, personal satisfaction. As I'm sure you've guessed we used Luke and Paul to con Charity. But of course we never expected them to show up at the Cobdon Theater that night. Certainly we never expected them to steal the tape we were making." She waved an airy hand. "And when I say we, understand that your friends were completely unaware of my involvement in this. I am after all a rising star on the London stage. I couldn't have them recognizing me."

Her expression brightened. She smiled again, another quick twist of her lips. "Well, that's the story, more or less. Oh, except to say that we learned of your plans to help Luke the first night you and your sexy Brazilian friend arrived here. We felt a little con might be in order, throw you off the scent, so to speak."

"Yes, I figured as much."

"Did you? Well, enough said, then." Ava left the stone to take the gun from Jonathan. "Kill her," she ordered without preamble.

For a moment Rielle was too startled to react. She'd expected Ava to gloat some more, to prolong the tale, not to mention the mental suffering.

But such was not to be the case. Already Jonathan was advancing on her, his pale eyes alight with anticipation, his red lips drawn back over his teeth, his fingers curled and ready.

He wore gloves now, she noticed obscurely. Thick white gloves to blur the bruises on her throat. The autopsy would read Death By Strangulation, but the killer would not be caught. She'd be just another statistic, and all of Aunt Lavinia's dark prophecies about her life of crime would be borne out.

Gloved fingertips grazed the skin of her neck. Wind rushed down the staircase, blowing up dust and cobwebs. Lightning flashed and thunder shook the castle walls. Shook Rielle. No! She would not die. Not like this. Better to fight and be shot than to be choked by a madman.

He was close now, very close. His eyes were a crazed gray glow in the shadowy chamber. His breath touched her cheek. Gathering every scrap of her strength and courage, Rielle brought her knee up hard between his legs, half expecting him to grab her anyway.

It surprised her that he didn't. And suddenly it seemed all hell broke loose in the dungeon.

She heard a gunshot; she was sure of it, a bullet zinging through the gloom, bouncing off the wall. Then something else flew past her. She couldn't absorb it all. Couldn't even see, and that seemed odd indeed—until she realized that she was no longer standing, that someone had yanked her away from the pillar and thrown her to the ground.

Adrian!

She scrambled to her knees. Blond hair visible through a cloud of brown dust. And a pair of anxious blue eyes staring into hers.

"Luke," she managed to croak, waving at the soot that stung her eyes. Where was it coming from?

Grunts audible behind her. Two men struggling in the shadows. Adrian and the Phantom.

"Do something," she hissed at Luke, still waving at the dust clouds as she staggered rather dizzily to her feet. "Help him."

"Love to. Where is he?"

Rielle gave her old friend a shove in the right direction and, grabbing a torch from the stone column, would have followed him if she hadn't suddenly remembered Ava. And the gun.

She spun around, peering into the darkness, her fingers tight about the base of the torch. No sign of the woman. But she had to be here.

Behind her she heard Luke swear, heard something slash through the air. Another blazing torch. Jonathan was swinging it at his assailants, holding them off with the flames, snarling at them like a wild animal. But there was still no sign of Ava.

Had she run? Deserted her Phantom? Not likely, Rielle decided, edging cautiously around the column. So where, then...?

The thought came to an abrupt halt as a piece of rope wound itself with suffocating force around Rielle's throat.

"Bitch," Ava snarled in her ear. "Call them off, or you die. Do it," she growled, clearly anticipating resistance, "or I swear to hell, I'll kill you here and now."

Rielle couldn't breathe; the rope was that tight. And getting tighter by the second, she realized in desperation.

"All right," she gasped. "I'll do it. I'll call..."

Without warning, she twisted her body around and jammed her right elbow into Ava's stomach. A yelp of pain and surprise broke from the woman's throat. The rope fell away, and Rielle was thrust roughly forward.

The gun!

She snatched up the torch again before Ava could recapture her, positioning it over one shoulder like a baseball bat, certain that horrid gun would be pointing at her by the time she got herself turned.

But there was no gun. And no Ava, her shocked senses informed her. The woman had to be a phantom herself to keep disappearing like this. Where had she gone?

A great long thunderbolt cut through dust and shadows and gloom to illuminate the woman's figure scrabbling hastily about the dirty stone floor. In a fit of fury she pounded her fists against a nearby rock, leapt to her feet and grabbed the videotape.

She'd lost her weapon, Rielle realized. And loyalty be damned, she was going to desert her Phantom after all.

The Phantom!

Rielle spun back to the struggle behind her, which was really more of a standoff at this point than a fight. "Adrian!" She shouted his name as he circled a wary Jonathan and tossed him the torch she held.

Now the Phantom had no choice. He swung his own torch in Adrian's direction, wielding it like an ancient sword—and exposing his back in the process. Easy prey for Luke, who pounced immediately, tackling him by the knees and sending him sprawling to the ground. One solid punch to the jaw from Adrian's deceptively powerful fist, and the Phantom was out.

Adrian was across the floor and hauling Rielle into his arms before she was even aware he'd moved. Not a gentle embrace by any means, there was a decided edge of terror in it. And all the strength and warmth she could ever want.

But it wasn't over yet. Ava was gone, and she had the tape, proof of the Phantom's identity. They had to stop her.

"Which way did she go?" Adrian asked while Luke set about binding Jonathan's ankles and wrists.

"Up the stairs." Rielle wound her fingers around his wrist. "No arguments, amigo," she said firmly. "I'm coming with you."

To her amazement a smile touched the corners of his mouth. He brushed the hair from her dusty face. "Do you think I did not already know this, *querida?*"

Giving her no chance to answer, he took hold of her hand, heading for the staircase—and whatever dark horrors lay beyond.

AVA RAN UP the wide stairs, cursing the gown and robe that hampered her. Thunder crashing all around, shaking the darkness. Her head pounded with the sound. Broken, like her dreams.

It wasn't right. She wasn't finished yet! More victims waited. But she didn't have her Phantom anymore.

She wanted to cry, to scream. To kill them all. She had the tape, but they had her Phantom. Hers. And maybe that couldn't be proven in a court of law, but he would surely wind up locked away in some impenetrable asylum. A psychotic creature forever caged—and no longer able to do her bidding.

Not fair, she raged as she ran up more stairs, a narrower set this time, and into the tower. Still nowhere near the great hall, though she thought she could hear music. Requiem for Odessa. How fitting.

Her robe got snagged on a piece of stone. She ripped it free. Run, her brain shouted. Get away!

They would follow, she knew. But they would go out into the night and she was going up, to the top of the tower. Safety there. And danger, too. She could feel it, like army ants, crawling on her skin.

Midnight coming, and the music, her frenzied mind told her. Unimportant now, but she'd wanted it to mean something. Wanted to become what Odessa was already. A symbol of evil. Such a glorious thing, to be the personification of evil. And in a way, she *was* a Metamorph, wasn't she? An actress. The Phantom's "voice." She had controlled life and death for a time. And would again, she vowed fiercely.

Footsteps behind her—and voices. They were coming.

Where was the tape? She clawed at the deep pockets of her robe. Still there. Safe in her possession.

She kept running, through the darkness, past blackened passageways and empty chambers. Cool, damp air rushed down at her. Open door ahead. And beyond it a huge room, barren, with part of the wall caved in near the window.

She was trapped!

She looked around frantically. "No," she breathed, and clutched at the pocket of her robe and the tape buried deep inside. "No!"

"There is no way out, Ava."

Adrian's quiet voice reached her above the wind and the thunder and the roar of the sea beyond the ruined wall. She whirled to face him, to face both of them, still clutching her robe pocket, a snarl forming on her lips. Fools! Did they really think she would let them win?

She backed away, toward the crumbling wall, stepping carefully over mounds of rubble. Crash of waves behind her. Water hitting the rocks below.

"This proves nothing," she cried suddenly, her fingers like claws around the pocketed tape. "I'm not on here, and what magistrate would take the word of three crooks over mine?"

"Perhaps none," Adrian agreed.

"In which case," Rielle put in quickly, "you have nothing to worry about."

Ava paused, feeling the tape beneath the rough material of her robe. Was she so sure her image had not been captured by her own video camera? Had she ever looked? Except for Sybil's death, all of the murders were on this cassette. She'd watched it a hundred times or more, and yet she'd never really checked out that most important, most incriminating detail.

Movement in front of her! She snapped her head up, continued to inch backward. They had drawn very close, damn them. Where could she go? Damp gusts of wind hit her spine, made her hair blow wildly about her face. Only the sea, unforgiving and cold, and a thousand deadly rocks lay below. No sanctuary to be found there.

But she wouldn't let them take her, would never let them take the tape.

"Ava, no!"

She heard Rielle shout as she turned sharply and stumbled forward. Footsteps on the stones. Of course they would try to stop her. Nothing noble in the act—they wanted the tape.

She laughed at the thought, a coarse, bitter sound, perhaps a little crazed, and scrambled up onto the ledge. Triumph in her eyes when she looked down at them.

The wind whipped the woolen robe about her legs. She laughed again, louder this time, and clawed at the tape in her pocket. All she had to do was drop it. The victory would be hers. And the solstice.

She heard Adrian talking to her, heard Rielle, too. They were coming closer. But the tape was stuck, caught on a seam. She yanked hard at it. Still stuck. And what was that other thing now? That strange light she could see out of the corner of her eye? Colors of green and gold and softest red visible as a glow out on the water. Such a beautiful aura it had.

Midnight bells tolled in the distance. Midsummer magic.

A jolt of shock went through her. The faerie island!

She glanced back at Rielle and Adrian. They had stopped. They saw it, too, that gentle, ethereal glow far out at sea.

The wind seemed to pull at her, tugging hard at her robe. Did it call to her? Try to tell her something?

Dismay mingled with wonder, confusing her. The faerie island had risen. Did that mean Odessa had been defeated?

Ava swayed on the ledge. She didn't believe in these things. Not real, any of this. Destroy the tape! That mattered. Save herself!

With a violent yank she tore the cassette from her pocket, then gave a sudden shriek as a blast of wind seized her. Motion in her peripheral vision. Adrian and Rielle, rushing forward. But the cassette! It was gone! She'd dropped it on the floor!

Her fingers scratched at the air. Lightning shot through the night sky. That strange mystical glow lingered on the horizon, fading now, but she knew she'd seen it.

"No!"

The scream was torn from her lungs. Nothing to grab, and now the wind had her. She couldn't regain her balance. The hands that reached for her were too far away.

The stone ledge seemed to crumble beneath her feet. The glow intensified for a moment, and then it vanished.

The magic was gone. Her Phantom had been caught. Her dreams were shattered. And she was falling, silently, through the wind and the darkness and the salty spray of the sea.

Tumbling through the night to the deadly rocks below.

Epilogue

The limousine glided smoothly through the early-morning mist, a powerful white sedan sailing along the autobahn at a more than respectable speed.

Through the smoked-glass window, Rielle watched the fog-shrouded countryside roll by. A week had passed since Ava had fallen to her death from the castle tower. A week since the Phantom had been caught and taken away under heavy guard to a London hospital for psychiatric evaluation. Scotland Yard had the incriminating tape in its possession, Luke was in the process of working a deal with them, and the Midsummer Festival was, for one more year at least, history.

A smile touched Rielle's lips as more lush scenery rolled by. In her mind she heard voices, not like those belonging to the Phantom, but explanations. Simple, straightforward and entirely reasonable in retrospect.

"Humming, you say?" Reuben stared at her long and hard in the sitting room at Brede Manor, puffing thoughtfully on his pipe. Then his face brightened. "Yes, of course, I remember now. The music. I was out for a stroll before breakfast when I heard it. Rather a catchy tune this 'Mellow Yellow.' And you say the Phantom used it to draw you to the edge of the cliff?"

That was about the size of it. Endanger her life and lure Luke to Morgate. A simple enough plan.

More memories crowded in, the other guests telling her things, starting with Noah's bitter "All my life I despised the riffraff my father dragged home from the theater. Cheap tarts and pimps, that's what they all were...."

Rielle shivered in the warm confines of the limo. A man with deep psychological problems was Noah Bishop. But at least he didn't seem homicidal.

Her thoughts turned to Ivan Ragozcy.

"...Better known as Spencer Roe and, best known as Sidney Rawlins," was how he'd put his blithe explanation to her. "Writer of Gothic horror novels. Real monster-in-the-shadows stuff. Ah, but then to be a good fiend, you must first walk in that fiend's shoes, don't you agree? And so, love, I become my own main characters for a time as part of my research. Simple as that."

Rielle couldn't help laughing a little as she sank back into the soft leather seat. Strange people, every last one of them, but not murderous phantoms. Not even criminals. Well, except for Fagan and Reuben who, although neither would come right out and admit it, were smack in the middle of a juicy little mail-order con. Their product: Gypsy herbal cream.

"For what it's worth, my child," Fagan had assured her Monday morning, "the only people I've ever really cheated were true cheats themselves." He'd given her a mischievous smile then and patted her arm. "Of course those days are far behind me, you understand."

Understand? Yes. Believe? Rielle laughed.

"Ah, yes," Fagan had continued. "Creams and lotions and maybe soon a Gypsy herbal tea. Caffeine-free, of course. Quite relaxing."

Well, if he needed a guinea pig for that last product, he might consider using Gretchen. Stiffer than her, people didn't come. But then she wasn't really being fair, was she? Gretchen had sound reasons for her austere demeanor. And for despising any and all things related to the stage.

"My son took up with an actress once, miss," she'd said. "A lot like Sybil Fawkes, she was, too. Cold and heartless.

He's been fighting the bottle ever since she left him two years ago."

That was it. Everything explained in just a few short hours. Even Jonathan's limp. That bit of fakery, Rielle thought in mild self-reproach, being something she should have spotted straight away.

Injured left leg, indeed. One inch of bone removed. But it was the sole of his right shoe that was thicker. And a thickened right sole didn't correct a limp; it *gave* him one.

Rielle shook the thought away as the limousine glided to a smooth halt just inside a wire fence. Seconds later the door opened, and the chauffeur appeared.

"We are here, *Fräulein,*" he announced courteously. "The *Herr* is here to meet you."

Rielle stepped from the rear of the luxury vehicle. It was early Sunday morning, and she hadn't seen Adrian since they'd returned to London on Tuesday. He had to leave for Germany, he'd explained in a distant tone that wasn't difficult to recognize. He had a race that weekend in Hockenheim. Did she understand?

No, but she wasn't about to admit that to him. He'd never claimed to love her; she'd never assumed he would.

"Ms. Marchand?" A man's very pleasant voice called her back to the present.

She focused on him. Blond hair, British accent, dressed in black pants and a short-sleeved white shirt with the name of Adrian's racing team emblazoned on the pocket.

He smiled. "If you'll come with me, please, I'll escort you to your seat in the Paddock Club."

She'd come this far, hadn't she? Of course she would come with him. Upstairs to the exclusive hospitality suites that resided above the pit lane. Very posh.

"All has been arranged for you," he continued with impeccable courtesy. He didn't say by whom, but that was obvious enough, wasn't it?

"Some of the drivers are still out on the track," he said with a smile. "Warming up, though the race itself doesn't begin for several hours yet." He stopped suddenly on the stairs, glanced down, then nodded. "I'm sorry," he apologized. "It seems we're going in the wrong direction."

Oh, really? Rielle leaned against the railing, not moving. "Where exactly is it that we're going?"

His smile widened. "To the motor home."

"And why are we going there?"

"Because, *querida,* it is the only place where we can be alone."

She managed to hold her ground, even managed to continue leaning calmly against the railing. Her gaze remained fixed on her guide. "I see you're a ventriloquist," she said to him. "Very talented."

A pair of strong hands circled her waist, doing what she refused to. Turning her to meet the sexiest pair of brown eyes she'd ever seen.

He was wearing his red racing suit. His dark hair was damp with perspiration and curling over the open collar. A smile played on the corners of his mouth and in his eyes, and his hands, his deft, beautiful hands, were still clamped firmly about her waist.

"Come, *querida,* " he said, and to her surprise brushed his damp lips across hers. "We cannot stay here. Unless you wish to have a confrontation with the international press."

A shiver passed through her. "Thanks, but I think I'll pass."

They made it through another wire fence just ahead of a gaggle of autograph-hungry fans. Holding tight to her hand, Adrian led her past a collection of round tables to the door of the motor home.

They didn't go inside immediately. It was a cloudy summer morning, warm and humid with the smell of pine needles, rubber and fuel strong in the air. A light breeze blew in from the forest behind them, ruffling Adrian's hair, and Rielle found herself reaching up to touch the damp curls.

"I missed you, you know," she murmured with her usual candor. "I thought I might never see you again. Well, except maybe on television," she added with a smile.

Shaking his head, he took hold of the hand that continued to play with his hair and brought it to his lips. "This
would not have been possible, *querida*."

His eyes locked on hers. So serious he looked. Not troubled, exactly, but she could tell he wanted to say something, and he didn't want to be misunderstood.

She waited patiently, staring at him, determined not to
push. She knew what she wanted, what her own expecta-
tions were. Time now for him to talk, to tell her whatever
needed to be said.

"It is difficult to do this," he said at last, his fingers still
curled around hers. "I think sometimes it is better not to
care for anyone."

"Easier, Adrian," she corrected softly, "not better."

Now his lips curved into a small smile. So familiar, that
hint of amusement playing on the corners of his mouth. She
wanted to reach up and pull that sexy mouth down onto
hers.

"Gosto de ti," he murmured, drawing her closer to his
warm, hard body. "I love you, Rielle. This is all I know and
all I have been able to think about since we left Morgate. I
love you, but this feeling frightens me. And I do not like to
be frightened."

Her eyes sparkled with delight. Smiling, she slid her arms
loosely about his neck, aware of the tension in his muscles.
"No one does, Adrian. And how lucky for you that you
have no reason to be. You know I love you, more than anyone in the world. But I wouldn't cling to you. I couldn't."

"You are very strong," he said, stroking her cheek with
his thumb.

"One of the few positive by-products of my jaded past."
She grinned. "That and my ability to take life one day at a
time."

He lowered his head slightly, and she felt his lips move
against her temple. "One day at a time. I like this idea. I
think I will have to take you home with me to Brazil. Introduce you to Emile. In November, perhaps, when the racing
season is over. Maybe by then we will also know about

Luke's fate." He lifted his head to look into her eyes. "Is Scotland Yard still holding him?"

"They're still questioning him. I figure by November he'll probably be working for them."

"This would be interesting."

She hesitated for a moment as another thought occurred to her. Disturbing, yet difficult to articulate. Still...

"Adrian, did you see it?" she asked, and thankfully he didn't pretend not to understand.

"The faerie island?"

"Yes."

The barest hint of a smile crossed his mouth, and he pulled her close against his hard, lean body. She felt his lips rub across hers, heard his quiet "I believe in the power of love, *querida*."

And that was answer enough. For everything.

Around them the wind swirled in slow circles, though Rielle scarcely noticed it. Then Adrian's mouth closed on hers, and even the noise of the crowd began to subside, the throb of high-powered engines fading away to nothing.

Nothing except the silky rustle of pine needles in the nearby woods. And the delicate tinkle of crystal that floated eerily through the misty morning air....

HARLEQUIN
Season's Greetings

Christmas cards from relatives and friends
wishing you love and happiness. Twinkling lights
in the nighttime sky. Christmas—the time for
magic, dreams ... and possibly destiny?

Harlequin American Romance brings you
SEASON'S GREETINGS. When a magical, red-
cheeked, white-haired postman delivers long-lost
letters, the lives of four unsuspecting couples will
change forever.

Don't miss the chance to experience the magic of
Christmas with these special books, coming to
you from American Romance in December.

#417 UNDER THE MISTLETOE
by Rebecca Flanders
#418 CHRISTMAS IN TOYLAND
by Julie Kistler
#419 AN ANGEL IN TIME
by Stella Cameron
#420 FOR AULD LANG SYNE
by Pamela Browning

Christmas—the season when wishes *do* come true....

SG91

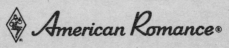

American Romance®

HARLEQUIN HISTORICAL

CHRISTMAS

STORIES · 1991

Bring back heartwarming memories of Christmas past
with HISTORICAL CHRISTMAS STORIES 1991,
a collection of romantic stories
by three popular authors.
The perfect Christmas gift!

Don't miss these heartwarming stories,
available in November
wherever Harlequin books are sold:

CHRISTMAS YET TO COME
by Lynda Trent
A SEASON OF JOY
by Caryn Cameron
FORTUNE'S GIFT
by DeLoras Scott

**Best Wishes and Season's Greetings
from Harlequin!**

XM-91R

HARLEQUIN

Romance

A Christmas tradition...

**Imagine spending Christmas in New
Orleans with a blind stranger and his aged
guide dog—when you're supposed to be
there on your honeymoon!**
**#3163 Every Kind of Heaven
by Bethany Campbell**

**Imagine spending Christmas with a man
you once ''married''—in a mock ceremony
at the age of eight!**
**#3166 The Forgetful Bride
by Debbie Macomber**

*Available in December 1991, wherever
Harlequin books are sold.*

RXM

HARLEQUIN

Romance

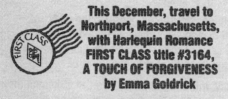

This December, travel to
Northport, Massachusetts,
with Harlequin Romance
FIRST CLASS title #3164,
A TOUCH OF FORGIVENESS
by Emma Goldrick

Folks in Northport called Kitty the meanest woman in town,
but she couldn't forget how they had duped her brother and
exploited her family's land. It was hard to be mean, though,
when Joel Carmody was around—his calm, good humor
made Kitty feel like a new woman. Nevertheless, a Carmody
was a Carmody, and the name meant money and power to
the townspeople.... Could Kitty really trust Joel, or was he
like all the rest?

If you missed September title #3149, ROSES HAVE THORNS (England), October title
#3155, TRAPPED (England) or November title #3159, AN ANSWER FROM THE HEART
(England) and would like to order any of them, send your name, address, zip or postal
code, along with a check or money order for $2.99 plus 75¢ postage and handling ($1.00
in Canada) for each book ordered, payable to Harlequin Reader Service to:

In the U.S.	In Canada
3010 Walden Avenue	P.O. Box 609
P.O. Box 1325	Fort Erie, Ontario
Buffalo, NY 14269-1325	L2A 5X3

Please specify book title(s) with your order.
Canadian residents add applicable federal and provincial taxes.

JT-B12R

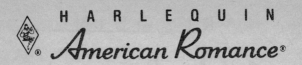

HARLEQUIN
American Romance®

From the Alaskan wilderness to sultry New Orleans...from New England seashores to the rugged Rockies...American Romance brings you the best of America. And with each trip, you'll find the best in romance.

Each month, American Romance brings you the magic of falling in love with that special American man. Whether an untamed cowboy or a polished executive, he has that sensuality, that special spark sure to capture your heart.

For stories of today, with women just like you and the men they dream about, read American Romance. Four new titles each month.

HARLEQUIN AMERICAN ROMANCE—the love stories you can believe in.

AMERICAN